Baron's Crusade

Baron's Crusade

**Book 8 in the Border Knight Series
By
Griff Hosker**

Baron's Crusade

Published by Sword Books Ltd 2019

Copyright © Griff Hosker First Edition

The author has asserted their moral right under the Copyright, Designs and Patents Act, 1988, to be identified as the author of this work. All Rights reserved. No part of this publication may be reproduced, copied, stored in a retrieval system, or transmitted, in any form or by any means, without the prior written consent of the copyright holder, nor be otherwise circulated in any form of binding or cover other than that in which it is published and without a similar condition being imposed on the subsequent purchaser.
A CIP catalogue record for this title is available from the British Library.

Baron's Crusade

List of protagonists (Fictional ones are in italics.)

Sir Thomas of Stockton, Earl of Cleveland.
William of Elsdon- Sir Thomas' son
King Henry III of England (Henry Winchester)
Richard, Earl of Cornwall (King Henry's brother)
King Thibaut of Navarre, (Theobald of Champagne)
Pope Gregory IX
Duke Peter of Brittany
Hugh, Duke of Burgundy
Amaury de Montfort
Simon de Montfort
Henry of Bar (French Nobleman)
As-Salih Ayyub (Meledin- Muslim ruler)
As-Salih Ismail- Muslim ruler of Damascus
An-Nasir Dawud- Muslim Lord of Kerak
Al-Muzaffar Mahmud, Emir of Hama
Al-Mujahid, Emir of Homs
Al-Adil II- Saladin's nephew and the ruler in Cairo

Following the death of Saladin, his Empire was broken up by warring sons. Saladin was a Kurd as were his sons but some went south and took over the land of Egypt. The others stayed in the north and east where they led the Kurdish side of the family.

Contents

Baron's Crusade 1
Sir Thomas 6
Prologue 6
Chapter 1 7
Chapter 2 20
Chapter 3 32
Chapter 4 44
Chapter 5 59
Sir William of Elsdon 67
Chapter 6 67
Chapter 7 78
Sir Thomas 88
Chapter 8 90
Chapter 9 97
Chapter 10 107
Chapter 11 117
Chapter 12 129
Chapter 13 140
Chapter 14 153
Chapter 15 167
Chapter 16 178
Chapter 17 191
Epilogue 206
Glossary 208
Historical Notes 209
Other books by Griff Hosker 211

Baron's Crusade

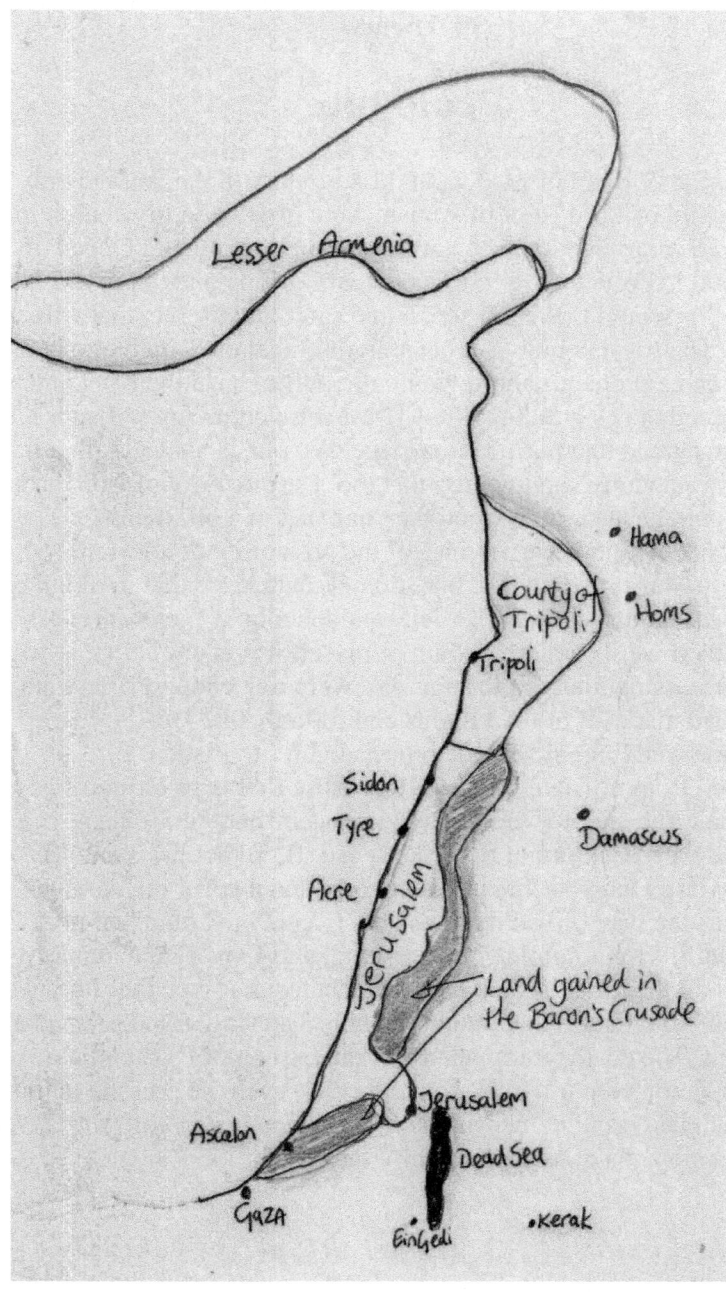

Baron's Crusade

Sir Thomas

Prologue

My son, Sir William of Elsdon, and Lady Mary of Annan, the only surviving child of Lord Kerk of Annan, were married in my church in Stockton. The marriage had been arranged by the King and Queen of Scotland and I was not certain if King Henry of England approved, but I knew that this would make my son's land safer and for me, that was all-important. The royal couple had been grateful that the daughter of Lord Kerk now had a protector and it would not hurt to have the King and Queen of Scotland as grateful allies. However, neither my wife nor I would have agreed to a political marriage. We ourselves had fallen in love and I wanted my son to enjoy that too. Despite the situation, he and Mary had both been smitten when they had met in York. King Alexander had held out the promise of the possibility of a fortune belonging to Mary's family but that did not matter to either William or me. As it was held in Jedburgh Abbey and the monks there were less than friendly towards either William or myself it was unlikely that we would be accessing it any time soon. We were rich enough. Our wars and raids had made all of my knights comfortably off.

After the wedding, the couple returned north to Elsdon. I remembered from my own marriage that those first days of marriage were special. The couple would get to know one another. It also allowed me that most rare of pastimes; peace. I did not have to raid nor go to war. King Henry seemed to have forgotten me, for the moment, and that was the way I liked it. I was able to enjoy my land and my people. I built, I went hunting and hawking, and I invested a nunnery. In short, I did all the things which had been denied me since that fateful day at Arsuf when my father had been slain. The Holy Land seemed a lifetime ago. The death, at my hands, of the Bishop of Durham, now seemed an action committed by someone else, even the crusade in the Baltic which had brought me Margaret seemed to be the stuff of legend and now I enjoyed a quiet and peaceful time.

Chapter 1

I now had seven grandchildren and William and Mary would soon produce more; when I had been a sword for hire, I had never thought I would become a grandfather. Now that I had children and grandchildren then I had a complete life. I knew that I was lucky but it had not always been so. King John had almost ruined my life and despite the fame, I had gained at Arsuf, King Richard had not been the friend he should have been. King Henry, the new King, had also shown that he put himself before his country and my son and I had frequently been used as pawns by the King. It did not sit well with me and I was happy to stay in the north where I knew and trusted the people and the lords who followed me, and I was well away from the politics which I despised.

Mary was with child just six months after the marriage and my wife fretted about the position of the manor which was close to the border raiders. "Elsdon is a wild manor and the Scots are too close for my liking!"

I shook my head, "Mary is Scottish!"

"Do not be obtuse! You know what I mean and the Earl of Fife is not only her enemy but the enemy of our son and of you."

I sighed, "And we have beaten them at every turn. We now have good lords of the manor there and the King and Queen of Scotland are our friends."

She changed her tack. I had noticed that women were very adept at this. "Then think of the medical attention she could receive here. We have a doctor in the castle. The midwives of Stockton are amongst the finest in the land. Bring them home just until they have the child. Besides, the journey north to see our new grandchild might be too hard for a lady of my years!"

I burst out laughing, "Do not make me laugh! You will outlive me and you are fitter than some of the men at arms."

"Thomas?" When she used her gentle voice then I knew I was done for. Her hectoring voice made me argue but when she was gentle then she knew I would accede to her request.

I shook my head, "Very well, I will make the offer but if our son rejects the idea then I will not do more."

"That is all that I ask."

Baron's Crusade

In the event, my son surprised me and he brought his pregnant wife south to Stockton. My wife had been correct about the medical care and Richard, named after Mary's father, was a healthy bairn and I was happy. They had their own quarters in my castle and I saw the red-faced child every day. Everything about the situation was perfect. Perhaps Fate had determined that my son and his wife should be at my castle, for a month after the birth I received a message from York. King Henry was visiting York and had asked to meet with me and my son. We were told that the Archbishop of Canterbury would be there too and I was immediately suspicious. Why would the leading prelate in the country come north and why would he wish to speak with me and my son? What I could not do was refuse to attend. I knew the problems of annoying a king!

I did not take many men; we took our squires, pages and just four men at arms. My most experienced men at arms and archers were close in age to me and had seen almost sixty summers; I did not take them. I had to obey the King's command; they did not. My wife gave me a long shopping list and so I took my steward with me. Geoffrey knew what my wife liked far better than I did. Our squires and pages had fought together when we had defended Elsdon and the Coquet Valley from the Scots. They conversed easily as they rode and followed behind William and me as we headed south. With two of my men at arms before us, for security, William and I were able to talk as we rode.

"Do you think, father, that King Henry wishes to reward us for our services on the border?"

I laughed, "You are still young, William, and do not know the way that kings work. We serve a purpose and, as such, are useful but our King fears his barons. It was they who rose against his father and the Great Charter bound King Henry and his powers. No, this will not be to reward us. As I discovered with King Richard, kings can soon forget what knights do for them and I do not look forward to this meeting for I do not think that we will see any benefit from it. This visit will result in some service we will owe the crown and that will, inevitably, mean I will have to leave my valley and, if truth be told, I grow weary of such journeys. I have seen over sixty summers and I do not relish campaigns as much as I did when I was young."

My son was shrewd, "From what Ridley the Giant and your senior men have told me you never enjoyed campaigning. You did what you did to get back the manors our families had once owned."

"Perhaps, but now we have them."

"And yet to retain them we have to keep on the good side of King Henry."

I nodded, "Now you are learning. This should not affect you. Whatever happens in York you should be able to return to your manor with your wife and son."

"That is unlikely to happen, father, for why else would I be summoned to accompany you? I have been included too. Whatever the King requires of you he will require of me."

He was right, of course, and the thought depressed me even more. Just when I had a life I could enjoy, the wilful King would disrupt it.

Going to York was always difficult. Each time I saw the Bootham Gate, the entrance to York from the north, my heart sank for my firstborn, Alfred, had been treacherously slain at the Sherriff's stables. Although his death had been avenged, each time I dismounted and allowed my horse to be led away I relived that moment when I had lost my child. It still hurt, even now.

The Sherriff of York had been my squire and despite the fact that the royal visit took over most of the castle my son and I, along with our squires and pages, had fine accommodation for Ralph remembered the kindnesses shown by my wife and me. It was Sir Ralph who greeted us. He had not campaigned for some years and it showed. Where William and I were still relatively lean, Ralph was a little portlier than when he had been my knight. "The King has brought many guests, my lord. He and the Archbishop are with the Archbishop of York. They have, it seems, much to discuss."

"And have you any idea why we have been summoned?"

He shook his head, "Your guess is as good as mine, lord. You know how close the King is. Come, I will take you to your quarters and then I shall broach a hogshead of wine. The King brought a couple, in lieu, no doubt, of any payment for his stay." He shook his head, "When a King visits the coffers empty!"

I laughed, "Aye, it was ever thus!"

We left our squires and pages to organize the rooms and went to the Great Hall. As we entered Sir Ralph groaned, "I forgot about our French guest."

I looked into the hall and saw a man whose back was to us. "French guest?"

"Simon de Montfort, the putative Earl of Leicester. He came after the King's arrival and is waiting to speak with the King."

The French baron turned and rose as we entered. I could speak French. All those who wished to get on at court could speak the language of the King but I was reluctant to speak it here in the north of England. I determined to speak English. I suppose I must have frowned or it may have been that de Montfort was sensitive to such facial expressions for he spoke in heavily accented English as he tried to win me to his side. I was one of the two most powerful earls in the north of England.

"Earl, it is an honour to meet you and your son. Your victories in the north were truly inspiring." He seemed to be genuine in his praise. I saw no lie in his eyes.

"You are most kind, my lord." I knew that he had not been confirmed in his title yet. I was unsure of his actual title and 'my lord' seemed to be the safest form of address.

Sir Ralph poured wine and we chatted. I had expected a pleasant conversation with my son and former knight but de Montfort's presence meant that our conversation was more stilted and formal than I would have liked. I did, however, learn much. De Montfort had also been promised the Earldom of Chester in addition to the inherited title of Leicester. The earldom of Chester had belonged to his family until King John took it from them. Now, in return for de Montfort's elder brother being allowed to keep his French and Norman lands, Simon de Montfort had given up claims to France to recover their English estates. King Henry knew how to play barons off against each other. He had given himself an ally and that, perhaps, explained de Montfort's presence.

The King and the two archbishops arrived just an hour after we had begun to enjoy the wine. The King had always been a religious man. He had spoken often to me of his wish to go on a crusade and so I was not surprised to see him with the two most senior churchmen in the land but I still wondered why Canterbury had come north. The smile the King gave me was genuine. I hoped that he truly knew how much he owed the crown which sat upon his head to me and my men.

"Sir Thomas, it is good to see you and your brave son. Once more you have saved the north of England from the privations of the Scots!"

"I serve my King."

He smiled, "And you will continue to do so." He turned to Sir Ralph, "Sherriff, I would have a conference with Sir Thomas and his son, I pray you take Sir Simon to the Minster. Let him rejoice in the church we have raised to God!"

Simon de Montfort did not wish to be taken away from this conference and he objected, "But King Henry, I have seen it already!"

"Then see it again!" The King's voice had lost its humour and was cold and commanding.

Sir Ralph knew that the King wished for privacy and he smiled as he said, "There are some parts which even pilgrims do not see. Come, Sir Simon. It will give us an appetite for the feast we hold later." Sir Simon nodded and Sir Ralph spoke to his senior servant, "Abelard, when you have ensured that there is wine and food for our guests have all the servants retire beyond the doors until they are needed."

"Aye, lord."

The King and the two archbishops made themselves comfortable and the King waited until Abelard and the others had left before he spoke, "Sir Ralph is a discreet man. He is a good Sheriff."

I was not certain if the last words he spoke were a statement or a question. "He is a stout man and reliable. I am certain that the Archbishop would concur."

Walter de Gray, the Archbishop of York, knew the value of an honest Sherriff and he smiled, "He is the most trustworthy man in the north, Sir Thomas excepted."

"Good. Now that we are alone, we can speak. I will let the Archbishop of Canterbury give you the background while I enjoy some of this most excellent-looking ham."

Edmund Rich had only been Archbishop for a relatively short time. Walter de Gray was a more assured prelate. I could hear the nervousness in the voice of the former prebendary of Salisbury as he spoke. I knew that the three previous choices for Archbishop had been quashed by Pope Gregory and I wondered if that accounted for the hesitancy I could hear in the Archbishop.

"Know you that the King has a great desire to go on Holy Crusade?" I nodded. "And Pope Gregory is concerned that the agreement to leave Jerusalem in Christian hands runs out in less than five years." I did not know that. "His Holiness has imposed a tax to fund another Crusade to go to the Holy Land and ensure that Jerusalem does not fall into Muslim hands once more." He paused and looked at me. I knew about the tax. Every church in England sent money each month to York.

I was confused. It was obvious that all three men sought some comment from me but this had nought to do with me. My days as a crusader had ended when I had brought my wife back from the Baltic. I played for time until my mind, slowed, no doubt, by the wine, could grasp the point they were trying to make, "And who will lead this crusade, my lord?"

"King Thibaut of Navarre also known as Theobald of Champagne."

I had heard of this Frenchman who was also Count of Champagne. He had a reputation as a good leader.

The King wiped his hands on a napkin and then drank some wine. He looked at the goblet, "A somewhat indifferent wine." Then he looked at me, "The Pope and I have had our disagreements of late and I would heal the breach between England and the Church of Rome."

Baron's Crusade

I expected him to say that he would, therefore, be joining the Crusade. If he did then there could be a problem as Navarre was a smaller kingdom than England and I could not see King Henry acquiescing to a junior king. I merely nodded to show that I understood his motives. Was he consulting me as a senior Earl?

"To that end, we would have you visit with the Pope and deliver a letter from us and then join the crusade on our behalf."

My mouth must have dropped open for I could not believe what I was hearing. My son spoke for me, "King Henry, my father is no longer a young knight and he has served on a crusade twice. He was the hero of Arsuf!"

King Henry smiled, "And that is why, Sir William, you will accompany your father. You are young and your deeds on the border have shown us that you are a knight who is the copy of his father."

It was one thing to send me but quite another to force my son to go, "Your Majesty, my son has recently become a father. His place is in his home!"

King Henry's eyes became cold, "And your son married a Scottish heiress without our permission." His flattery had been the honey and this was now the stick. This crusade will expunge any wrong that was done and will result in my royal blessing for this marriage, more I will also confer the manor of Seggesfield upon him. I am sure that Alan of Bellingham can hold Elsdon for him and your son would be closer to you." He smiled but it was a smile without humour, "That is generosity enough."

"And just the two of us would represent England, Your Majesty?"

He laughed, "Of course not. There are other knights who wish to go on a crusade under the standard of England. You will have others to join you." He smiled and added, "My brother, Richard, Earl of Cornwall, is also anxious to go on a crusade but it will take us time to organize an army which is large enough to represent England. Give me a year, that is all, and when my brother arrives then you can come home." He picked up the goblet and was about to drink from it and then pushed it away. "I must see if the Sherriff's man has opened the wine I brought!"

I turned and looked at William. His resigned eyes told me that we had no way out of this and he shrugged. I took a drink of the wine. It tasted fine to me. "And when do we leave, King Henry?"

"I will return to London. The knights and their men who will accompany you will return here to York. That is the length of time you have to prepare for Archbishop de Gray will arrange the shipping and the equipment you will need. Archbishop Rich will send the funds. You just need to bring your son and your retinue." He smiled again, "See how all is well planned? And now we had better see de Montfort. I expect that he will have seen enough of your church, de Gray."

I did not want to sit in the Great Hall and listen to a baron plead with the King, for the putative Earl of Leicester was obviously a supplicant; I wanted to speak with William but one did not leave the presence of a king.

Simon de Montfort and the Sherriff returned. I could see that the young knight wished to have a private conference with the King but the ruler of England was his own man and he made de Montfort speak before all of us. I felt sorry for him.

"Your Majesty, I come here to ask for the hand of your sister, Eleanor, the widow of William Marshal, in marriage."

I could see that Archbishop Rich knew nothing of this but the look on the King's face told me that he knew. "Yet my sister took a vow upon the death of her husband." He looked at Archbishop Rich, "It was in your presence I believe, Archbishop."

"Aye, it was, Your Majesty, and as such is a solemn vow not to be broken lightly."

Simon de Montfort coloured, "I have met with the lady and she and I are determined to be wed."

I saw the King's calculating mind, "I am mindful that my sister is young and has yet to bear children. Yet she did make the vow and the breaking of such a vow would need papal approval." He turned to me. "Sir Thomas, when you deliver my letter to the Pope, perhaps you could ask him for dispensation to allow the marriage to take place." I nodded. "There, Sir Simon, you would have your answer in less than three months. That is not too long to wait, is it?"

He obviously thought it was but he was in no position to argue, "No, King Henry."

"And then, perhaps, we can see how you can repay us." As usual in such royal dealings, there was a price to be paid! The King had known what de Montfort would ask and he planned his next move before de Montfort had reached York. My visit to Rome would serve two purposes. "And, perforce, this must remain a secret until all is settled." He glared at all of us in the room and we all nodded. We could say nothing.

Before the meeting ended, I made a plea to the King for I knew not the knights I would be leading, "I would ask, Your Majesty, that you impress upon these knights that we need good horses and that, if they have them, they should bring archers as well as well mailed sergeants."

His dismissive hand showed that he was not a military man and had not even thought of that, "Of course. You are the expert."

"And losses, such as armour and horses will be made good?"

This was always a problematic area for horses were expensive. The King did not war himself but he knew the cost; King Henry knew the cost of everything! "It has been our policy hitherto and there seems little need to change it." I knew why he was so generous. It was not his coins that he would be giving to me! The money would come from that raised in all of the churches in England.

That evening, as we ate, there was a muted atmosphere around the room. Only the King seemed in good spirits. That was because he had achieved his objectives. He had a hold over Simon de Montfort. His brother, Amaury, was one of the most powerful barons in France and an alliance could only help the King. He had offered the hand of peace to the Pope and it would cost him nothing. In fact, he would benefit financially as the ships which were being hired turned out to belong to the King.

Simon de Montfort sat next to me. I did not know the man but I suspected his motives. He had to have chosen Eleanor, widow of William Marshal and sought her out. Was he putting himself in line for the throne? I knew that the de Montfort clan was ambitious and so when he spoke with me, I was guarded in my responses. My son, William, was busy speaking with the King and de Montfort kept his voice low and conspiratorial.

"My lord, how will you be travelling to Rome? By sea?"

Although I had been taken by surprise at the King's orders, I had already planned our route. I shook my head, "The sea and the pirates around the Straits of Hercules mean that a journey across land would be preferable. We will travel by ship from York to Calais and then travel across France."

He smiled, "That is good for I will give you a letter to take to my brother Amaury. He will give you an escort across France and then a messenger can return directly to me with the news."

I was relieved. I did not wish to send one of my own men back. "And if the news is not good?"

He gave me a sly look. "My brother is not without power and influence. There will be a way. I am convinced that the news will be good."

"Then all is well."

"I envy you, Sir Thomas. If this matter was not so pressing then I would join King Henry's young knights on this noble venture. I would have your reputation. If a man makes his name early then his route to the top is assured. It is a lifetime ago and yet men still speak of the hero of Arsuf. What was it like?"

"The battle or the crusade?"

"The battle. I would know how King Richard defeated these Muslim warriors. They just use the bow do they not and mounted bowmen can be easily defeated?"

He had heard of the Turkish horsemen but he did not know how effective they could be. "King Richard did not defeat them. He won Jerusalem and then returned home. This crusade which is demanded by the Pope will, at best, keep Jerusalem in Christian hands for a short time only. And they have other mounted men who are as skilled as any knight in Christendom."

His words reflected the views of many knights but I knew different. I thought back to the battle. I still had nightmares for we had thought we had defeated them when the enemy sent men armed such as we.

The men who charged us were not horse archers. These were armed as we were. They had spears and mail. Their helmets, bayda or egg helmets, had a full mail coif hanging down so that they looked to have a mailed head. They wore a cuirass beneath their flowing robes. With a lance and a curved sword, they had a shield which looked like ours. These were the best that the Seljuk Turks had.

"They are fanatical warriors, Sir Simon, and their weapons and armour make them hard to defeat. More, the land conspires against us. There is little water and an army must carry all of its food with it.

He looked at me with new eyes. "You surprise me, Earl, I thought you would have relished the glory and fame."

"I lost my father that day and he lost all of his oathsworn knights. Do you think that was a reasonable trade?"

"No, Sir Thomas, and now I think I begin to understand yet I would still take the cross and ensure my place in heaven!" He smiled.

The King had been listening and said, I suspect, for the ears of de Montfort for he had already spoken of this to me, "You may tell the Pope that you are but the vanguard of the English contingent. It will take time to rouse English lords. I have hopes that my brother, Richard of Cornwall, might well lead the next contingent but do not say. Be vague."

I saw the effect it had on de Montfort. He could marry the King's sister and travel with the King's brother. It would move him into the highest echelon of English nobility and guarantee that his name would be known.

King Henry knew how to be slippery and evasive. I was not sure I could emulate him. I believed in God but I was not convinced, despite the Pope's words, that heaven was guaranteed to Crusaders. I had seen too much evil for that to be true.

We did not speak again with the King before we returned home, the next day. He sent one of his pages with the documents we would need. When Sir Simon brought his missive, for his brother, I knew that we would need a chest for all of the valuable papers we had to carry. We left the documents with the Sherriff. We had not mentioned our mission to our pages and squires. We would do that once we had left York as the road had few ears. Geoffrey and the servants rode behind us with our purchases and as we rode, I told the pages and squires what we had been asked.

"It goes without saying that you need not come with us. In fact, Henry Samuel, I doubt that your mother would allow you to come."

"But, lord, grandfather, I am your page and I am my father's son."

"And that is why she may not want you to go. Fighting just sixty miles from home is less dangerous than the Holy Land. Believe me, I know!"

I looked at the other three. Matthew, my son's squire, grinned, "I think I speak for all of us when I say that the chance to go to the Holy Land on Crusade and have all of our sins forgiven is a price worth paying. We would go and I believe we will be the envy of all of the squires and pages who stay at home. As for Sam, my lord, if he comes then we will watch over him."

"And while that is noble of you it is not me you have to convince but the Lady Matilda. We will leave that for now. We have much to do and very little time to do it. The journey through France will be hard enough but we will go from the cold of England to the heat of Palestine. It will be hard on the horses. I intend to buy horses for us to take. We have to take servants and they will be those who choose to go on crusade. This is not like the wars we have fought in England. We will be away for, probably, more than a year. Think about that!"

They were young and they thought not about such matters. To them, it was an adventure and I remembered what I had learned when I had gone with my father. I, too, had not foreseen the dangers and I was the only one who could tell them the truth. No matter what I said they would assume I was exaggerating.

William smiled, "I know how they feel. As much as I wish to stay with my wife and son this is an opportunity I know comes but once in a lifetime. To take the cross, the Pope has decreed, guarantees a place in heaven. It is not as though we have to capture Jerusalem. It is in our hands already. We just need to hold on to it! I doubt that we will even need to draw our swords."

I sighed at his naiveté. "Son, I doubt not the hearts and arms of knights, men at arms and archers who will fight, but it is the leaders I fear. Each will have their own plans and they are all self-serving. King Richard fought with his fellow kings as much as Saladin and one of his allies imprisoned him. That cost England dear! Do not expect nobility, honour or glory. They will not be there. We do our duty and, as soon as we can, we return home."

I was prepared for the squall which would hit me in Stockton but not the full-blown gale. "You cannot be serious husband! Has King Henry lost his mind? Sending an old fool and a boy to do that which is the work of an army! Does he not know that you have earned your place in heaven twice over while he squats like a toad in London!"

I smiled but shook my head at the same time, "Peace, wife. I trust all of our people but if such a tirade should reach the ears of King Henry then things might go ill!"

"I care not! His father was a fool and an evil fool at that. His son is merely incompetent and after what this family has sacrificed for the crown! It is too bad! You shall not go!"

I held her hands in mine, "We can rant and we can rave. We can complain but it will do no good for we are ordered to go by the King. William and I were commanded directly by the King. For the rest, I leave it to them. I care not if William and I go alone; we will have fulfilled our obligations but we two have to leave or we risk losing all." I waved my hand around the hall. "Remember when we came back? We had nothing. You are right we have earned the stones, walls and towers which guard us but they can be taken away on the whim of a King. The Great Charter means nothing to King Henry. It will take another king, as yet unborn, to do anything about the injustices which remain. It will avail us nought to complain. Now let us make the best of what is, you are right, a bad job. I will see my men and ask them who wishes to accompany me. William's can stay at Elsdon. Alan of Bellingham will have need of them. Lady Mary and young Richard can stay here with you. So long as my family is safe then I am a happy man."

She suddenly burst into tears and threw her arms around me. "You are the best of men! I shout, not at you, but the King! All you have ever thought of is your family, your people and your country!" She nodded, "You are right and we should bear our tribulations with nobility but I know one thing, Henry of Winchester will never go to heaven!"

I spoke with Ridley the Giant, Henry Youngblood and David of Wales before I spoke with my men. I told them of my obligations and pre-empted what I knew was coming, "I will not take you for you are fathers and grandfathers. Besides which, I need you to watch over my family."

Henry said, "Lord, we should come. We are the last two of the men you brought from the Holy Land. We were young men then, as were you."

David nodded, "Aye, lord, if you return then we should too."

I could tell, from their voices and faces, that they did not relish the journey and that they hoped I would change my mind. They were not knights and did not understand my obligations. I said, "I take no man with children or a wife! And you two are grandfathers. I am the leader of this conroi and I have to go. I only take those without obligations and ties to others. Ask our men who wish to come with us. That is if any wish to travel across a continent and endure the heat and arid land that is Palestine!"

They both laughed and Ridley said, "It will be harder to persuade them not to come. Perhaps you are right, my lord. You would have me buy horses?"

I nodded, "You and Alan would be best. He knows horses and you know their purpose. Middleham now has some horse breeders who seem to know their business and it is not far. William and I will need three each. Worry not about the cost for the money for them will come from the King, eventually!"

Ridley the Giant nodded, "When I have spoken with our men, I will ride. I think you are correct to leave your better horses at home, none are young and that is what you need, strong horses which are young and can adapt to the climes."

I left my two captains to speak with the men and then went to Alan Horse Master. "I would have you go with Ridley to Middleham. We need many horses." I handed him a leather pouch filled with coins. We were not poor and I knew we would be recompensed by the King. It was, after all, not his money he was spending; it was the churches!

I went, after speaking with Alan, to my church. I needed to pray to the Warlord whose body was buried there. Many people would have regarded it as sacrilegious but I was praying to God and using my great-grandsire to pass my message on. It gave me comfort knowing that all of my family was buried here, all save my father. He lay in the land to which I would be travelling. That was one positive to take from this ill-considered venture. When I came out, I saw Matilda, my daughter-in-law, and Henry Samuel waiting for me. Matilda had been crying and Henry Samuel had his arm around her.

"What is this, Matilda? Tears? I told Henry Samuel that he would not be travelling with me. Your son is safe."

She shook her head and, when she spoke, her voice was on the edge of breaking with emotion, "No, my lord, it is not right that my maternal instincts should stand in his way. We both know that Alfred would have taken him to war. It was his way and he is his father's son." She smiled and kissed her son on the cheek. "He is the image of his father." Turning to me she said, "All that I ask is that you try to keep him safe. I know that you will do your best and I know that war is a fickle mistress. I will pray for him each night." Curtsying to me she kissed the back of my hand and then went inside my church. She would speak with her dead husband, my son.

I turned to Henry Samuel who had disobeyed me a little. I had not wanted to take him but he had persuaded his mother, "Sam, your mother needs you."

He forced himself upright, "Grandfather, it is a hard choice I have made but I have to have faith that I am a worthy warrior and can come through the trials and tribulations of a crusade. More, my uncle will need me at his side to help to protect you. Family will be more important than you can know. It was you who almost saved your father, my namesake. If I can save your life then it will be worth the hurt I have caused my mother. Whatever you say, I am going."

The meal that night was a quiet one. We were all behaving as though we were walking on a sea of eggs. For my own part, I was taking in my children, their spouses and their children. Who knew when we would see our families again?

Chapter 2

Of course, it was inevitable that my knights and the lords of my manors would hear of the crusade. It was not from my lips but the whole of my valley knew whither I was bound. They came to offer to travel with me. Even Sir Edward who had been wounded and now would war no more offered his services. When he spoke with me, I saw death in his eyes. His son and a future knight, Henry, confided in me that he had the coughing sickness. "I fear, Sir Thomas, that when you return my father will be with God."

"Thank you for telling me. I will speak privately with him before I leave."

This was the saddest of ends for any warrior. Edward had been at my side since I had returned from the Holy Land and was as dear to me as any of my children. I was touched by the affection I saw from all of my men. I was a lucky man to have such loyalty. I would not have had to order any man to go on crusade. I could have asked while King Henry had to order and that was one of the many differences between us. I made certain that, despite all of my preparations, I spoke to all of them and especially Edward as I was not certain that I would be returning.

The preparations should have taken weeks but we had only days. The sheer number of men who wished to come with us also made it difficult as I had to tell most of those who offered their services that they had to stay at home and, in the end, I chose just two captains, seven men at arms and seven archers. Along with three servants, they were my whole retinue. There was logic to my choices. We were going as a token and a symbol of England. To that end, we did not need large numbers. In addition, we would have knights sent by King Henry. They would have men with them. I needed a conroi which I could manage. We would be part of a greater whole. The final factor was that they had to be single. That meant that they were, generally, my younger warriors. There were three exceptions. Padraig the Wanderer, Richard Red Leg and Cedric Warbow chose to come. All were either unmarried or their wives and, in Cedric's case, children had died. I was grateful for the three of them. The grey hairs they shared were a measure of their skill. They had forgotten more than most of my young men knew. Cedric and Padraig would be my captains.

I worried about our armour. When I had been in the Holy Land last, we had all worn mail hauberks. Now some knights wore plates to protect their knees. I knew the heat and, as plate would make our armour even heavier, we took just mail. The surcoats we had would be too heavy and thick but we had no choice for there was no time to have new ones made. I would have to hope that we could have thinner ones made once we reached Italy or Palestine. I sat with William, our squires and pages and my three senior men in my Great Hall. It was there I explained what we would take and our route.

"We have to visit with the Pope. It would be quicker to join the muster at Marseille which is where the King of Navarre is gathering his men but the King's command means that we will have a longer land journey. We will have to join with those who leave from the southern part of Italy. The only advantage we have is that is a shorter voyage. The further one sails in the Blue Sea the more chance there is of meeting pirates!" I saw the pages' eyes widen. "The crusade will begin in Acre. With luck it will not involve fighting but, if we have to fight, then I will be under the orders of the King of Navarre. To that end, Cedric, you will command any English archers and, Padraig, any English men at arms. I know not which knights have been secured for us but when we meet, they shall know that I command them. I have no time for politics. Richard Red Leg, you know horses. I wish you to keep a close watch on our mounts, especially in Palestine. If we are afoot then we will die."

It was the first time I had mentioned the possibility of death and I saw John and Henry Samuel look at each other. My squire, Mark, asked, "But if we do not fight then…"

I laughed, "The enemies who are Muslim are not our only foes. There are bandits and sub-sects who wish us harm. This is not the army which was led by Saladin. There are factions and rebels. It is why we still hold Jerusalem and the Holy Orders are not always on the side of crusaders." I said no more on the matter but it had been Templars who had almost done for me when I had been a young knight abandoned by King Richard.

All too soon it was time to leave. The day before we left, I visited with Edward. His son had no reason to lie to me and I knew that I would never see Edward again. There had to be a parting which would satisfy us both. We had stood in battle side by side and back to back. We had held each other's lives in our hands and so there had to be honesty.

"Farewell, old friend."

"Farewell, my lord, but I wish it was not so. I would rather die in battle than this way, piece by piece; coughing up blood and pissing my breeks."

I nodded, "You know then?"

"They try to keep it from me but Father John is an honest man and I know. Take me with you, lord, and let me die with a sword in my hand."

"If there were just the two of us then I would say, aye but I have my son and grandson. I lead men for King Henry. We both know that battle finds any weakness in a man and you would not wish another to die trying to save you."

He nodded; resignation on his face for he was an honest man and knew I spoke the truth, "Then I ask you to pray for me at the place they crucified our lord."

"Know that I will and when I see the Pope, I will ask him to intercede for you."

He smiled and said, "You are a good man, lord. Do not throw your life away for Lackland's son. He is not worth it! This valley needs you and your son."

"I intend to do all that I can to return but if God chooses to take me and William then I have left two other sons, and the knights of my valley, Sir Peter, Sir William of Hartburn, Sir Geoffrey Fitzurse, Sir Robert of Redmarshal, Sir Gilles of Wulfestun, Sir Richard of East Harlsey and Sir Fótr of Norton, will all watch out for them. We trained them, did we not?"

"Aye lord, we did and they are all good men."

We clasped arms before I left. We were warriors and there were words in our eyes and our hands as we parted. I would pray that he had a peaceful end.

We rose in the early hours for I wished to be on the road before dawn. The grandsons I left, Alfred and Thomas, were most upset that they were not joining Henry Samuel and my granddaughters were upset that we were going at all. It was hard leaving my home. Little Geoffrey was too young to complain but he was upset that his grandfather and uncle were leaving not to mention Henry Samuel who was everyone's favourite. My wife was stoic when we parted for we had said goodbye the night before. Then she had wept and we had told each other those things which are normally kept for a death bed. Strangely they made me feel better. We had been married for a long time and our feelings were kept hidden. That last night they were bared and we were both the better for it.

We crossed the river on our ferry and our long train with ten sumpters headed down the road to York. I intended to push on and reach it in one day. William and I had three good horses. We each had a couple of coursers and a good palfrey. The journey to York would allow us to get to know them. We had spare horses for the others but they would have a long sea voyage to Calais to help them to recover. I had no doubt that we would end up buying more horses along the way. We kept the same formation all the way to York and I intended it to be the same all the way to the Italian port. Cedric had four archers before us as scouts. The others were with the baggage. William and I along with the squires followed the scouts and Padraig and the men at arms followed behind me, Richard and two of the men at arms were at the rear. Our experience stiffened the column and the three veterans would counsel and advise the youngsters. They would return different men; if they returned at all.

It was late when we reached York and the knights promised by the King had yet to arrive. In some ways that pleased me for we had more time to rest our horses and to choose the best of the ships for our men. There were eight ships waiting for us and, as I had expected, all belonged to the King. It was not a navy; it was a way to make money. I guessed that I would have the largest entourage and so I commandeered the largest two. I was lucky in that the two captains looked to be the most trustworthy and the most experienced. Captain Jack and *'Petrel'* looked to be both veterans of the sea. A good captain would ensure that our animals arrived in port safely and in the best condition! While we were at the river, we purchased all that we might need for the journey. The closer one came to the Holy Land the higher would be the prices. Rope, leather, bits, bridles and stirrups were all purchased. Our archers had a good quantity of arrows as well as fletch, arrowheads and bowstrings. Alf Fletcher, one of the archers I had brought, was the son of a Fletcher and he could make arrows if they were needed. Each of my archers had a spare bow made of English yew for that wood was the best for bows.

Padraig and Richard Red Leg also advised the men to buy a good round of English cheese. I smiled when I heard them advising the younger men, "Foreign cheese is fit for pigs only! It stinks and is soft! A good, well-wrapped cheese will last three months or more. Trust us, you will get no decent cheese once we board the ships!"

They thought I could not hear them for Alan son of Paul said, "But I thought that lords and kings ate foreign cheese!"

Richard shook his head, "Aye they do! I think that must be penance. It is why I will never be knighted!" That made the other men laugh.

The knights promised by the King did not reach us for two days. It did not bother me that we were leaving later than the King wanted. They were his knights and the delay in our departure would be down to his choice of men. They arrived not long after noon which told me that they had spent the night within fifteen miles of York. It told me much about their character for they could have pushed on and reached us sooner had they been keen. They were accompanied by the younger brother of the Earl of Norfolk who was the King's representative. Hugh Bigod was a close friend of the King's. He was not even twenty and yet entrusted by the young King with the delivery of the knights.

He gave a bow and swept his arm behind him, "My lord, I bring the knights who will serve King Henry and yourself in this noble crusade." I saw that all of them, the seven knights, thirty-eight men at arms and twenty archers all wore a white tunic with the distinctive cross of Jerusalem upon it. Perhaps they thought I would be impressed by such attire. There were also three young priests. I hoped they knew how to heal! I frowned at the young nobleman. "They are late! Were they waiting for their fine surcoats to be finished?"

I saw the faces of the seven knights fall at my disapproving tone. They were slightly older than William and he was young for a knight.

"The King wished them all to look the same. He has fifty surcoats on the sumpters for your men, too."

I waved a dismissive hand. Such frippery was unnecessary. My men would ride to war wearing the family surcoat. "And has he sent the coin which we will need?"

"The King said that the Archbishop of York has the monies collected in the north and that he is to use that to pay your expenses."

The King and the Archbishop of York would have ensured that they made a profit from the monies collected in the south. Between them and the Chancellor, they knew how to extract every coin that they could. The people of England had paid the crusade tax for the last four years and now the King could, legitimately, tell them that it had been used to send English knights on crusade. Perhaps there was too much of the cynic in me.

"Very well and will you be coming with us, Master Hugh?"

He looked embarrassed as he replied, "As much as I would love to go to the Holy Land, I must wait until King Henry goes."

And that would be a long time coming!

I was introduced to the knights. All were English and all served one of the lords living in the south. None were from the same manor. Had the lords whom King Henry had approached sent me their poorest knights or were these genuine crusaders? Time alone would tell. Two were from the north, Sir Robert of Kendal and Sir Stephen of Malton. The latter might be known to Sir Ralph. The rest were from the south of the country. Sir Richard of Tewkesbury and his men might be of some use as they often had to fight the Welsh but all the rest came from such manors as Lewes, Norwich and Dunwich. At best they would have been to a tournament.

"Welcome, my lords. I am sorry to see that despite my request you have brought but twenty archers. I needed three times that number and so your archers will have to work three times as hard. The captain of archers is Cedric Warbow. The men at arms will be commanded by Padraig the Wanderer. There will be no argument about the command. Any archer and man at arms who objects should stay in York." I glared at the men at arms and archers daring them to object. "You are all late and this is our last night in port. We leave before dawn when the tide is high."

After they had gone Hugh asked me, "Why were you so hard on them, my lord? They go to do God's work and they serve the King!"

"And none of that matters on the battlefield. When these men fight, they will have to obey my orders instantly. They will need to heed my every command. If they do so then some may survive. They do not have to like me but they need to obey me."

"Then I am glad that I will not be with you."

I laughed, "Then we are in agreement over that!" I took his hands in mine and turned them over, "These hands are not calloused. You have not spent enough time with a sword in hand. If you wish to be a knight then work at it. Being a knight does not just mean wearing mail and a fine surcoat. It is having a weapon in your hand and knowing how to kill the enemy who seeks your life! When you can do that then return to me and I will tell you if you are ready to go on a crusade!"

I left a shocked young noble. I had been deliberately harsh with all of them. It was partly anger at the enforced delay but it was also to save their lives. The Archbishop had brought a chest with gold and silver. I thanked him for the chest, "Many people suffered to pay this tax, lord. Use it wisely."

"Have I ever done other?"

He smiled, "No, lord, your motives are beyond reproach. Go with God." He made the sign of the cross and gave me an inlaid wooden cross. I saw that the four ends were marked with Whitby jet. "This has been blessed too and may offer you some protection although the Muslims treat Christians harshly."

"They learned from us, Archbishop, but I thank you for this gift."

Sir Ralph was waiting for me at the gate, "A word?"

"William, take the horses to the ships and begin loading."

My son waved cheerily, "Aye, father. Farewell, Sir Ralph!"

"You take care, young William!" When we were alone, he said, "I had some unwelcome news from the knights who came from the south."

I frowned. If the news concerned me then why had I not been told directly rather than this second-hand method? Sir Ralph continued, "Malcolm, the Earl of Fife and your avowed enemy, is with the crusade. He took a ship from Southampton to sail directly for France and the muster."

"The Earl of Fife?"

"Aye, it seems he sees this as a way of garnering support when he tries to become King of Scotland. He has family who live in France; they are his allies and there has been communication between Scotland and France. The longer that the royal couple are childless the greater his chance of success. Everyone, it seems, considers this crusade has the greatest chance of success." He smiled at the scowl on my face, "Everyone it seems but you. By taking part he gains honour and support from the Pope. He boasted that he will be away for less than a year."

I nodded, "That is the same message given to me by King Henry but none of them has fought the Turk and the Egyptian. I have. None have experienced the treachery of the Templars, I have. For my part, I do all that I am asked but I will return home once Richard, Earl of Cornwall arrives with the main English contingent. Once I am sure that Jerusalem is secure then I will hurry back to England and my home. I will have a clear conscience."

"I thought you should know."

I smiled, "And it is good news that you have brought me."

"Good news?"

"Aye, for if the Scottish snake is in the Holy Land trying to kill me then my family is safe!"

As we headed down the river, I told William the news. "Can he hurt us? We are on a crusade and protected by the Pope and the King of Navarre."

"He wished to have your bride and her fortune for himself. He will not be worried about the niceties of protocol and honour. He will not face us openly but we watch for the knife in the night. I will see Padraig and Richard Red Leg. They will ensure we are safe."

Even though we had left before dawn we had had a twisting and turning river network to negotiate and, by dark, we had barely cleared Whitby to the west. As soon as we hit the cold sea the winds made our movement more violent. My three veterans and I were the only ones immune from the mal de mer which afflicted everyone, to the great amusement of the crew. The green-faced warriors hurling the contents of their stomachs overboard brought them some satisfaction; I know not why. I looked astern at the other ships. The one which followed us, **'Stormbird'** contained half of my men and then the knights and their men were spread around the other ships. I knew it was a mistake not to have at least one of the knights on my ship, *'Petrel'*, but I was selfish. I wanted my family and my men around me. We would have a journey across France and Germany to get to know one another.

When darkness fell few of our men were ready for sleep; most were too busy vomiting and so the four of us with stronger stomachs had plenty of room to sleep. I always slept well at sea and the motion, extreme though it was, sent me into a deep and untroubled sleep. I awoke at dawn and stepped onto a deck which was littered with the bodies of my men. Their colour and appearance might lead one to believe we had been attacked but the Captain put me straight on that.

"When they emptied their stomachs for the last time they just collapsed and fell asleep. They will be fine now. We couldn't light the galley last night, my lord, so it will be cold fare but we have some fresh bread, Yorkshire ham and Wensleydale cheese."

I rubbed my hands, "Provender for a king." I looked astern and saw only *'Stormbird'*. "The other ships?"

"We lost them in the night. The wind has dropped and we are a little too far east for my liking but it is a good wind from the north. It might be a chill wind but it will take us where we need to go. I dare say the others will catch up but it doesn't really matter. We all know the destination, Calais. With this wind, we might be there by dawn tomorrow. Anyway, I will get your food sorted out. "Nob, food for his lordship."

"Aye, Captain!"

Cedric, Richard and Padraig woke and joined me in the lee of the bowsprit as the food and beer arrived. While we ate, I told them of the threat from the Earl of Fife. "I am not worried about Scots, my lord, but there are Italians and Frenchmen who are quite happy to slit a throat for the price of a bottle of wine. However, have no fear, we will keep them all away from you."

William rose. He had not been as ill as the others. He had at least one sea voyage under his belt but that had been a relatively calm one. "I am sorry about last night, my lord."

"You have it out of your system now but we appear to have lost our consorts. Not an auspicious start to our crusade." I lifted out the Archbishop's cross. "I am not certain that God smiles upon this venture."

They all made the sign of the cross. It did not do to be flippant.

We ate and we drank although, in William's case, it was less than we ate and, gradually, the men and our squires and pages rose, albeit unsteadily. They drank some beer but few could face food. We stood to allow them the benefit of the lee and I stared ahead, "I am glad that our mail is wrapped in sheepskins. This salt air would have Mark and Matthew scrubbing rust for a week."

Just then there was a call from the lookout who was perched precariously on the crosstrees of the mainmast. "Sail to the south and west. Five points off the starboard, Captain."

The Captain nodded and, cupping his hands, called to me, "It may well be one of the other ships."

I was looking astern and I saw, behind *'Stormbird'*, more sails to the north, "Captain, that may be the others astern!"

"You have good eyes, my lord, that is *'Swan'* you see."

The lookout shouted, "Captain it is three ships and two are attacking the other!" He paused, "The one under attack is the *'Maid of Staithes'*."

I hurried to the stern, "What does this mean, Captain?"

"The *'Maid'* is a small and lively little vessel. She could have been driven ahead of us. I will wager these are Frisian pirates. I hope the crew have their wits about them. Let fly the staysail. Let us see if *'Petrel'* can live up to her name!"

It was Stephen of Malton and Robert of Kendal who were aboard that vessel. As I recalled they had just fifteen men with them and their squires. The crew of our ship went to a locker and took out a piece of triangular canvas. They scurried up to the bowsprit and quickly attached it. One had to lean far over the bow and I was certain that he would fall but the crew knew their business and as soon as it was adjusted and the wind caught the extra sail, I felt the power as the ship seemed to fly over the water. Our consorts would join us but we were the only vessel which might frighten off the enemy.

"Cedric, get your bows. Padraig, have the men armed." Half of our men were on *'Stormbird'* along with most of our spare equipment. I had two squires, three pages, my son, three archers and three men at arms. It was hardly an army. They might have been seasick but the squires did not forget their duty and they fetched our swords and daggers from our chests.

"Will you need your helmet, Sir Thomas?"

"No, Mark. I need to be able to see well!"

With the sword on my belt, I went to the bow. The lookout had been a little premature. The two pirates had closed with the *'Maid of Staithes'* but not yet boarded her. The captain of the *'Maid'* was using every trick he knew to avoid them grappling him. Perhaps one of his lookouts had seen us. We were certainly closing so fast that I hoped we might be in time.

"Cedric, we have but three archers, use your arrows well. When you are able, try to get the man on the helm."

"Yes, my lord."

I saw that the two ships which had attacked *'Maid of Staithes'* were lower in the water than our ships and had oars. The Frisians were still wild people. The King of Denmark and the Count of Flanders were the two rulers who were supposed to control them but there were so many small islands and inlets in their land that the pirates who lived there were still able to act as their forebears had. It was in their blood. We were now less than two hundred paces from them and the two pirates had finally clattered into the side of the ship whose wily captain had done all that he could to buy time by tacking, turning and using the wind.

I saw that my bowmen had their arrows already nocked. "Cedric, does the wind help us?"

"Aye, we are just within range, lord. Should we try?"

"It might discomfit them!"

He nodded and turned to his men, "Draw!"

The three bows creaked as the archers drew the strings on their yew bows back.

"Release!"

The three arrows soared and the time between my command and the arrows being released had seen us draw twenty paces closer. Of the three arrows, two found flesh and one of the two sent a Frisian over the side. Faces turned to view the threat and in that turning helped Cedric and my archers to target more flesh. This time three men were hit, including the steersman who clutched his shoulder.

We had closed to within a hundred paces and the Captain shouted, "Take in the staysail and shorten sail. Sir Thomas, we will be alongside before you know it."

I turned to my men at arms. "Padraig, Richard, Rafe, we, with William will board the other vessel and clear the stern. Mark, you and your brother will stay here with the pages and defend our stern. Cedric, watch our backs!" Henry Samuel had their shields, swords and helmets. This was not the action I had expected from them. Mark and Matthew flanked them. The twins would look after the pages if they could.

"Aye, lord."

I saw that there were two seamen with grappling hooks waiting to secure us to the Frisian. I drew my sword and climbed up onto the gunwale while holding on to the forestay. I smiled to myself. I was getting too old to be leaping across a dark and chilly sea. The change of sail had slowed us and our frenetic ride became easier. Cedric's arrows concentrated the Frisians' attention on their stern and the pressure on the *'Maid of Staithes'* had lessened. More, they had not noticed the five of us standing on the side. As soon as we touched, I leapt down to the Frisian deck for the pirate had a lower side than our cog. I landed softly on the body of a man slain by an arrow. As much as I wanted to go to the aid of the beleaguered knights, we needed control of the vessel first.

I ran to the stern and saw that there were just two men left alive. Both were sailors and, as I approached, they leapt into the sea. There was a boarding axe by the body of the wounded helmsman. I picked it up and hacked through the rope which fed the steering board. I had disabled the ship. The wounded Frisian helmsman looked up and spat at me. I did not know if he understood English but I said, before I turned, "I give you your life! Be grateful!" Before I turned, I saw that *'Stormbird'* had closed rapidly and was about to attack the other pirate which was attacking the other side of the *'Maid'*.

I ran to follow William and my men at arms as they raced to charge into the men trying to clamber up the side of the *'Maid'*. There were more than twenty pirates. The men on the cog had done all that they could to deter the enemy. I saw that they had poured pig fat over the side to make it slippery and harder for the pirates to climb. The first five pirates died without knowing that their vessel had been boarded. We were ruthless. I swung my sword sideways into the back of the huge Frisian with a pot helmet and a double-handed axe. If I had been facing him, he would have been fearsome but with just an old byrnie my sword hacked through the ancient links, into his side to rip through to his vital organs and almost slice him in two. Tearing my sword free, I raised it again to hack into the head and spine of the next Frisian who had thrown a grappling hook towards the gunwale of the *'Maid'* and was trying to climb up the side. His scream was like that of a vixen in the night and rose above the cacophony of battle. It made the other Frisians turn. Cedric and our archers had moved closer and even as the pirates turned more were slain. The others raised their arms in surrender. There were just nine survivors.

I looked up at the side and saw Sir Stephen. "This vessel is ours and *'Stormbird'* will board the other pirate soon. Be of good heart."

He waved, "I will, Sir Thomas, and I thank you!"

I turned to my men. "Throw the weapons, mail and helmets overboard!"

"Aye, lord."

"Cedric, cover them."

"Any of them moves an eyelash they will die, lord!"

Captain Jack shouted, "They are pirates, lord! Hang 'em all!"

Baron's Crusade

I shook my head, "We go on Holy Crusade and these, for all their evil, are Christians. I would not begin our venture killing those who have surrendered. We have disabled their ships and will take all that is of value. They will be warier in future of attacking English ships."

Attacked on two sides the other pirate surrendered too. With her steering board disabled and what little treasure they had taken, we left them for the rest of our ships had arrived. After commanding all the other captains to sail closer to us we left the two rudderless pirates to drift. They would be able to repair their vessels but it would be a long time before they would go a-viking again!

Chapter 3

We reached Calais not long after dawn the next day. I feared for the men at arms and archers who had been on *'Maid'* but, as we watched them lead their horses down to the quay, I saw that although some were wounded, all had survived; that was thanks to the skill of Captain Jack and the other captains. William and I went directly to speak to the two knights. Their squires had also suffered wounds and one had his head heavily bandaged.

Sir Stephen and Sir Robert both took a knee. Sir Stephen spoke, "My lord, we both owe you a life. The Sherriff of York was correct; you are the greatest knight of your age. You attacked ten times your number with just four men." He rose and shook his head, "I had thought we were dead until then."

"Yet you fought on. Perhaps this trial was sent to us to show your mettle. Your men fought well as their wounds show. We have many months of travel and that will also set us challenges and problems which we can solve." They both nodded, "Have your men walk their horses while the ships are unloaded. The voyage was not long but they will need to become accustomed to the land again."

Our early landing meant that we were able to leave the English enclave before noon. Calais and the land around it were still English. This was an English town. The documents from the King and the seal of Simon de Montfort were the assurance of safety, as were the white surcoats with the cross of Jerusalem worn by the knights of King Henry. All but my men wore them. My fear was not the Normans nor the Flemish but assassins sent by the Earl of Fife. To that end Padraig had one of his men at arms sleep behind our door when we had lodgings.

Montfort was a four-day ride across Flanders and we had to stay in four towns on the way. We did not manage to all stay in one place except for the two monasteries we found. Abbeys, monasteries and nunneries were obliged to accommodate pilgrims and crusaders. I knew we would be safe from the Earl of Fife in such religious establishments for even an evil man like the Earl feared for his soul.

When we reached it, I saw that Montfort itself was a powerful-looking castle. It had been built by Duke Robert of Normandy and dominated the landscape. We had been spied from afar. The white surcoats of the knights and their men at arms would have told those within the castle that our intentions were peaceful. A steward greeted me and the letter from Simon de Montfort gained me entry to the Great Hall. My son had more about him than the other knights and it was he who found accommodation for our men; the castle would be full for Amaury de Montfort had plans. I just took Henry Samuel with me and the letters.

Amaury de Montfort was younger than I was but not by much. He had chosen France over England and, when he spoke, it was in French. I did not mind. I was more comfortable with English or Norman French but I could manage. He was a hospitable man and wine was brought for both myself and my page. I knew that my grandson would not abuse the privilege. When he had finished reading the letter he nodded as he folded it.

"This is a happy meeting, my lord, and that is not something I expected to say to the knight who has been the bane of my people for so many years." I smiled. It did not require a reply. "I am heading to Marseille to join the King of Navarre on Holy Crusade. We will be fighting together perhaps?" He pointed to the standard which was prominently displayed. It was the fleur de lyse; the royal standard. "King Louis has asked me to carry the standard for France. Some of your men wear the cross of Jerusalem; does that mean they, too, are heading for the Crusade?"

"Yes, Lord de Montfort, as am I. The visit to Rome is but a stop along the journey."

"Then you will be joining with the German contingent which is departing from Emperor Frederick's ports in southern Italy?"

"That is my intention."

"I fear the detour will mean that you have a long journey ahead of you. It will take at least fifty days to reach Rome and then a further five to reach Taranto. The King and my brother have inconvenienced you."

"It is my duty and it will help my young knights to prepare for what lies ahead. Have you been on a crusade, my lord?"

"I was with my father on the crusade against the Cathars; he perished there and so I know the dangers although I know that the Holy Land will bring different dangers." He smiled, "We will leave in a few days' time and we can travel together. I hope you will be comfortable until then."

Shaking my head, I said, "We will leave tomorrow for King Henry is anxious for me to speak with the Pope sooner rather than later."

I do not think that the Norman was happy about my decision but he offered me a conroi of knights to escort us as far as Lyon. He also gave me a squire and a page who would return to England with the Pope's answer for his brother. Henri and Jean proved to be of great use to us on the journey for they knew the land of Swabia. The conroi of knights would wait for their lord at Lyon and we would take the road through

Swabia towards Italy and Rome. Amaury de Montfort was, however, a generous host, and my knights and I were invited to a feast before we left. It proved useful for as our squires and pages served us, they picked up nuggets of information from the other squires. There was a good chance that we would be fighting alongside the Lord de Montfort and it always helped to know something of the character of one's companions.

As we left, early the next morning, Lord de Montfort promised to tell King Thibaut that we would be joining him. I needed the King of Navarre to know that King Henry had heeded the Pope's summons. To me, it did not matter but King Henry was trying to tell the world that he supported the Crusade, even if he would not physically join it and even though he had sent the smallest conroi that he could. He was using my name to make up for the paucity of numbers. The presence of Norman knights, the knights of the man who would carry the French banner in the Holy Land, ensured that our journey to Lyon was comfortable with accommodation in castles, monasteries and abbeys. When we left them after Lyon, I knew that we would have the hardest part of our journey ahead. We were lucky that it was summer and there was little snow in the high passes over the Alps. I had been told that the Carthaginians had climbed them in winter! It was a hard six weeks before we descended into the plains of Italy and we could move more easily and quickly along the coastal road. The obstacle which was then in our way was the heat. In many ways, it was good as it helped to prepare us for the even hotter clime of Palestine! Yet it slowed us down more than I would have liked.

The arduous crossing of the Alps had done one thing, it had shown me the character of the knights I would lead. Stephen and Robert were the only ones who bore the hard climb stoically. The others moaned and complained at every obstacle, rockfall, cold wind and hard lodgings. Their men did not and that heartened me. Our squires and pages had already told me that Amaury de Montfort was a rash and reckless knight and I learned, as we crossed the Alps, that at least four of the knights I would lead had a similar disposition.

William had grown during the march. He was able to help me by speaking with the knights and explaining warfare and the way I expected it to be fought. None had fought in a war of any kind. William was a veteran by comparison. There were just the four stubborn knights who refused to believe all that my son said. They were misguided enough to believe that a noble charge, boot to boot, by English knights would drive an enemy before them. They did not listen to my son as he told them how good the Turkish archers would be. He had no experience himself but I had and he knew the efficacy of arrows. I just hoped that our crusade would be a relatively peaceful one and that we would not be called upon to fight a battle; if we were then I would not return to England with all of King Henry's knights. We halted a day short of Rome and we were in papal lands. As crusaders, we were greeted and treated well. I spoke with the abbot of the monastery in which we stayed the night before we reached the Holy City. As it turned out he had been born an Englishman but as he chose a priestly career Brother Adrian became the Abbot of this small monastery. I learned much as we dined. It was frugal fare which my new knights found beneath them but I knew we would have far worse in the future.

As we were both English he confided in me, "The Pope and the Emperor Frederick are at loggerheads. There was a war and now there is a truce but His Holiness cannot forgive the Emperor for failing to heed his call to crusade."

I nodded, "And this may well cause problems for me and my men as we travel through Imperial Italy!"

He nodded, "There is hope that there may be German lords who are travelling south and you might be able to accompany them."

I also learned of the enmity between the Pope and the rebels who were making life difficult for the Eastern Emperor, John Doukas Vatatzes. The Pope, it seemed, wished crusaders to go to the aid of that Emperor. It was useful information and helped to prepare me for the papal audience.

I was astounded by the home of the Pope. It seemed to me to be both a palace and a fortress. It was fit for an Emperor and that told me much about the papacy. It was as political an organization as any country and the papal army was armed and mailed much as the knights I had with me. We were closely scrutinised on our approach for, despite the cross of Jerusalem, we were strangers and Emperor Frederick had used subterfuge to attack before now. I had sent William ahead with Matthew to alert the Pope of our imminent arrival as I knew there was a protocol to such meetings. My foresight helped us for William and I were admitted within just an hour of my arrival. It would not be a private meeting; I had not expected one. It was, however, smaller than I might have envisioned. There were just six men in the room.

One was an English cardinal, Robert Somercotes, and, so it was rumoured, he was a possible future pope. I noticed that he studied me closely. The Pope was a well-educated man and I daresay he spoke English but he used French. It was one language which all in the room could speak and put all of us on an equal footing.

The Pope waved for me to approach his throne, which was the largest I had ever seen. I bowed and kissed the ring on his right hand. William had the two documents we were to deliver. "So, my son, what brings you all the way from England to the home of the Church?"

"Two reasons, Your Holiness, one is to deliver this missive from King Henry of England." William stepped forward and handed it to the pontiff. I saw him examine the seal closely to ensure that it had not been broken. When he was satisfied, he took out an ornate stiletto and sliced it open. He read it twice and then nodded. He handed it to Robert Somercotes who examined it in detail.

"The King of England has sent an army, Sir Thomas?"

I knew this was a trap and I had to answer diplomatically. "No, Your Holiness, there will be more barons who will be coming but the King has sent us as an assurance of his commitment. More men will be leaving England next year for that is the year you wish the crusade to begin."

"And by the time they reach the Holy Land, they will arrive late." He smiled. "I am not criticising you, Sir Thomas. That you have raced to get here shows great zeal and, I believe, this will be your third crusade?"

Robert Somercotes hurried over and whispered in his ear. I saw the Pope frown. "I understand that one crusade does not count as it was atonement for the murder of a Bishop."

I glanced at the English Cardinal. He had played his cards early. He was no friend of mine. Was he an enemy to the King? "And I was given absolution by Bishop Albert."

"Nonetheless, I command that you seek absolution at the Church of the Holy Sepulchre where you shall spend a night in vigil." I nodded. I would pay twice for an act I would repeat in a heartbeat. "And when this crusade has achieved its end will you take part in the crusade against the enemies of the Eastern Empire?"

"If my King commands me then I will do so."

"But not if the Pope commands?" I did not answer what I believed to be a rhetorical question. "That bridge will be crossed later. And you said there was another matter which required my attention?"

William stepped forward and handed the letter from Simon de Montfort. This time, when he read it, he frowned and turned to his English Cardinal. "Here we have another Englishman who seeks to flaunt God's laws."

It would have been disingenuous of me to point out that de Montfort was a Frenchman.

"I cannot decide such a matter now. I will send an answer when time permits."

Baron's Crusade

I nodded, "There are two of Lord de Montfort's men who will take your answer, Your Holiness, for I am anxious to get to Taranto and take ship for the Holy Land."

He smiled, "I see hope in you, Sir Thomas, despite what must have been a black heart when you were young. It is fortunate that there is another contingent of knights and they will be leaving tomorrow. It is a company of Teutonic knights and they are led by Burchard von Bouland. You should get on for he has just come from the Baltic. You may use the ships which were prepared for the men of the Empire." He scowled, "Once again the Emperor Frederick has let us down."

"There was another matter, Your Holiness, of a more personal nature."

"I am intrigued. Speak."

One of my knights, Edward of Wulfestun, is dying. He has the coughing sickness. He came on the Baltic Crusade with me and I would ask for you to intercede for him. He is a good man and deserves to go to heaven."

The Pope smiled, "I thought you would ask for something for yourself. That you ask for another speaks well of you. I will pray for him."

With that, we were dismissed. I did not get the opportunity to speak to the English Cardinal so I did not know why he took it upon himself to bring up the Bishop of Durham's murder but he must have made enemies in Rome for he was murdered by poison within three years. We were told we could use the lodgings of the Teutonic Knights. I did not expect to know any of the knights with whom we would ride for it had been a lifetime, over thirty years, since I had fought alongside the Sword Brethren.

Rome was the largest place we had seen since York and once my audience was over, we spent the afternoon making purchases. A port of embarkation would charge the earth for basic necessities. I allowed William to make my purchases while I sought out the commander of the Teutonic Knights and the Sergeant with whom we would be travelling. They had a hospital in Rome and they were there. I was not sure how I would be greeted. The military orders of knights tended to look down their noses at mere knights. The one exception had been a Knight Hospitaller I had met when I was a young knight but the Templars I had known had been arrogant to a man!

In the event, I was pleasantly surprised. There must have been an effective network of spies and messengers controlled by the Church for I was expected and more, I was welcomed. I had Mark and Henry

Samuel with me and they, too, were given a warm and fulsome welcome. I soon discovered why.

"You are most welcome, Englishman, for we have heard your name before. We fought with the grandson of Jarl Birger Brosa and we were regaled with stories of your heroism, not only in the Baltic Crusade but in the Holy Land. Three Crusades," the Commander shook his head, "I feel humbled. Had you chosen a military order you would surely have been grandmaster by now!"

"Thank you, Commander Burchard von Bouland, you flatter me. I was a sword for hire and it proved convenient to fight the enemies of the church."

"And now you fight on behalf of your King." He noticed my squire and page. "I see a resemblance between you and this young page."

"It is my grandson, Henry Samuel."

"Have your men fetched here for there is room enough. We have had it expanded recently for more of our brethren will be making the journey from the Baltic. We will go to fight the heathen in the Holy Land."

I sent Mark to fetch the rest of the men and our knights. The ones who were with William would find us when they had finished in the markets while the rest waited at St Peter's Basilica.

As he led me to an inner courtyard filled with olive and lemon trees, he shook his head, "After joining the order I have one regret and that is I did not father children."

He gestured for us to sit and we were brought iced wine. "And were you always a Teutonic Knight?"

"No, I was a Sword Brethren. This garb takes some getting used to but I still serve God and use my sword to smite his enemies and to kill heathens."

As with most military orders, the commander was zealous. "So, we have ships to take us to Acre?"

"We do, for my order has barracks in the castle and a Hochmeister, Herman von Salza. He is a very experienced warrior. All of the orders are sending reinforcements to join this crusade. This is a momentous time. We hold Jerusalem and our enemies are divided. If King Thibaut is a good leader then we can reverse the losses of the past forty years. We have now built a huge castle, Starkenberg, in French you call it Montfort. It is my new home for I am appointed castellan!" I smiled, "You are amused at such a thought?"

"No, Sir Burchard, it is just that we travelled from Montfort Castle in Normandy and I travelled with some Montfortian knights. I was amused by the coincidence. You should know, coming from the Baltic, of the heathen idea of the three sisters who spin." He nodded. "This seems to me to be just such an example."

He laughed, "Englishman, I can see that we are going to get on. You are honest and have a wit which is lacking in most of my companions!"

The hospitality of the military order was all that I had hoped and we left, as dawn was breaking, for what promised to be a long and arduous journey. In truth, despite the heat, it was a most pleasant ride along the spine of Italy. We quickly learned that riding in the early hours and resting for four hours in the middle of the day meant we travelled further and hurt the animals we rode, less. I had forgotten such tricks. When we came to Palestine those tricks might save lives. Burchard and I were older than the rest and, for some reason, did not need as much sleep. We spoke of Sweden and Lithuania for I had enjoyed my time there and, like Ridley the Giant, it was where I had met my wife. Fótr, who was now one of my nights, had left it to follow me. Our lives were different for Burchard had no family and had dedicated his life to the Sword Brethren and now the Teutonic Knights and yet we had so many similar experiences that we could have been brothers separated at birth. We had both known evil leaders who had led the order and, in my case, a country, down a disastrous path. We had both lost friends in battle. I knew that, even though he would be far from my conroi in the Holy Land, at Montfort, I had a friend there and that gave me comfort.

He also had with him some most interesting warriors. One of them, Conrad von Schweistein, had been a doctor. Sir Burchard told me that he was a gifted surgeon and had operated upon the skulls of men hurt in battle. Surgeons could earn a fortune and I wondered why he had chosen this life.

Burchard said, "Ask him."

The warrior, who looked younger than he ought for one with such a reputation, was happy to answer. "My family was slaughtered by the heathens when my town was raided. I was at the court of the Emperor Frederick earning a fortune as a doctor when that happened and I realised that all of my money meant nothing. I was tending to warts, carbuncles and hangnails when there were men dying fighting for Our Lord. I decided to dedicate my life to God. I can wield a sword as well as most men and I can wield a scalpel better than any. I can heal and I can fight. My life is fulfilled." He was an inspiration and gave me hope that, this time, the Crusade might actually succeed.

When we reached Taranto, I was glad that the Pope had arranged our ships for there was a veritable maelstrom of men trying to take passage to Palestine. Ours were earmarked and we were fewer in number than the men promised by Emperor Frederick. We had plenty of room for our horses and I was able to spread my knights out amongst the ships. Only Robert and Stephen had bonded with William and me and I was disappointed in the attitude of the others. If they were a measure of the quality of King Henry's knights then England was in trouble.

William and I travelled together again and our fleet headed south and east through the Greek Islands and the blue Mediterranean. There were plenty of pirates in this sea but they would not risk taking on such heavily armed ships bearing the standards of the Teutonic Order. The Byzantine ships of Emperor John were a much easier target. We had a fast voyage, or so the captain assured us. Fourteen days was considered as fast as one could expect in summer. It was late summer but we had no storms and, the waters, compared with the sea off the east coast of England, were positively benign.

Acre was the strongest Crusader stronghold in the whole of Outremer. A narrow causeway and the sea protecting three sides meant it would be hard to take. Every inch of land was taken and that was its weakness. If it was besieged it would need to be supplied by sea for it to survive. All of the military orders had chapter houses in the citadel and that aided us for Sir Burchard arranged our accommodation. The King of Navarre had yet to arrive and the accommodation was relatively empty. Despite our longer route, we had beaten the main body of crusaders and that was crucial so we could acclimatise quicker. The second night saw my conroi, son and myself dining with the legendary Hochmeister, Herman von Salza. It was a sad meeting for the great man, and I could tell that he had done great things, was a shadow now of the man he had been. He had been the go-between who had facilitated communications between the Pope and the Emperor Frederick. The situation was now so bad that the Hochmeister was returning to Italy to attempt to heal the rifts between the two men. I know that he hoped to rekindle the alliance but his eyes told me that he was going there to die. I never saw him again for he left on the ships which had brought us, but it encapsulated the situation in the Holy Land. If the Christian world had really decided to take the land, they could have done so but too many of the leaders had their own plans and ideas.

He was a mine of information and told us much that I either did not know or had forgotten.

"We are lucky at the moment, Sir Thomas. The sons and nephews of Saladin fight amongst themselves and seek power. The most powerful in the north is As-Salih Ismail, the Emir of Damascus. He is the oldest of the emirs and he is a good warrior. He is the one I fear the most. Then there is the one who, ostensibly, controls the lands of Egypt, Al-

Adil. Thankfully he is weak and corrupt. He is the nephew of Saladin and I think that he will soon lose what power he has for there is another there, As-Salih Ayyub, who will eventually wrest power from his cousin and then we will see which of the two powerful leaders survive."

I nodded and William said, "That does not sound so bad."

"Ah, but I did not mention the Assassins or the Hashashini as they are also known. They are a secret order who have strongholds in Syria and Persia. They are deadly killers who are hired out to kill other leaders. They charge a fortune for they always succeed. Even Saladin feared them and paid them not to kill him. If they are given your name then you are a dead man." He shook his head, "I remember a Frankish count who approached their stronghold in Syria. He spoke with their leader, the Old Man of the Mountains, and said that as he had more men than the assassins he would win. In answer, the Old Man of the Mountains ordered one of his men to throw themselves from the battlements to die on the rocks below. He obeyed and the Count withdrew. That is their power. I pray you never cross their path."

We left two days later so that I could fulfil the promise I had made to the Pope and beg forgiveness at the Church of the Holy Sepulchre. I would also pray there, as I promised, for Edward and his soul. For all, I knew he could already be dead. I had no desire to stay in Acre and Sir Burchard also wished to visit the holy city and its shrines before he returned to the northern outpost. It was a happy happenstance for it meant we could travel together.

We headed south down the narrow coastal strip. This part of the Holy Land was as busy and overcrowded as I remembered it. The fertile parts were so congested that people had to live cheek by jowl. Although the knights I had brought with me were impressed by the castle, as we headed east, towards Jerusalem, I saw disappointment creep across their faces. The disappointment was augmented by the reddening of their skin thanks to the sun. They rode with their coifs around their shoulders and soon paid the price. I had bought white hooded cloaks for my men and they were both cooler and protected us from the searing heat of the sun's rays. We travelled just twelve miles that first day for I wished our men to grow used to this land and its heat.

Sir Burchard smiled that night as we camped. The red-faced knights and their men at arms would suffer all night and for the next few days. "Your experience has helped your men." I nodded. He lowered his voice, "If you have to lead these knights in battle, Sir Thomas, I fear that more would die than live."

"And that is my fear too, Sir Burchard, for I am in unknown territory. I was chosen, I suspect, because of my prowess and skill in leading knights in battle but hitherto I have led my own knights, most of whom I have trained. I know that my knights and men at arms will obey my orders instantly and, more, I know what they will do when they fight. These knights and their men at arms are unknown to me. Perhaps we will not have to fight. There may be peace."

"And if that was likely my order would not have invested so much gold into my new home."

My son looked to the east, "The Ayyubid are close then?"

Sir Burchard nodded, "Before I left, I spoke with the Hochmeister. He gave me a much better picture of this land. The journey we are undertaking is one hundred and twenty miles from Acre to Jerusalem. That sounds like a great distance yet it is less than thirty miles east to the land ruled by the Ayyubid."

I saw some of my knights stare in horror and finger their weapons. William said, "Then we are in danger?"

"Your father would know better than I for I have never fought in this land."

I shook my head, "I remember a few words of the language and some of the terrain is familiar but all I know of the leaders of the Muslims is what the Hochmeister told us. What I would say is that we have one-third of our men watch each night for our horses are like treasure. When we stop for water then we have a local drink it first, for they would happily poison it to kill a Frankish knight." I stood and addressed all of my knights. "Tomorrow we rise three hours before the sun has risen and we stop two hours after it has begun to warm the land. When we camp and men sleep, then two knights and their men will stand watch. Tonight, it will be my son and me, tomorrow night it will be Sir Robert and Sir Stephen. I know that some of you will think such a duty is beneath you. It is not and it is my command!"

As we had more men than the others, I was able to let half of my men rest during the watch and I sent William to have an hour of sleep. He complained that I needed it but I did not. After he had gone to sleep, I spoke with Padraig and Richard who stood a watch with me. "I want you to watch this road carefully as we ride, for we will have to return this way and we will not have the luxury of a conroi of Teutonic Knights with us."

"Aye, lord, this is ambush country and no mistake. I like not riding at night but I see that it is necessary."

"That it is, Padraig, for to ride during the day for long periods would merely ensure that we walked having killed our horses."

Our second day took us closer to Ayyubid land and further from the safety of Acre. Our squires and pages were given the task of watching the horses. I rode my new palfrey, Willow, but I made certain that we walked almost as much as we rode. It was not easy in spurs but carrying a mailed knight in the heat of Palestine was not easy for any horse. I was tired when we made our second camp but there was still much I needed to know. I learned, from Sir Burchard, about the politics of the Muslims.

"Their leader is Saladin's nephew, al-Malik Al-Adil. He is the hope of all of us for he gave us Jerusalem and the lands to the east of the Jordan as a buffer against those of his own family who wish to usurp him. It is that fear which has allowed us to strengthen this land but if he should lose control then the floodgates would be opened. From what the Hochmeister told us then I think our allies' days are numbered. The Seljuks and the Khwarzamians are a threat to the Egyptian Ayyubid. The Khwarzamians lost their land to the Mongols and now seek land here in the west."

As we began our third hot ride, we learned that heat was not the only enemy. We were ambushed. When the arrows plucked our two scouts, men serving Sir Hubert of Lewes, from their saddles, we knew that peace was still an illusion this close to the border.

Baron's Crusade

Chapter 4

Our first losses were equally distributed between the Teutonic knights and my conroi. Two Teutonic sergeants fell. I could not worry about the Teutonic knights I had to get my own knights and men at arms in some sort of defensive position. We had had no time to practise and it had cost us.

"Archers dismount. Men at arms and knights, dismount and protect the archers! Shields!"

I pulled up my coif and donned my helmet before dismounting. I was gratified to see that my men at arms, archers, squires and pages obeyed instantly. A heartbeat later the men of Malton and Kendal did as ordered. Most of the other knights and men at arms made the mistake of delaying; they looked at each other; perhaps they thought their white surcoats with the cross of Jerusalem would save them. Sir Hubert of Lewes was even worse for he reacted to the death of his men. Raising his lance, he shouted, "Charge!"

I knew not who he would be charging for there were few targets to be seen, all that we saw were the arrows as they soared from behind rocks, scrubby trees and bushes. The enemy arrows continued to rain down upon us. These were not bodkins but they were accurately released and if they struck flesh, either man or horse, then they would do great damage for the Seljuk bows were powerful ones. They would find any flesh not protected by mail and I was glad that our pages and squires had mail and good helmets. Sir Hubert's page and squire were not so lucky. Seljuk arrows threw them from their saddles and I saw the heads of the arrows protrude from their backs; neither had worn mail. The only good part about the reckless charge was that it focussed the attention of our attackers upon Sir Hubert and his wild charge.

Cedric Warbow managed to organise the archers and he used volleys of arrows which were sent towards the place he thought the enemy archers were hiding. Sir Burchard sent twenty sergeants in a flanking attack up the side of the valley. My men and I did that hardest of tasks. We endured arrows, for all of Sir Hubert's men were slain. Sir Hubert was a brave knight and he plunged through the scrub and I saw him raise his sword. When he raised it again it was bloody but it was to no avail; I saw a spear rammed through his side and he fell from his horse. Some of the squires and pages were hit and I heard plaintive cries.

Sir Henry of Dunwich shouted, "My lord, must we endure this? Our young pages are being hurt! Let us charge the enemy!"

I roared, "Stand firm and have the pages and squires shelter behind shields. This will pass." I saw the swords of the sergeants rise and fall. Cedric and the archers adjusted their aim and when I saw horse archers fleeing eastwards then I knew that we had won. We waited until the Teutonic sergeants returned before we moved. Our three priests ran to the bodies but it was too late for Sir Hubert and his ten men. After checking their bodies, they hurried to the squires and pages who had been hurt.

The sergeant brother who had led the attack on the enemy reported to Sir Burchard and the Teutonic commander then came to me. "That could have been worse. We had minor wounds and more than thirty of the enemy were killed but," he waved a hand at my dead, "for you this is a disaster."

Shaking my head, I said, "Better here than when we were alone and isolated. Your presence saved us. When we camp, I will speak with my knights. They have learned, this day, that this is not a tournament where death is a possibility. This is war, where death is a certainty when you make a mistake."

We buried our dead and the priests said words over them. The priests had done well for they had not panicked and the men who had wounds were tended well. I saw that Father Paul had taken charge during the attack and he became the priest I went to first. We managed a bare ten miles that day. I wondered if I should have waited at Acre for the rest of the army then I realised that would merely have delayed the deaths. Whenever we were attacked this would have been the result. I gathered the knights around me as the rest of the men made our camp.

I looked at each lord squarely in the eyes, "Today's disaster need not have happened and Sir Hubert and his men have paid for his mistake with their lives. Sir Henry, you were worried about your pages and squire. Why were they not sheltering behind shields as the rest were?"

"There is no honour in that and they seek glory." He sounded almost sulky and petulant.

"With that attitude, all that they will achieve is sudden death. Do you think that Sir Hubert had a glorious death? He died alone and a man with a spear, probably little more than a peasant, ended his life. These were not the best that the Muslims have to offer. These came here on the chance of ambushing inexperienced, red-faced knights who did not know how to fight and they were almost proved right! These were horse archers and they have thousands of them. Their arrows are not bodkins and cannot penetrate mail; at best they are an irritation for well-armoured and disciplined men."

Sir Edward of Tewkesbury said, "But they can hurt our horses!"

"Then use caparisons! They will minimise the losses. Do not ride your war horses! Keep them with the baggage. This is not a game and it is not a tournament. I know not what the King said to you but if he misled you into thinking this was some holy tournament then he was wrong; return home now!"

I could see that I had shocked all of them, "We could not do that, lord! Think of the shame!"

"Sir Hugo, the shame is thinking that this crusade is anything other than an attempt to steal this land from the people who live here. The Christians were not mistreated before the Crusaders came to this land. The Holy City could be visited by pilgrims. When you see the castles of Outremer ask yourselves their purpose; why were they built? None are close to the pilgrim routes. Montfort is there to protect pilgrims as is Kerak de Chevaliers. The ones around Jerusalem and Damascus, Antioch and Acre are there to make Franks, us, rich!" They were silent. "We will be attacked again. My orders are simple. Listen to my voice and that of my son! Do so and we will keep you alive!"

I saw in the eyes of most of them, understanding. That disastrous ambush might have been the saving of the other young knights for they saw their fate. All that they had seen of our enemies were the bodies we had left by the side of the road. These were not mailed warriors; they were a band of raiders sent to harass the knights of Outremer. It was in the interests of their leaders to foster conflict between the Muslims and the Christians. The truce still had a year to go and yet, already, it was clear that it would not be renewed voluntarily. The ruler in Cairo was Al-Adil, an old man clinging to power and others were flexing their muscles to make a play for power and take over this sleeping tiger. All was not lost; we had the horses and arms of the dead men and four Muslim horses had been caught by the Teutonic Knights. Our doctor, Conrad von Schweistein, tended to the wounded although, in truth, the three priests we had with us could have dealt with the minor wounds the men had suffered.

I rode with Sir Burchard. "That has been a harsh lesson for us, Sir Thomas. I had thought that it was the borderlands which were dangerous. Here we are close to the sea and yet we were attacked."

"And I, too, was complacent. I had forgotten the tactics that they use. Mail is uncomfortable to wear in this heat and makes it harder to move and yet it is now obvious that it is vital against the arrows which come from hidden attackers." I pointed to the small horses we had taken from the dead Seljuk archers. "Look at their mounts. They cannot carry a mailed man yet they can outrun any of our horses. I fear it will be hit and run until we can draw them to battle."

Baron's Crusade

That there would be a battle was now clear to me and it made my heart feel like lead. I had hoped that life would be dull in the Holy Land and that we could do our duty and then return home. I wondered if the Pope's command to me had been a curse. Perhaps when I visited the Church and begged forgiveness then our fortune would change.

What surprised me about Jerusalem was the paucity of Christian defenders. The only defended part of the whole city was the Tower of David and the couple of hundred defenders were too few to be able to hold it against a determined assault. We were lucky that our foes were in such disarray. When Sir Burchard and I tried to gain admittance to the Tower we were refused. We were told that the castellan was busy. It did not bode well.

After admittance to the Tower had been refused, I went, first, with William and Sir Burchard to the Church of the Holy Sepulchre. This was a holy place as it was the church built on the site of the crucifixion, it was a revered place and I abased myself before the altar and begged Christ to forgive my sin of murder. I had been absolved already but this place, so close to where Christ had been crucified, would guarantee that forgiveness would be forthcoming. I also said a longer prayer, not for myself, but for Sir Edward. Surprisingly, when we left the church, I felt lighter in my heart. I knew that the Bishop of Durham had deserved to die and I did not regret killing him but murder, and murder it had been, did not sit well with me. For the first time, I felt real absolution and I felt that here, unlike in Rome, I had spoken to God and that he would intercede for Sir Edward. William, too, was deeply affected by the sights we saw.

As we headed back to the hospital of the Teutonic Knights, he said, "I still wish I was at home with my wife and son, father, but this visit has made me feel closer to God and that cannot be a bad thing for a knight, can it?"

"You are right. We are both warriors and know that death is just around the corner." I was thinking of Alfred as I spoke. "Now I feel that God will be waiting for us when we reach heaven for we will have done all that we can to keep this Muslim threat at bay."

We parted the next day for we were to return to Acre and Sir Burchard and his knights were heading for the borderlands. "I am pleased that we have met, Sir Thomas. Our threads have been bound together in blood. I pray that you and your men return home to your homeland. For myself, this is where I shall die. If we do not meet in this life then I hope we meet in heaven."

I smiled and clasped his arm, "But not for a long time, eh?"

He laughed, "You have the right of it there, Sir Thomas."

Baron's Crusade

The ride back to Acre was uneventful. My knights had been changed by the attack. They did not now resent their duties and when their men watched, the knights were as vigilant as any. They were more watchful and alert. When we passed the graves of our dead their faces showed that they knew how close they had come to death. The minor wounds their pages and squires had suffered were now healed but all of them had scars inside their heads and they would take much longer to remove.

The rest of the army had arrived when we reached Acre. We were lucky that the commander of the Teutonic knights remembered us and we were allowed to stay in their hospital although it was now four men to a cell and we felt overcrowded. The alternative would have been to find accommodation in the town and that would have eaten into our funds as well as risking all sorts of thievery and disease.

I was summoned, not long after we returned, to meet with King Thibaut and the Duke of Burgundy. Peter, Duke of Brittany, was also there. In the background, I saw Amaury de Montfort who was standing with other senior lords like Henry of Bar and Guigues of Forez. De Montfort obviously wished to be part of the leadership of this crusade but he was patently excluded. The King and two dukes were the real power.

"You lead the contingent sent by King Henry?"

"I do, Your Majesty."

"The handful of knights with you are a mere token."

"We are the advanced guard, so to speak, King Thibaut and already we have paid the price of joining this crusade for one of my knights and his men perished in an attack on our ride to Jerusalem. Be patient, Your Majesty, the rest will be coming."

The Duke of Brittany, who also held the title of the Earl of Richmond and was about the same age as me, smiled, "King Thibaut, do you not know of Sir Thomas?" It was obvious, from the blank look on the King's face, that he did not. "He is the hero of Arsuf and this is his third Crusade. King Henry has sent us his best, first."

King Thibaut smiled, "I thought that a legend and that the squire who defended his father was long dead. If the knights who follow you are your equal then this Crusade will have a happy outcome."

I nodded, "As I told you, Your Majesty when we travelled with a company of Teutonic Knights to Jerusalem, we were attacked and I lost one of my knights. The land is not as safe as one might think."

The faces of all became much more serious. "I was told that all was peaceful because of the discord between As-Salih Ismail and Al-Adil."

Baron's Crusade

The Duke of Brittany shook his head, "It is as I said, Your Majesty, we need to be more aggressive and head for Ascalon sooner rather than later. We need to make that fortress as strong as Acre."

The King waved a dismissive hand, "It is too hot. We will stay here a while and then when we have more men, we will do God's work." He stood, "And now I will retire to my room. The heat of this land I find oppressive and I find solace in writing poetry."

He left but, before I could rejoin my men, Peter of Brittany sought me out. "Sir Thomas, let us speak awhile. I had hoped you would have travelled from Marseille with the main body for I wished to have conference with you."

I nodded as he led me from the hall. "I had to deliver a message to Pope Gregory."

"So I understand from Baron de Montfort." He shook his head, once we were out of earshot of others, "The King sits and writes poetry to his wife, you know when we should be prosecuting this war."

"Will prosecuting the war not escalate tension, my lord?"

"The attack on you and your men is evidence that there is tension enough. They were Seljuk Turks?" I nodded. "And I have heard that the Ayyubs in Egypt are allying with one of the emirs in the north. If those two chose to bring an army north then neither the Holy Orders nor King Thibaut would be able to stop them. We have to prevent this alliance."

His words were reasonable and sounded correct, "But what could we do?"

"You know Ascalon?"

I nodded, "I fought there but that was before Saladin destroyed it."

"Yet the foundations still remain and if we rebuilt the fortress then we would control the road from Egypt to Damascus and there is more. Since the Mongols defeated the Khwarzamians those warriors have begun to hire themselves out as mercenaries. They could shift the balance of power."

"Duke, I am the leader of fewer than ten knights. There were more than two thousand knights gathered around Acre. Surely there must be another who could aid you?"

"I know that you do not lead large numbers and when the rest of your contingent arrives, I know that they will be led by another."

"How do you know that?"

"The letter you delivered to Amaury from his brother spoke of the rest of the English contingent. They will be led by Richard, Earl of Cornwall, the King's brother."

I knew I had been used for King Henry had told just me about the real English crusaders; we were a token force to placate the Pope. There had been no need for me to come except that it gave Richard of Cornwall the time to gather stronger, better-armed forces and, perhaps, for King Thibaut to be defeated which would allow Richard of Cornwall to garner the glory. Perhaps I was cynical but my dealings with the Kings of England had jaundiced my view. Shaking my head, I said, "This still begs the question, my lord, why me?"

"Your skill as a general. Who else has fought in Palestine, Sweden, Lithuania, Wales, Scotland and France? When you have led you have never been beaten. It is your mind I need. We are of an age but my experience is limited to skirmishes in France, Normandy and Anjou. You served in this land. Serve me and you will be rewarded."

I sighed for he was trying to suborn me, "Duke Peter, all that I wish is to be back home with my family."

"Then give me until the rest of the English arrive and it shall be so. I will expedite your return."

The two of us were looking out across the battlements on the western side of the fortress; there lay the ocean. I felt as though I could see my home. If I served under Duke Peter, I would still be fulfilling my oath to Henry and to the Pope. I would be fighting in a crusade and I felt that I could trust this man. Certainly, his words had shown me that he was a thinker and was not reckless. He understood strategy.

"Very well, Duke Peter. I shall go and tell my men that we will follow your standard."

My knights could not have cared less about the banner we followed but William was concerned for he was a thinker and we sat by the harbour while he explained his misgivings, "Father, we need not follow any banner. You are the Earl of Cleveland, why should we obey the orders of any lord?"

"Because we are part of this crusade and King Thibaut commands. If we were not part of the Breton knights, we would be with another, de Montfort, Henry of Bar, Hugh of Burgundy. I am happy for it to be Duke Peter for he seems to have some grasp of the inherent threats which lie in this land."

I could see that I had partly convinced my son. "When Richard of Cornwall reaches us then we can go home. I would not follow his orders for he is even younger than our King and has less experience in battle than Henry Samuel!" William smiled. "And we will be rewarded. For myself, that means nothing as there is nothing more I wish, neither money nor land but you and the knights I lead are young and it would be foolish to come home without some reward."

When I spoke to my captains they concurred. They had already spoken with other men at arms, archers and even crossbowmen and learned that Peter of Brittany and his Lieutenant, Raoul de Soissons, had a good reputation and were seen as leaders that men could follow. The die was cast. It did not take long to realise that we had made the right choice for King Thibaut sat and wrote poetry. His leaders, the Duke of Burgundy, Henry of Bar and Duke Peter urged him to move to Ascalon but he seemed reluctant.

At the start of September, a new contingent of knights arrived. This time they were Scottish. I did not see them arrive but I heard that they had not entered Acre, instead, like me, they had journeyed to Jerusalem. It was when we set off for Ascalon that I heard that one of the lords was Malcolm, Earl of Fife. I knew not why he had taken so long to arrive but I suspected that it had involved treachery of some kind. My enemy had found me.

It was the end of October before the King stirred himself. An army of four thousand knights headed down the coastal road to Ascalon. We were not going to war. We were going to build a castle! One advantage of being attached to such a senior lord was that we were not relegated to the back of the huge column of men. We rode in the van and drank water which was fresher than the ones at the rear had and we did not have to endure the dust of this dry land. I rode with Duke Peter and Raoul. William rode with my knights. Mark and Sam were delighted they were privy to the conversations they overheard.

"At least we moved, Duke Peter."

"True, Sir Thomas, but I wish to do more than simply rebuild a castle. I want to hurt our enemies. Raoul here has heard of a heavily protected caravan which is heading to Damascus from Egypt. It has weapons and armour, as well as supplies. It is intended for An-Nasir Dawud who hopes to usurp the Emir of Damascus! An-Nasir is Emir of Kerak and is an ally of As-Salih Ayyub. If the caravan gets through then one faction will be stronger than the other. We need them to be as they are now, vying with each other for power, and if we can stop this caravan getting through then neither faction has greater power and we might succeed."

I shook my head, "If King Thibaut had any wit about him, he would strike now for it seems that every Muslim is fighting against every other."

Raoul laughed, "Aye but the Emir of Damascus is on our side, at the moment we need him!"

"This caravan should be stopped then."

"You read my mind, Sir Thomas. When we reach Ascalon the three of us will plan how we can thwart this attempt to weaken our ally."

When we reached Ascalon, I saw that the Egyptians had tried to destroy its defences completely. My grandfather had been at Ascalon when the Templars had foolishly charged a breach in the walls and suffered a massive defeat. Saladin had realised the danger of the fortress and when he defeated the Franks the castle was razed to the ground. Fortunately, they had not removed the stone; instead, they had just filled the ditches with the stones. It would not be as hard to rebuild as I had thought. Of course, knights did not dirty their hands with such labour. That was the work of men at arms, archers and crossbowmen.

When I sat with the two Bretons warriors, I suddenly found memories flooding back. The road they spoke of was close to the place where Robert of Blois had met his end. He had been ambushed by Muslims. I had barely escaped with my life and had been saved by a fierce Muslim warrior who had believed my story. Raoul had a map and when I saw it, I recognised some of the features. I nodded and pointed, "There are two places we could use to attack the caravan. One is here where there is a rocky ridge above the road and scrubby trees which would hide us and the other is here, a mile further north. Here the road passes close to a stream, or what passes for a stream in this part of the world."

Duke Peter laughed, "I knew your knowledge would come to our aid. Raoul, you take half of our knights and wait on the riverside. I will take the other half along with Sir Thomas and his knights. We will wait at the other ambush site."

"Duke Peter, we might have to wait for days."

"I know, Sir Thomas and the alternative is for us to sit here and drink. There is a cooling breeze from the sea, I grant you, but would you not rather wait where you can hurt our enemies and forestall a defeat?"

I liked the Duke for he was confident and that could win battles, "Aye, Duke Peter, you are quite correct."

I told my three captains of our plans to raid while they continued to build Ascalon's walls and they were, as I had expected, disappointed and resentful. "Sir Thomas, we are not labourers!"

"I know, Padraig, but this is necessary. Can you imagine the danger we would face if this An-Nasir Dawud was able to defeat the Emir? The Ayyub of Egypt would join forces with the Emir of Kerak and we would have an army of a hundred thousand men to face."

They saw the sense in my words, "Aye, lord, but you be careful. Remember the Earl of Fife is close and we are not there to protect you."

"Richard Red Leg, you three are the only ones who know our plan and I do not believe that the Earl will know where we ambush the caravan as that is only known by three people. I confess that when he joins the army there will be a problem but let us cross that bridge when we have to and not before."

We headed east the next morning well before the sun had risen. I rode Flame for I knew I would need a courser. The Duke led a hundred knights, including mine. If the King was concerned about our destination he said nothing, while the other barons appeared to be more concerned with securing better accommodation. We rode until mid-morning and rested in the shade of some olive trees. Raoul and his forty knights left us in the early afternoon. They would wait by the stream. The Duke had chosen the harder place to wait and it showed much about his character for unlike King Henry he would tackle the harder battle. It was getting on for sunset when we reached the road. It would have been useful to have archers but they were needed to rebuild Ascalon.

William and I built a hovel, much to the amusement of the Breton knights. I did not mind their mocking looks for we would be slightly more comfortable than they would be, sleeping in the open. This was Palestine and there was no frost but it was November and there could be rain. The Duke had brought servants to cook for us. I thought it a mistake as it would alert other travellers and the last thing we needed was for news of the ambush to reach the caravan.

"Tomorrow, Duke Peter, I will take my son and squires and we will scout out the land around here."

"There is no need, Sir Thomas."

"There is for I like to know what is around me. Are there horse archers waiting to ambush us? My grandfather had a scout, Masood, and I wish we had one just like him. We do not fit in with the land. We wear mail and ride warhorses while the locals do not and they can blend in easier than we can."

"You know your own mind, Sir Thomas."

"And that is why I have lived so long. We will leave well before dawn."

Mark and Matthew had grown since I had taken them from the tannery. It was not just physical growth; they had both learned skills. Both were good archers and they had learned from Cedric and my men. They knew how to track. It was they found the trail which led high up along the ridge. We kept away from the skyline so that while we would not be seen if there were enemies, then we would see them first. We did not see the tracks of any horses and that was a relief. We stopped when the sun began to make the metal of my mail too hot to touch. We found a stand of scrubby trees and used their shade.

Henry Samuel was curious, "Grandfather, what if the caravan comes this day and we miss the chance to ambush it?"

"Then we will not garner the reward that the others do but I do not think that it will come this day." I shrugged. "I have nothing to base that idea upon save a feeling. We have ascertained that we are alone and we will leave as soon as it is cool enough. First, I will walk up that small peak and spy out the road below us. Would you like to come, Sam?"

He was eager to join me, "Aye, grandfather!"

I took off my spurs and helmet. I would not need them and I slipped my coif around my shoulders. The white hood on my cloak would keep my head cool. I took it steady as I climbed because I had to. I was no longer a young man but it was good practice anyway as slow and steady movements were harder to see. The path twisted to the right and then double-backed upon itself to climb higher. I saw the road below us and then, to the northeast, a castle. It was not a Frankish castle but it had two gates and a tower. I pushed Henry Samuel to the ground and I lay there to spy it out. The yellow flag which flew above it told me that it was Ayyubid as did the arms and armour of the four guards I saw on the walls and in the tallest tower. The gates were open and I saw no frenetic activity. They did not know that there were a hundred knights within five miles of it. We backed down the slope and then stood.

"This changes our plans. We will need to warn the Duke."

"Does this mean that we will not ambush the caravan?"

"We may still attack but the Duke might not wish to split his forces. He is the leader and it is his decision."

I deemed, by the time we returned to our horses, that we could risk heading back to the Duke even though it was not the cool of the evening. Flame had not been hard-pressed thus far and he could cope with an extra effort. I told William my news as we headed back to the camp. We arrived before dark. I told Duke Peter what we had learned and my recommendations and he did not seem put out by the fact that there was a castle nearby.

"I am not surprised for the caravans must use such places to rest. This gives me hope, Sir Thomas, for it means that they will pass us when they are looking forward to the shelter the castle offers. You have done well and have justified your inclusion." He pointed to my knights. "They were most discomfited that you did not take them. I think they feel like they are your oathsworn."

I was surprised. They had changed since we had come to Palestine. Sir Stephen approached me, "My lord, why did you not take us with you? Have we disappointed you?"

"No, Sir Stephen, in fact since the attack by the horse archers all of you have impressed me but what I did needed stealth. Have you ever scouted out an enemy?" The other knights had joined us and they all shook their heads. "And that is why I took just my squire, son and pages. You need small numbers to find the enemy and you need those who can move quietly and without leaving a trail. Now be of good cheer. We have the opportunity to strike the first blow for the Crusade. Within the next days, we will be fighting the enemy and then you will be truly tested. Do not let his apparent lack of mail fool you. They use other means to protect themselves and their weapons are the equal to ours, but they are different. Now rest and make your peace with God."

The Duke had brought two of his retainers with him. They looked after the horses and he sent them, the next morning, to keep watch on the road to the south of us. I had exerted myself enough the previous day and I used my cloak to make a shelter from the sun and I dozed. Henry Samuel and William thought I was asleep and I heard their words.

"Grandfather is the oldest man on this crusade, uncle. The climate does not suit him. He was out of breath when we reached the top of the peak."

"Do not worry about my father, Sam. He has steel for bones and he will keep going longer than any of us. This land was the land which forged him. When he was knighted, he was little older than you and, abandoned by King Richard, he had to learn to use his wits. I am still learning by watching him and you should learn by watching me. This is not the place for a ceremonial page. Here we are all fighting men. If the Turk comes then you will have to fight and neither my father nor I can watch over you."

I heard his voice which sounded very small, "I am not afraid for the blood of the Warlord is in my veins too! It is the Turks who should worry!"

I wondered if the blood of the warlord was a curse. And in that instant, I knew it was not. Had it not been for the blood of Alfred, the Warlord, I would not have defended my father and then I would have died. There would have been no Alfred, William, Thomas, Isabelle and Henry Samuel, not to mention Geoffrey and Richard. It was not a curse. It was a blessing and, comforted, I slept.

It was Mark who woke me, "Lord, the scouts have returned and the caravan approaches. I fear they have more men than we do."

I smiled, "Have courage and trust in God and your sword. Go and saddle Flame!" As he ran off, I took the waterskin and drank deeply. I looked at the sky and saw that it was late in the afternoon. The leader of the caravan would be rushing to reach the castle before dark. We had more than a chance.

I hurried to the Duke who was already mounted. When I reached his side he smiled, "We may have bitten off a larger piece of meat than I expected. They have more than a hundred guards!"

"Yet the last thing they will expect is an attack by the Franks. When we charge sound the horn to summon your lieutenant, Raoul. He can cut off their escape to the castle."

"I would not play chess against you for you are always two moves ahead of me."

William, Mark and my knights appeared. Flame looked eager for war. While Mark held his reins, I mounted and took the spear from Henry Samuel. I turned to my knights. "We charge in a wedge. William and I will lead. Squires and pages form the third rank!" I nudged Flame close to the scrubby brush. Already the horses were neighing for there were camels approaching and these horses had not been trained to approach that most disgusting of animals. It could not be helped but the Turks would know that there were horsemen close by.

Peter of Brittany might only have fought in skirmishes but he knew his business and he shouted, "Sound the horn three times!" That was the signal for our knights to attack and for Raoul to come to our aid. It would take him some time to reach us but I hoped that the shock of our dual attack would make the Muslims panic. They were riding tired beasts and the animals would be desperate for water.

I spurred Flame and he leapt through the thinly branched scrub. I had my shield held close to me and protecting Flame's head for there would be archers with the caravan and the last thing I needed was a wound to my horse. There were just sixty knights who charged with us but with our squires and pages, the number who fell upon the caravan was more than one hundred and thirty. The camels were protected on two sides by horsemen but that meant that only half of the enemy faced us. I pulled my arm back and rammed my spear into the side of a surprised mailed warrior. He was a noble for he had mail about his head and the scimitar which hung from his belt was damasked. His shield was small and I had time to aim for his face. His shield was slow to rise and my spearhead rammed into his mouth and I saw it emerge from the back of his skull. As he fell, he tore the spear from my hand and, in an instant, I had my sword drawn. The horse archer who rode close by was already drawing his composite bow. Had he released then the arrow was at such a close range that it would have torn through my mail. As it was my swinging sword took him in the chest. I shattered his bow and then laid open his organs. He fell to the ground and was dead before he reached it.

Baron's Crusade

I passed the camels and headed towards the line of warriors on the other side. I hoped that William and my knights were with me but in such a battle all that a knight could do was fight the enemies before him. The warrior's spear was headed for my face but I still had good reactions and my shield blocked the blow. I swung blindly in a long sweep. I caught his horse's mane which made the horse flinch but my blade slipped beneath his shield to rip open and eviscerate the Ayyubid.

I yelled, "Wheel!" and jerked Flames' reins to the right. As I rode back up the slope, I saw that the enemy had broken and were heading up the road. They would meet Raoul and his men. "Knights! On me!" I shouted in English so that my men would know that the command came from me.

I heard William shout, "Sir Richard, heed the command! Leave the damned camels!"

I spurred Flame. The knights I led were keen but only William and I had horses which were as good as those of the Duke. We led the pursuit. This was not war, this was slaughter. I swept my sword to hack across the backs of those who fled before me. The ones I missed were killed by William. I knew not where Mark and Henry Samuel were but I prayed that they were safe. This was a great victory but only if we all survived. I saw that we were heading for the castle. If they closed the gates then we would have to besiege it and that would be costly. I urged Flame on and found myself overtaking the oathsworn of the Duke of Brittany. I heard a wail from ahead as Raoul de Soissons led his knights to attack the side of the leading warriors. I spied a warrior with mail and a horsehair plume on his helmet, He rode a fine horse and I knew him to be a leader. If I could catch him before he entered the castle then I had a chance.

He had a good horse and my mail was heavier but Flame had his bit between his teeth and we inexorably closed with the Muslim warrior. The men on the walls were shouting in panic as they saw me closing and I saw the doors beginning to shut. The man I was chasing had to be important for the men on the gates hesitated and, in that hesitation, lay defeat. I caught him as he closed with the gates. I brought my sword down across his back. Even had I not sliced through his mail I would have broken his spine. As he fell from his horse I clattered through the gate and kicked one of the sentries in the face with my boot. My son William's sword hacked into the side of the head of the other guard and I shouted, "Hold the gate!"

Sir Stephen and Sir Robert were close behind and with four of us in the gateway we dared any to try to close the gates. Behind us, we heard the dying screams as the Duke and his men slaughtered the dismayed guards from the caravan. Our squires and pages, along with the rest of my knights were the next through and once they were there I shouted, "Mark, Matthew, you and the squires hold the gates. Knights, let us take this castle!"

I confess that the joy of battle was upon me and I spurred Flame to charge through the castle. It was not built as a Norman castle. There was no keep but I knew there would be another gate and I headed directly for it. The men who stepped into our path and tried to stop us were doomed to failure. We were mailed and well-armed. Swords sliced and hacked as we carved our way to the northern gate. There we stopped and I ordered Sir Henry and Sir Hugo to close and hold the gates. By the time the Duke arrived, we had a hundred prisoners and there were twenty dead warriors who had attempted to breach the gate. The rest surrendered for there was no alternative.

I took off my helmet and lowered my coif for I was both hot and tired. There had been little danger in this fight but I was tired. The Duke dismounted and clasped my arm, "You have not lost your touch, hero of Arsuf. Other men would have blanched when the gates began to close but you rode at them as though you were Hercules himself. You and your brave knights deserve much honour and treasure and I will ensure that you receive it."

I looked around and saw that all of my knights, squires and pages had survived and had no wounds, I bowed, "For that, my lord, we thank you!"

My men had exceeded all of my expectations. William looked at me, grinned and nodded. We had a small conroi but in two actions we had ensured that they would fight as well as any knights of Cleveland. In future, I could go into battle knowing that I had men riding behind me upon whom I could rely! We stayed for two days and took animals and treasure, not to mention many weapons back to Ascalon and the rest of the army.

Chapter 5

Our return caused a celebration but also created tension and dissension. King Thibaut was already annoyed for the work on Ascalon was not progressing as fast as he had hoped. Although he approved of Peter of Brittany's motives, preventing weapons and armour from reaching our enemies, he did not like the fact that he had been excluded from the plan. The Dukes of Bar and Burgundy were also in high dudgeon for they had wished to participate in such a raid. I could see that the arguments and debates would go on for a long time and so I rejoined my conroi. On the ride back I had impressed upon my young knights the need to share the booty with the men they had left behind. None had more than eight and the cost would not be much. William and I had far more men but I did not begrudge them any of it. The treasure we had taken from the castle meant that all of us were rich men. In addition, we had horses and weapons.

William and I sat with Padraig, Cedric and Richard and spoke of the raid and the progress on Ascalon's walls. "We laboured, lord, and the knights just watched. That is why the work has barely begun. It will take six months or more to rebuild the castle. Is that what King Henry and the Pope would have wished for this crusade? Why bring warriors when they could have sent masons?"

Padraig was correct; the King of Navarre was vacillating. "Perhaps we can persuade the knights to help with the building work."

Richard Red Leg shook his head, "The holy orders will not labour, lord. We watched their sergeants toil under the hot sun while the knights knelt and prayed."

Cedric said, quietly, "And the Earl of Fife knows that we are here, lord." I had almost forgotten that snake. "His men spied us working and recognised the livery. The Earl himself came by and asked where you were." He grinned, "He learned nothing and called us English peasants."

Padraig laughed, "Which showed how ignorant he is for I am Irish or I once was!"

"Keep a good watch for them and be aware that there might be treachery."

"We have already arranged a man to sleep inside your tent, lord. Besides, they have not come prepared for the sun. Their faces are as red as a cooked lobster! Their skin has cracked and they look as though they are in pain."

William nodded, "That is God's punishment for their actions when they raided our lands! Father, I could challenge the Earl. That would end the problem."

"No, for that could be seen as helping our enemies, the Ayyubid. We will just watch and be patient. This is not Elsdon. Let us see how events unfold."

I confess that despite the presence of Declan of Dublin in our tent I did not sleep well that night. It was not for myself that I worried but Henry Samuel. During the attack on the caravan, he had behaved and fought as well as any knight. Mark told me how he saw my grandson taking on warriors who were far more experienced than he was. The expense of the mail he wore had proved justified for the arrows from the horse archers had not penetrated and he had slain three enemy warriors and captured two horses. The fact that two of the enemy had been fleeing us did not detract from his victory; he had done well. I knew that he would become more skilled on the battlefield but the tent, at night, was something different. I could sleep with one eye open but Henry Samuel slept the sleep of the innocent. I would have to keep him close to me and use my reactions and instincts.

The debates and arguments amongst the lords still raged the next day. I kept out of it. All work on the castle stopped and I feared that the crusade would degenerate into chaos. It had happened under King Richard and King Thibaut did not seem to have the same charismatic personality. That lack of authority manifested itself in the late afternoon.

Raoul de Soissons sought me out, "Sir Thomas, the Duke has sent for you."

"What is it?"

"A large part of the army intends to head south and to raid closer to Egypt! They wish to emulate our raid!"

"But that is foolish! We took out a caravan which was close to our castles and we used a handful of men. To travel south into the heartland of the enemy is foolish!" As I hurried to the King's tent I asked, "Who are the leaders of this dissenting group?"

"Henry of Bar, Hugh of Burgundy, Lord Montfort and the Earl of Fife. Almost a fifth of the knights wish to follow them. It is only ourselves, the King's men and the Holy Orders who see the danger of such an action."

"And what can I do?"

"The King wishes you to tell them of the folly of their actions. He said you are the most experienced knight in the army and your words might sway them."

Baron's Crusade

My heart sank. I might be able to persuade some but not the Earl of Fife, however, I would have to try and that way I would have a clear conscience. I headed to the hubbub. The noise sounded like Stockton Market! Men shouted and fingers were pointed as voices were raised. When Raoul and I appeared, it reached a crescendo.

King Thibaut shouted, "Silence! Let us hear the words of the knight who fought in this land before many of you were even born! Sir Thomas, speak!"

It took some moments for all the voices to be silenced and I spoke as reasonably as I could. I knew that if I condescended to them, they would resent me. "Trying to pin down the mounted archers of the Turks and Egyptians is like trying to catch quicksilver in your fingers. If you wish to battle the enemy then you need to choose your battleground; it needs to be close to aid and our castles. The land to the south of us is without either and, worse, it is filled with the enemy. Riding forth in the hope of catching them will result in disaster."

It was the Earl of Fife who spoke. I saw that his skin was all cracked and flaked, Padraig was right. They had been touched by the sun! He pointed an accusing finger at me. "This man is treacherous! He has raided the Muslims and yet he counsels us to stay here and to build the walls of Ascalon." I did not point out that I had done no such thing for he would not have heard me. This was a diatribe. "I know this man. He is a venal treasure hunter! Do not heed his words."

The Master of the Hospitallers, Bertrand de Comps stood, "Sir Thomas is right. We live cheek by jowl with the Egyptians and the Turks. A raid on a caravan, especially one which carries arms to fight against us, is a good thing but to ride south in the hope of a similar success is doomed to failure."

The Duke of Burgundy shook his head, "I do not agree with the Earl of Fife; from what I have seen Sir Thomas has honour but I do not agree with his conclusions. We have come on Crusade and all that we have done thus far is to squat in Acre and now grub around the ruins of a fortress. I came here to fight the Muslim horde and if the King of Navarre will not lead us then I will. The Duke of Brittany and the Earl of Cleveland have shown us that the Muslim arrow cannot penetrate mail. What have we to fear? Our blades are superior to those of our enemies! The men of Brittany and England have had their glory. Now it is the time of Burgundy and France! All who wish to follow my banner we leave at the third hour of the dark when it is cool!"

He and the other rebellious lords stormed off and it was only then that their true numbers could be seen. The ones who followed the Duke were half of the crusaders who had arrived with King Thibaut. The

Holy Orders, Bretons and the men of Navarre were the only men who had not followed the Duke.

Duke Peter said, "King Thibaut, we cannot allow the Duke of Burgundy to do this. It would be a disaster for the crusade. If we lose a thousand knights then we might as well go home for we cannot win a war with just three thousand knights."

"And how do we stop them, Duke? Do we draw swords and fight them? That would serve only our enemies." He turned to me, "I thank you for your efforts, Earl, and I am sorry for the words of the Earl of Fife; I know them to be untrue."

"Words cannot hurt me, King Thibaut, but I do not trust this man. When he raided our lands in England, he took women and children as slaves."

"Perhaps he is here for absolution."

"Perhaps." I did not believe it but King Thibaut thought the best of men. I knew that the Earl of Fife was here for one thing and that was treasure. He had not an ounce of honour in his body.

We were woken by the noise they made when the host left us to head south. I rose for I would not be able to sleep anymore. I feared mischief from the Earl of Fife. In the event my fears were groundless. I put the conniving Scot from my mind. It was the potential loss of so many knights which concerned me. I knew I had to do something. I went to the Duke of Brittany. He, too, was awake. We had slaughtered some of the animals we had captured at the castle and he was eating cold mutton for his breakfast when I found him

"Food, Sir Thomas?"

"Perhaps later. We must do something about this raid, lord."

"What can we do? The King is right. We cannot fight them to stop them."

"Then we must be there to protect them from themselves. I was not at Hattin but I was told of the battle. Their horsemen tempted the knights who broke formation and when they were isolated, they were cut down. It is true that horse archers cannot hurt knights but as Sir Hubert discovered, sergeants at arms and horses can be hurt. At Arsuf they led King Richard away from the main band so that they could send in more horsemen to surround the other knights. If we are close then it may prevent the Muslims from prosecuting their attack."

He wiped his greasy hands on a napkin and drank some of the local wine. "What you say makes sense but King Thibaut is a proud man. He will not wish to be seen to back down."

"Do your best, my lord, for if the King's neck is too stiff then good men will die."

Baron's Crusade

The three leaders of the military orders must have felt the same for they spent the morning arguing with the King. In the face of such pressure, he relented and agreed to follow the Duke of Burgundy's army but, by the time our men were roused and we began to move south, almost fourteen hours had passed. We were at the fore and I rode next to Duke Peter, "Lord, we move at a snail's pace and we move blindly. Let me take my conroi and close with the men who left us. We need eyes and ears before us!"

This time the King agreed and, leaving our spare horses with the baggage train, I rode Willow and led my men down the road to Jaffa and Gaza. I felt better with just my men. I had my own archers and Cedric as scouts and the other archers guarding the rear. We took our three priests with us. They asked to come and I was proud of them for they were unarmed. We rode through the night. I feared for the knights who rode ahead of us because they were riding into the unknown. This was new to all of them and none of them understood the power of the Muslim horse archers and their heavy cavalry. I did and I was afraid. I did not push our horses for I knew that they would need to be protected. The last thing we needed was to attack the enemy with blown horses.

I waved our pages forward.

"When we find the enemy, you will ride back to the King and tell him where we are. Do not hesitate! As soon as we sight them you turn and ride back. Our lives depend upon it."

"Yes, lord!"

"Yes, Grandfather!"

We rode through the night and I knew that the cooler conditions would help us but I feared that the main army would lag too far behind. We were like a monstrous mailed behemoth. Dawn broke and we halted. There was a village with a well and we took advantage of it. I checked that all of my men and their mounts were in good condition.

Dick, son of John rode in. He was the leading scout with Alf Fletcher, "Lord, the knights have met with the Egyptians and there is a battle." I cocked my head to the side. He nodded, "They are surrounded and they are losing."

"John and Henry Samuel ride back to the main column and tell them that the Duke of Burgundy and his men are in dire straits. The King must come sooner rather than later."

My grandson nodded, "We will not let you down, lord." He turned his horse and he and John headed north. He looked so young and, not for the first time, I regretted his participation in this ill-fated crusade.

When they had ridden off, I turned to my knights. "We now have that hardest of tasks. We have to try to save an army whilst fighting odds which would terrify St. Michael himself. You are English knights and I do not doubt your courage but listen to the horn of my squire When I sound the withdraw signal then obey, instantly. We are here to try to save as many of those who followed him as we can. The Duke of Burgundy has chosen his bed and I will not lie with him!"

For some reason that made my men and knights laugh and showed that they were not downhearted. We had hope.

"Cedric, keep the enemy occupied. Padraig and Richard have our men at arms as close behind us as though we were born from the same mother!"

My three veterans all chorused, "Aye, Lord!"

I turned to Mark who handed me a spear. William nodded and nudged his horse next to mine. He shouted, "Knights, form a wedge behind us." We had too few knights to make a difference unless we broke through their rear. That was my hope.

Cedric and the archers galloped off. There would be just twenty-five of them and they would have to give the impression that they represented a far greater number of archers. Cedric would clear our flanks and give us the greatest chance to break through and cause dissension. We had to buy time until the bulk of the army could join us. They would be hours behind us and the task looked hopeless. I took the spear which Mark proffered.

"Stay behind me and watch yourself!"

"Aye, lord!" His grin told me that my words were wasted.

I raised my spear and pointed it forward. The battle was some way ahead. We could hear the cries of the dying and the soon-to-be-dead. Haste would gain us nothing. We had to appear as though we were the vanguard of an army rather than less than one hundred men. We would be the insect which irritated and not the teeth of the wolf which could hurt. We soon saw the men fleeing the battle. These were the ones whose masters had died or whose masters they thought would soon be dead. I let them run for they were beyond rallying. Perhaps the King might give them steel but my handful of men could not. I saw the rear of the Egyptian army which had surrounded the men who had put their heads into the serpent's mouth. I knew we could not save many men. I hoped for a handful but whatever we saved would help Christendom in its fight against Islam.

Lowering my spear, I spurred my palfrey. She was no warhorse but she was a good horse with a stout heart and she responded. I knew that my son, next to me, was as brave a knight as I could wish and I would be protected on that side. My shield would bear the brunt of an attack from my left. The rest was in the hands of God, or if you were a pagan, then Fate. I looked ahead to see the standards of those closest to us. Whoever controlled that day determined that the men we would first save would be the men of the Earl of Fife and his Scotsmen. I pulled back my spear and drove it through the mailed body of the Mameluke who was to hack into the young squire sheltering behind his slain horse. I pulled back the spear as the Muslim warrior slipped from his horse to perish on the plain before Gaza. I saw the squire nod at me gratefully as he grabbed the reins of the Mameluke horse. One young warrior might have been saved. How many more could we rescue? I rammed my spear into the face of the next warrior who turned to try to deal with this threat to their rear. My spear hit him between the eyes and I think his death was quick. William was younger than me and had better reactions. Three men had fallen to his spear as he ruthlessly slew those with their backs to him. Matthew was behind him and he was using William's spare spear to clear Muslim horses. We were doing all that we could do. I saw Scotsmen, grateful that their enemies had been slain, grab their reins and gallop north as we punched a hole in the Egyptians' ranks. Cedric and his archers had dismounted and their arrows now began to appear above our heads. I know they saved my life for a handful of arrows hit the five warriors who had turned to block our attack. It gave us a chance for we drove deeper into their lines. Henry of Bar and the Duke of Burgundy had stout knights with them. Their mail made them hard to kill and they were blunting blades and making a solid defence. More of their sergeants fled through the escape route we had made. My wedge had worked. We had burst the Muslim dam. Now we would have to endure the repercussions.

The enemy had seen us and they reacted. I heard trumpets signal and swords were pointed in our direction. A few mailed askari turned to face us. The huge Egyptian who came at me wore a fish plate mail shirt and when my spear rammed at it, although it punctured his flesh, the head broke. Even as he tried to tear the weapon from his chest my sword was drawn and I had an easy kill as I sliced across his neck. I saw the Egyptian standard ahead. It was like Arsuf but in reverse. If I could take their standard then they would lose heart and our men might be saved. I spurred my horse towards the standard. I had to take the heart from the enemy.

I heard William's voice shout, "Father! No!" but I was committed; we had broken through the men who had been sent to face us and I galloped towards the Egyptian standard-bearer and his bodyguards. I was helped by the fact that they were closing with Henry of Bar. The Frenchman and his knights were dying hard. I saw that the standards of Burgundy and Montfort could no longer be seen. Either they were dead or had surrendered. I could do nothing about them but Henry of Bar could be saved. With William at my side and with my knights close behind me I tore into the ranks of bodyguards. These were the best that the Egyptians had but most were attacked from the rear and I slew two before they even knew we were amongst them. I used the point of my sword on one and laid open the back of another with my second strike. William slew one whose spear was rammed towards my side. He died before he could use the weapon. Stephen of Malton made his horse rear to clatter into the skull of the standard bearer and, as the flag fell, I hurdled the horse to attack the Egyptian commander. I hacked at his shoulder and my sword drew blood. I was lucky in that he rode a small horse and Willow was just a little taller. I reared her and her hooves pounded into the rump of the Egyptian's horse. The horse began to fall and I hacked at the warrior's leg as he tried to control his animal. I laid his leg open to the bone as he fell backwards.

It was then I sensed, rather than saw, the sword which came at my back. I reacted instinctively and slashed around with my sword. It hacked into mail and saved my life for it came away bloody. I heard William's voice as he shouted, "England, fall back! Mark, take my father's reins."

I lunged at the warrior before me and then felt a blow to the back of my head. I had never felt such pain. All became black and I could not see. Worse, I could not move my arm. It was as though time had stood still. My arms dropped, dragged down by the weight of the shield and the sword, but some instinct made me stay in the saddle. I felt a savage pain in my leg and pain coursed through my body. Willow's reins dropped and my horse stopped. I was deep in the enemy's lines and I could not see. The next blow would end my life, of that I was certain then, mercifully, all went black and I knew no more.

Baron's Crusade
Sir William of Elsdon
Chapter 6

As we charged into the heart of the enemy I was amazed by my father who appeared like a young knight rather than the veteran he was. He had seen more wars than any man I knew and yet he seemed to bear a charmed life. As he speared warrior after warrior it took all of my skill to keep up with him and protect his right side. This was where I missed Ridley the Giant. He would have guarded my father's left side. Sir Robert of Kendal was a good knight but he was not Ridley. My lance shattered before my father's spear and I drew my sword. That brief moment when I reached for my blade allowed Thorn to move a little further from me and I had to spur Thorn. A Turk, spear in hand, rode across my front in an attempt to spear my father. My last spurring of Thorn allowed me to close so that, by standing in my stirrups, I was able to bring my sword down on his head. I saw now that the enemy were wise to our attack and a plumed leader was waving his spear and shouting orders. The standard-bearer next to him was a clear target and I saw my father urge Willow towards him. He intended to take out the enemy leader for Henry of Bar and his beleaguered knights were close enough for him to reach. I could see what my father, blinded by his success, could not. He would be surrounded in moments, "Father, no!"

He had reached the Egyptian warrior and Willow reared to clatter down on the Egyptian horse. It looked, unlikely though it seemed, as though my father might succeed. Then I saw Sir Robert as he was speared from the side and that meant my father was exposed to his left. Mark urged his horse to reach the gap caused by the falling knight but he had too much ground to cover. The Egyptian who had slain Sir Robert was now behind my father. As another warrior rode at my father's sword side, I kicked Thorn on and my horse came between them. I took the blow from the spear which was intended for my father. The spearhead hit the side of my helmet. It was a well-made helmet and took the blow. I backhanded the warrior across the throat with my sword using all the strength that I had. In that moment two Turks flanked my father. I know not how he did it but he managed to, somehow, hit the one to his right with a blindly struck sword slash. The surprised warrior tumbled from the back of his horse but then I saw the second Turk smash his mace into the back of my father's head. Time seemed to stand still. Another Turk rode up and lunged at my father with his spear. My father's hands had dropped and I watched the spear slice through my father's chausses. I hacked into the man's throat as Mark reached the other Turk, the one with the mace who was raising it to end my father's life and almost cut him in two with a blow from his sword.

I realised that I should have shouted before. Now I found my voice as the enemy killed Henry of Bar and his oathsworn. "England, fall back! Mark, take my father's reins." My father was slumped forward, his body held by the cantle. I saw blood on his leg and there was a dent in the side of his helmet which was as big as my fist. It did not bode well for him.

Sir Stephen and Sir Richard reached me as did Padraig, Richard Red Leg and the rest of my father's men. We were a wall of steel. I shouted, "Matthew, help your brother! Get my father somewhere safe!"

"Aye, lord! We will not fail you!" Come, brother!"

"We hold them and give our squires time to save my father. Back your horses and await my command to break!"

I heard Padraig laugh but it was a cold and chilling laugh, "Aye, Sir William, and we will make these heathen bastards bleed for they have done for the Earl!"

A line of horsemen galloped at our thin line. We were helped by the fact that Henry of Bar's men were still dying as they protected the standard and the bodies of their comrades. I took the first spear on my shield and chopped down at the unprotected Muslim leg. My sword must have caught the horse for it reared and threw the maimed warrior to the ground. His body and that of his fallen horse broke the enemy line. Sir Stephen fought like a lion. His sword swung around at head height. He caught a warrior below the edge of his helmet and tore out the man's eyes. Padraig was wielding his sword like a club. He and Richard Red Leg were battering our enemies and were, seemingly, oblivious to the wounds they were suffering. I saw a spear lunge at Richard Red Leg's leg and when it came away bloody, I knew he was hurt.

Rearing Thorn I stood in my stirrups and looked behind us. Mark and his brother were leading Willow north. Behind us, the remnants of our conroi were fighting to keep the gap to the north open. It was time.

"England, fall back! Peter of York, take the reins of Richard Red Leg's horse and take him to safety!"

We would all have perished that day but for Cedric and the archers he commanded. Protected by Sir Robert's men at arms they were dismounted behind their horses.

"Release!" I heard Cedric's booming voice as our handful of archers sent their bodkin-tipped arrows over our heads. My archers were the most skilled in the Crusader army and I heard the arrows strike the Muslims who were just thirty paces behind us. I do not believe that any others could have been as accurate. Four more flights soared over us before we reached the line of horses and I slowed.

"Knights, turn and give the archers time to mount."

I wheeled a weary Thorn around and saw that the arrows of our archers had had a devastating effect. A handful of enemy horsemen had survived the arrow storm. They rode up to us but my knights and men at arms were angry. I saw Padraig spur his horse and ride into the midst of them. Sir Stephen followed as did Sir Richard. The ones who were not slain turned and fled. I saw, however, that the Egyptians had finally overcome Henry of Bar's men and the great mass of the enemy were now preparing to charge us. There were still isolated groups of Crusaders fighting but I saw that most were either dead or had surrendered. The battle of Gaza was almost over. I was stunned. A quarter, at least, of the crusader army was dead or captured!

"Ready, my lord!" Cedric's voice brought me to my senses.

"We ride back to the main army. We fight when they close with us."

We had not been beaten despite our losses and I heard them chorus, "Aye, lord!"

We did not gallop for our horses were too weary but we kept our weapons ready for the next attack which we knew would come. I could not see Mark and Matthew. I had to hope that they had taken my father's body to safety. He did not deserve to have it butchered and his head displayed by our enemies. I knew that would be the fate of Sir Robert. I saw, far ahead, Peter of York and Richard Red Leg. Richard would need attention but to stop would be fatal for both men. All along the flanks, Muslim horse archers were galloping along sending arrow after arrow at us. They were aiming at our men and that saved us for they could not pierce the mail.

Cedric stopped our archers and, dismounting, they sent enough arrows into the Turkish archers and their horses to discourage them. It bought us time. Godfrey of Richmond was at the fore and I heard his shout, "My lord, it is the King! The army has come!" I saw the standards fluttering in the hazy distance. Looking back, I saw that the Muslims were still closing and they were gaining on us. It was a race we could not win. Thorn was lathered as were the other horses. The Egyptians would catch us and spear us like hunted pigs. Our only hope was to make a last stand and hope that King Thibaut was less tardy than he had been, hitherto.

"England, dismount! We make our last stand here! Our horses are too weary and I am sick of showing my back to our enemies."

Padraig spoke for them all when he shouted, "Aye, let's show them how Englishmen can fight and die!"

"Wounded, hold the horses. I want a shield wall. Cedric, you know what to do!"

"Aye, lord!"

The horses would take little holding. I saw that I just had four knights left. The front rank was made up of my men at arms. Padraig stood on my right and Sir Stephen to my left. The Muslims saw us prepare and they halted too. Their leader formed lines. I saw at least a thousand men before us. Cedric and his archers had warned them of the skill of our bows and they halted beyond bow range. Then a horn sounded and the first line of two hundred and fifty men galloped towards us. The second two hundred and fifty would follow soon enough.

"Lock shields!" I held my sword over the top of my shield as Sir Stephen and Padraig locked shields with me and they, too, added their swords to the hedgehog of steel.

The ground shook beneath our feet as a thousand hooves thundered. Our mail meant that they could not use their horse archers to best effect and so they sent their mounted horsemen. Only some would be mailed and none of their horses would be protected. Had we had spears we could have held them off for a long time; we had none but I was confident that we could endure the first charge.

"Loose!"

The arrows soared above us and horses and riders fell. The arrows then followed as quickly as men could draw. My father's men were the better bowmen and they kept up a faster rate.

"Brace!"

We did not have enough men for three ranks and I knew that it was likely we would be pushed back but we were big men and we all wore mail. The Egyptian horses were much smaller than ours. This was all to do with timing and Padraig and I, along with our Stockton men at arms, were better. As one we lunged forward. Horses baulked as the long swords came for the heads of the animals. English horses would have towered above us but the horses' eyes were at a convenient height as they were smaller animals. As the horses turned so they exposed horsemen who were trying to control a horse, a lance and a shield. I felt my sword ram into the ribs of an Egyptian. As soon as it scraped off a bone I twisted and pulled. Entrails and guts were tugged from the body as I withdrew and then sliced sideways. The horses and their riders were so close that my backswing ripped open the thigh of the warrior whose horse had been killed by Padraig. As the warrior fell at our feet Padraig brought his sword down to smash through the turbaned helmet and head of the warrior. Their leader must have expected his front line to destroy us for the second line of horsemen was too close to the first and they had to slow. I saw only parts of this through the gaps left by dying horses and men. Cedric and his archers reaped a fine harvest as horsemen slowed and tried to avoid crashing into the rear of the ranks ahead of them.

Even though we were having success our men were still dying. Falling horses and their flailing hooves cared not if a man wore mail or not. I braced my shield arm as a lance was rammed at it. Sir Stephen hacked down across the lance and I forced the tip of my sword into the throat of the horse. As the blood spurted the horse fell to the side and the warrior was crushed by the hooves of a horse which followed closely. Behind me, I heard horns but they sounded as though they were miles away. My father's decision to try to save some of our army had been a good one but, in saving a few hundred, he had doomed himself and the rest of us to a desert death. The hero of Arsuf would perish in the disaster that was Gaza and with him King Henry's knights. My father's sense of honour had doomed us but I would not change the man he was.

An Egyptian trumpet sounded and the remnants of the first two lines withdrew. Before us was a mass of broken animals and dying warriors. Padraig spat out a tooth which had been dislodged in the last attack, "They will come at us from the flank, my lord!"

I knew he was right. The barrier of horseflesh before us negated the Egyptian's best weapon, the charging horse. They would merely come around the side. I nodded. "Turn back to back and face east and west. We will let the Egyptian dead guard one flank. Move any wounded to the horses. Pick up the discarded Muslim lances and spears; they will keep the horses away from us." I was clutching at straws but I knew that my father would not have given in until there was no hope left!

As the ones with wounds were shifted, I saw that Sir Stephen was wounded. His white surcoat was bespattered with not only the blood of his enemies but also his own for his cheek had been laid open to the bone.

"You are wounded, Sir Stephen."

He nodded, "Now I see the benefit of a full-face helm. I will get one when this is over."

My visor was raised to allow relatively cool air to refresh me. "Get one like this; I prefer them to the great helm." It was almost laughable that, in the face of almost certain death, we were still able to chat about helmets as though Sir Stephen would get the chance to buy one!

Egyptian trumpets sounded again. Sir Richard of Tewksbury said, "Why is not the King closer? Can they not see we are dying?"

I said, calmly, although I did not feel so inside, "They will get here as soon as they are able. If they gallop then the Egyptians will be able to destroy the rest of our army. We have to trust in God that he will save us!"

We ran towards the Egyptian dead to find spears and lances. It mattered not if they were broken so long as they were longer than a sword. Padraig was proved right. The last two lines of Egyptians did not ride directly at us but came in two columns, from the flanks. They had seen how few archers we had and they were dividing the arrows. Cedric and his archers would not be able to clear swathes of the enemy; they would have to pick off leaders and standard-bearers. More of the Muslim horde would reach us intact and more of my men would die; there were few enough as it was. I was at the end closest to the dead horses and Sir Stephen had my back. Padraig was next to me. Padraig kissed his cross before tucking it inside his surcoat. He said, quietly, "I shall soon join Sir Thomas. You have done your father great credit today, my lord. It was like fighting alongside Sir Thomas thirty years ago!"

"You will die when I say so, Padraig the Wanderer, and not before and that goes for the rest of you! We hold the enemy and pray that the King comes!!

The Muslims had no obstacles before them and this time they were able to gallop. The archers would still hit men and horses but there were so few on each side that it would barely halt, let alone, turn the tide. At least we had spears and lances this time. I knew that my blade had no edge to it. When I had to draw it again it would be like fighting with an iron bar! The Muslims were riding almost boot to boot but they were not as close to each other as a Frankish army would have been. Nor were they in a completely straight line. Some were ahead of the others, eager to close with us. Such tiny actions could decide if a man lived or died. This time I was the end man. No one protected my left save for the Egyptian dead. My shield was across my front, locked with Padraig's and I saw that four heavily mailed warriors had targeted me. Perhaps they saw me as the leader or it may have been because I was at the end and they wished to roll up our line. I know not. Four lances came at the two of us. My right foot braced the spear which rested on the top of my shield. The horsemen were able to lunge at the two of us and we had to endure the wooden lances smashing into us but in doing so they had to stand and expose themselves. There was a clatter and a crash as their lances hit our shields and knocked us backwards. This time we had other mailed men behind us and my back pressed against Sir Stephen's. The wooden lances splintered but neither Padraig nor I suffered splinter wounds for we both had a visored helmet. It was then that our borrowed lances came to our aid. Mine went into the ribs of the warrior the second from the end and drove upwards through his ribs to rip into his heart. As he fell, he knocked the end warrior from his saddle and my borrowed lance broke. I drew my sword and stepping onto the body of the dead Muslim I leapt towards the fallen man. I skewered him to the ground and then turned as Padraig slew the man who would have speared me. I whirled my sword at head height. It caught one horse on the muzzle and it reared.

I heard horns and I turned to look north. It was there that I saw the Duke of Brittany, with Henry Samuel and John close by, leading the Breton knights. They ploughed into the end of the Muslim line. The Egyptians were undone by their own attempt to outflank us. It was like the sound of thunder as the heavily mailed and armoured Bretons crashed and cracked into the lighter horses of the Muslims. The Duke had a thousand spears behind him and they tore into the remains of a mere two hundred Egyptians. The ones who survived fled and Peter of Brittany raised his sword in salute as they galloped by us. We had survived. Henry Samuel and John wheeled their horses to come to join us.

I took off my helmet as my men began to move amongst the enemy dispatching any who were too badly wounded to survive. I saw that barely twenty-five of us had survived. The three priests and the servants were tending to our wounded but there was no sign of my father's body and Richard Red Leg. Matthew, Mark and Peter of York must have left the battlefield or, and a cold chill came over me, perhaps they had been caught and butchered. Our defence would have been for nothing and we would have lost irreplaceable warriors without saving my father.

Henry Samuel threw himself from the saddle, "Grandfather?"

His words sent lead into my heart. I had hoped that he had seen Matthew and Mark, "Did you not see him? He was wounded, perhaps mortally, and Mark and Matthew took him to safety."

"We saw no one. We reached the King but it was the Duke of Brittany who ordered them to ride hard." He pointed to the next standards which headed in our direction, "See the King comes now with the bulk of the army." I looked up and saw the King leading the knights of Navarre. They were coming at a steady pace!

I cursed our tardy leader! Had he done as the Duke had done then he might have caught the whole of the Ayyubid army and defeated them. I put that thought from my head. We had to find my father, our squires, Peter of York and Richard Red Leg.

"Fetch our horses! We must find the Earl and Richard! They are lost somewhere!"

There might have been a time those who did not come from the valley of the Tees might have questioned my orders but not now and all went to their horses.

"Cedric, you and the archers escort the priests, our servants and wounded back to Ascalon. We will seek our men. Padraig, find us a couple of spare horses so that we can extend our search if we need to."

"We could help you, lord." Cedric's voice was concerned.

"I have enough to do what is necessary with the men who are here. Those who are hurt need to be tended for they have all fought like lions." Henry Samuel held Thorn for me as I mounted. We would not be able to ride hard as our horses had been pushed to the limit but we had to search. I turned in the saddle, "Spread out in a long line. Look for any sign of their passing."

Our squires and Peter were clever. They would know they had to try to do something to stop the bleeding on Richard Red Leg's wound. As for my father? I knew not if he lived or was dead already. Was I the Earl of Cleveland? I was not ready to be the lord of the Tees. I just wanted to find my father and get him to a healer; he had good mail and a well-made helmet. Although the blows which had incapacitated him had been hard, he had not fallen from the saddle. We found stragglers on the road heading north. They were the ones we had saved by our charge. They were not just the men who had followed the Earl of Fife, there were some men from France. Some had horses and some did not. They had banded together for mutual self-protection. We asked each group if they had seen my father but none had.

One Scottish knight, Sir David of Peebles, said, "I hope your father lives, Sir William, for his charge saved our lives."

I merely nodded for I was angry. That the Earl of Fife should live and my father die, seemed to me to be the greatest of injustices. After we had passed our tenth group of stragglers, I called a halt. "They have not come up this road." I pointed to the south and east where I knew there was water. "We head back towards the battlefield. They must have stopped sooner rather than later."

If any thought my order foolish then none spoke up. It soon became obvious that none had passed this way. It was John, my page, whose sharp eyes spotted the anomaly. "My lord, due east, I spy smoke."

Sir James of Evesham said, "And why should that mean anything?"

Padraig answered for me, "Because, my lord, there are two wounded men. It is many miles to Ascalon and Peter of York is a good man who knows how to tend to wounds. Richard Red Leg had a bad wound and it would need to be tended. Perhaps they stopped to light a fire and examine the wound or it may be that they are too badly wounded to carry on. Whatever the reason, it is worth investigating!"

I waved my men forward. We had to keep a steady pace as much as I might have wished to hurry and discover if this was our men. When we were a mile away it became obvious that it was our men. I recognised the horses. They waved at us and I began to prepare myself for the worst as we neared them. I saw that three men stood, Matthew, Mark and Peter. My father and Richard Red Leg lay covered by their cloaks. I dismounted and looked at Peter of York.

"They both live, my lord, and we have used a heated blade to seal the wounds and stop the bleeding. The wound on the Earl's leg was not dangerous but Richard Red Leg's was. He will need a healer. He was awake before we burned his leg. Now he sleeps."

"And my father?"

"Made neither sound nor movement when we burned the wound and I dared not try to remove the helmet for it is dented badly. The bleeding from his head has stopped." That chilled my heart for bleeding from a head wound could not be good.

I knelt next to my father and saw that Peter had lifted the visor. Taking off my own helmet and coif I put my ear next to my father's mouth. He was breathing but it was laboured. I put my mouth to his ear, "Be strong, father. We will do all in our power to aid you. God will not allow such a valiant warrior to perish like this." I saw the wooden cross with the Whitby jet hanging from his neck. It must have come free when he had been laid down. I unfastened it and put it in my father's fingers. The Archbishop of York had given it to him. I prayed that God would not let my father die.

We had to get back to Ascalon and the healers who were there. It was getting on towards dark and that might be our salvation for it would be cooler. The danger would be attacks from our enemies. I saw that Peter had found somewhere close to a tiny stream. I took a decision.

"Fill your skins with water. Then water the horses; let them drink deeply for they have a long ride ahead of them. If you have food then eat. Padraig, Peter, Mark and Matthew, rig two litters between the spare horses. When that is done, we will head north. First, we pray!"

All of us knelt and held our swords before us. Each man's prayers were silent but I know that each of them prayed that the two wounded men before us would survive the journey which was to come.

Padraig and Peter of York finished the first litter and it allowed Mark and Matthew to finish the other, "Lord, have something to drink yourself. It will avail us nothing if you succumb to this heat."

"You are right, Padraig." I drank deeply and handed the waterskin to Henry Samuel to refill. "We will need good men at the rear and in the van."

He nodded, "Then they will be our men. The others have come on in the last month but the battle today has taken much out of them."

"You are right." Peter of York had gone back to my father. "How is he, Peter?"

"I wish I knew, lord, for I know of no one who understands what goes on inside a man's skull."

I stood, "There is one but he is at Montfort and that might as well be on the other side of the world. We will get nothing done by waiting. Let us lift and secure my father. "

"Better we try Richard first, lord. Then we will see what problems are created."

"You are right, Peter, and I am not thinking straight."

"You have much excuse, lord.

Padraig shouted, "Master Henry and Master John, hold the horses. Mark, Peter, come and help us to lift Richard!"

Had we taken the hauberk from Richard it might have been easier but that could have awoken him and I knew that sleep would help the two wounded men to recover more quickly. We managed to put the sergeant on the litter and we learned what not to do. We were even more careful with my father for he had a head wound. When they were secured on the litters, we mounted. Henry Samuel rode one of the spare horses and John the other. They were both the smallest of any of us and they could watch the two men for signs of distress. I rode on one side with Mark while Matthew and Padraig rode on the other. If we were attacked then it would be up to the knights and the rest of the men at arms to protect us. I would not leave my father's side until we reached a doctor.

It was a long ride through the night. Others were also heading north from the battlefield. We were not the first to reach the camp at Ascalon. The Earl of Fife was already there. That would have been the moment for him to come to speak with me and thank us for our actions. Instead, he just stared at us and then went inside his tent. Cedric and the other wounded were also back in the camp and the three priests left the men they had tended to see to my father. They brought with them some of the healers from the holy orders. They were all Hospitallers and I knew them to be good men. After giving a cursory examination of Richard Red Leg they carefully removed the helmet from my father's head. I knew it was necessary but I feared that as soon as it was removed his life would end. It did not. They took off the bloody coif and I saw that the white arming cap was almost black with blood. He had bled a great deal and the senior Knight Hospitaller shook his head.

"This is not good, Sir William. He lives and we can bandage his head but none of us has the skill to probe beneath the skull. His leg will heal and we can keep him alive with water, wine and broth but someone with more skill than we have will need to finish the work on Sir Thomas."

"Is there any?" I knew the answer but I hoped that there would be one who was closer than Montfort.

He shook his head, "The only one is the Teutonic Knight Conrad von Schweistein and he is close to the land of the Turk at Montfort."

There was but one answer. If I could not take my father there then I would have to fetch the doctor thither.

Chapter 7

We had the two invalids placed in our tent and Padraig and I, along with our squires and pages, slept there. The healers told us that while Richard would recover, he had lost the full use of his left leg. He could ride and fight but he would never be able to fight on foot. He woke in the middle of the morning and I heard Padraig explain to him that he was lucky. There would still be a place for Richard in my father's castle; no man was ever rejected because of a wound but the decision concerning his future as a warrior would be his. He was silent after Padraig had finished. I was awake and, after checking up on my father and seeing that he was still comfortable, I went outside for men were returning from the south.

The disaster of the battle of Gaza was not as bad as it might have been. That was down to two things; my father's sacrifice and the Duke of Brittany's determination to save what was left of the army the Duke of Burgundy had led south. I spoke with the returning knights and discovered that barely one hundred and forty knights had survived. There were many prisoners who would languish in Egyptian captivity. The Duke of Burgundy and Amaury de Montfort were two such prisoners. It also became clear that Ascalon would be abandoned and we would return to Acre. Once I discovered that I hurried back to our camp and woke the others.

"Until my father recovers then I command this conroi. The army is leaving Ascalon. The King will make his way here but we will leave. I intend to vacate this camp tonight. Sir Stephen, I want two wagons procuring for our wounded. When the bulk of the army arrives then wagons will be in great demand; added to that the road will be clogged. I will go and speak with the commander of the camp and explain my reasons." I did not allow for debate and all went about their business.

The captain of the camp was an old knight who had served the King of Navarre for many years. Raymond de Maine was an old-fashioned soldier and I liked him. "It is good that you ask but you of all people do not need to do so. Your father's actions might have saved a great number of men. I am sorry that it has come to this for the healers have told me that they can do nothing. I will pray for your father. King Thibaut will return by dawn and then the camp will break. I fear that his plans for a swift end to this crusade will come to nought."

We left the camp by the north road and that meant we had to pass by the camp of the Earl of Fife. He must have been waiting for us to do so for he came out and said, loudly, "Typical of an Englishman! He runs when danger draws close."

Padraig's hand went to his sword but I said, "Hold. There will be a time for swords but it is not yet." I turned to the Scot. "You have neither honour nor nobility. If you had either you would have begged forgiveness for the pain you caused my people. My father lies at death's door because he came to your aid."

"I did not ask him and I have done nothing to be forgiven for. You took our land! I will take it back one day!"

Sir David of Peebles was close by and he suddenly burst out, "I will follow you no longer, Malcolm of Fife, for Sir William is right you have no honour. I will take my men back to Scotland to seek another lord who is worthy. You are not."

I saw the effect of the Scotsman's words. Other Scottish knights could not disguise the disgust they felt for the Earl. A chorus of them added their voices to David of Peebles.

I leaned from my saddle, "When you reach Acre, Earl, and my father has received attention then you and I will decide this matter by force of arms. You choose the weapons. If you do not relish the prospect then scuttle back to Fife!"

His face told me that he was afraid of such combat and he turned on his heel and went back into his tent. My men all cheered for they knew that this was a victory.

It was a long and slow journey back to Acre. I did not wish for a rough journey and we stopped often to rest the horses and for our three healers to attend to the wounded. My father remained in what the priests called God's sleep but they gave him water and broth. It took a long time to do both. We reached Acre just after the first of the wounded men who had come from the battle. Only my father needed the attention of the Hospitallers. Mark, John and Henry Samuel became his guards.

I told the castellan of my plan to ride to Montfort. He counselled against such an action. "We have heard that the emir whose caravan you raided has been to Damascus to demand that the truce be ended. The whole of the border is in turmoil. It will be a most dangerous journey."

"Nonetheless I must go but I will take only my men at arms and archers. The rest I leave here under the command of Sir Stephen of Malton."

That meant I would only have three men at arms and six archers. Along with Matthew that would be a very small number to go through what was now considered the front line of the war against the Muslims. I chose Flame as my horse but had Thorn as a backup. I waited only until the Duke of Brittany returned. I needed him to know what I was about and to ask him to keep an eye on the Earl of Fife.

The Duke was genuinely upset about the wound to my father. I saw in his eyes that he thought my father would die. "He was a brave man and the crusade will miss his sage advice."

"He is not dead, my lord, and I will bring a healer who can save his life. We are in the Holy Land and God's presence is everywhere. You are right, my father is a good man and with the help of Conrad von Schweistein and Almighty God, he will be saved and we will go home."

"Then I will watch over him."

"And I urge you to prevent the Earl of Fife from doing him or the men I leave here harm."

He looked shocked at the vehemence of my words and the message I gave, "Surely, after having his men and his own life saved the Earl will be eternally grateful to your father."

I shook my head, "No, lord, for this a feud which has its origins in the borders. When I return, I shall end it here on the field of combat."

"The King will not allow it."

"The King's vacillation led to my father's wound. He is no king of mine and I do not obey his commands. This is not Navarre!"

"You tread a dangerous road, Sir William!"

I laughed, "And that has ever been the way of my family."

We left in the late afternoon and endured a couple of hours of heat before the relative cool of the evening made the next few miles easier. We found a village which had been settled by the families of the first crusaders. They lived a perilous existence close to the fortress of Acre and Montfort. They were the children of men who had married local women. We paid for our beds and food. I did not wish to risk the mountain road to Montfort at night and so we broke that journey up over two days. As the crow flies the distance was not a great one but the road was not the best and the heat of the day exhausted horses. Despite the fact that time was slipping away I knew the dangers of not showing the land respect.

We spied Montfort for a good hour before we reached it. It was a spur castle on the top of the ridge and I could see why it had been chosen as a castle site. I had no doubt that we had been seen before we saw the castle. It was not a place where an enemy could approach unseen. We must have been recognised for the gates were opened to admit us and I was taken directly to Burchard. "What is amiss, Sir William? Your presence here, without your father, does not bode well."

I shook my head, "No, Master, for there has been a disaster." I told him of the battle and my father's wound.

Baron's Crusade

He shook his head, "Sergeant, go and fetch Brother von Schweistein." The sergeant left us and the Commander shook his head, "That is the trouble with some of the lords from France. They see this land as a land of plunder. I fear this crusade is doomed." I nodded. He added, quietly, "You know that as good as Conrad is, he may not be able to save your father?"

"I do but my father is strong and he is a fighter. He will not give in to this."

"It may be God's will."

Shaking my head, I said, "I cannot believe that for this is my father's third crusade. God will watch over him, surely." His words worried me and I was not sure if I was right. Perhaps God would take him. Refreshments were brought but I paid little attention to them. I was waiting for the doctor.

Conrad arrived, "The sergeant said there is a head wound to Sir Thomas. I take it you wish me to try to heal him." I nodded. "Describe the wound."

I did so and he shook his head. "If he is alive when we return then there is hope but you must brace yourself for the fact that he might be dead. Head wounds are like that. How long ago did you leave him?"

"It took three days to reach here."

The Master of Montfort smiled, "We can have you back in one night. The road is harder when you do not know it and it is a hard climb to get here. I have men who can guide you back far quicker. Rest during the day and I will send men back with you this evening. I have despatches which need to go to the new Hochmeister in Acre."

Conrad said, "I will need to gather what I need. I will see you at dusk, Sir William, and I promise that I will do all in my power to save the life of your father." He left.

The Commander of Montfort took me by the arm, "And before you rest, I have intelligence to give to you. This is for the ears of the King and the Duke of Brittany."

"I fear that the losses the army has suffered means an end to this crusade."

"Not so for I have learned much in the time I have been here."

It was a complicated story he told me. Saladin had held the Muslim factions together but, since his death, the power had been dissipated amongst others. The Egyptians in the south were a threat but, in the north, there were minor leaders who fought with each other. Al-Muzaffar Mahmud of Hama fought against his neighbour Al-Mujahid of Homs, and the Master believed that the King of Navarre might be able to exploit the dissension. In addition, As-Salih Ismail, Emir of

Damascus was an enemy to An-Nasir Dawud, the emir whose caravan we had destroyed.

"For the first time, it is the Muslims who fight amongst themselves and not the Christians. This defeat at Gaza may prove to be a blessing in disguise for those who might have resented King Thibaut's orders will now be more likely to stay within the fold. If we can exploit this heaven-sent division then there might be hope and light in this dark night."

The Master's words gave me hope and I slept slightly better, that day than I expected.

It was good that we had brought spare horses. We rode all night. It was cool and the fact that it was late November meant that the nights were longer than the days. We watched the sun rise behind us and illuminate Acre, just a few miles away. I shook my head, "I could have reached you a day earlier if I had pushed our horses harder!"

Conrad shook his head, "The man who led us was born in this land and knows every inch of the road between Montfort and Acre. I would not have risked the road but I trusted Raymond. This was meant to be, Sir William. If the healers feed your father and give him water and wine then he will stay alive. The brain is a complicated organ and the stillness of bed rest can only help but do not get your hopes up. Even if I save his life, he may never be able to function as a man. You understand that?"

I stopped Thorn, "What do you mean?"

"I do not know all that there is to know about the way the brain works but I read some of the writings from the doctors in Constantinople. They think that the brain controls different functions. One part the eyes, one the voice, one the arms and so on. Thus, part of the skull might be damaged but the rest might be healthy. Do you see?"

I thought back to the dented helmet. Suppose the part of the skull which had been damaged was the part which gave speech, hearing, or sight. I felt a sudden chill. If I lost the ability to see then I am not certain I would wish to live.

Conrad said, quietly, "Let us not see a pit of despair. I have yet to examine Sir Thomas."

When we reached the hospital, I was pleased to see not only Mark on guard but two Bretons. The Duke of Brittany had kept his promise. The three priests we had brought were inside with my father. I went in and saw that, whilst my father lay still, his fingers still clutched the Archbishop's cross. Conrad shooed us away so that he could examine him and speak with Brother Paul and the other priests. I was selfish and I did not do as I ought to have done and spoken to the King first.

Instead, I spoke to my men, knights and Mark. I learned that the Earl of Fife had taken ship and returned to England. More than half of the knights who had survived the battle of Gaza had left his service. But Sir Stephen felt the real reason he left was that he did not wish to face me in battle. Richard Red Leg was using crutches and he came to see me while we awaited the diagnosis from the Teutonic Knight.

"The leg is weak, my lord. They will have to call me Richard the Gammy now, but I should be able to ride. If your father would continue to have me as a sergeant then I will end my life beneath his banner!"

Padraig had spoken to me on the journey to Montfort and I knew that all of my men at arms wished Richard to continue to be one of them. I knew that it would bond them even closer.

I nodded, "And if God chooses to take my father then you can serve me."

Richard made the sign of the cross, "Fear not, Sir William, your father will live. I feel it here." He tapped his heart.

Conrad seemed to be inside for a long time and when he emerged, he was wiping some blood from his hands.

"Well?"

"There is hope. Before I can operate, I need to find a goldsmith for parts of the skull are missing. He will need a metal plate fitting for some of the bone is missing. Gold would be best. Have you any gold to melt?"

Padraig nodded, "Aye, lord, for we took gold from the heathens at Gaza. We were going to share it before going home but Sir Thomas is welcome to it and more."

Conrad smiled, "It will not need much. I am too tired to operate today but tonight you should all pray for tomorrow I will try to save the life of Sir Thomas. Now, I pray you leave us, for I have measurements to take." He looked at me, "Did you place the cross in his hand?"

"I did."

"He clings on to it and God watches over him; there is hope, Sir William."

While Padraig fetched the gold, I went in to see my father. Henry Samuel sat at his side. Mark had told me that my nephew had not left the chamber since I had left. My father was so still that he looked dead and yet Conrad's words had given me hope. His hands, still clutching the cross, felt warm as I held them. "Father, I would have you live! You have another grandson you need to watch grow. You have one here who has shown how we feel about you. Live so that you can see the others grow." I stood, "Come, Henry Samuel, the priests will watch over him.

You need to eat and sleep. Tomorrow is the day when he will need all of our prayers. This is not a request, it is a command!"

He came although he looked tearful. The blood on Conrad's hands had been worrying. I ate a hearty breakfast before I sought out the Duke of Brittany. I told him what I had learned. He nodded. "This may be the news that the King needs. The defeat at Gaza has laid his spirits low; more than that Amaury de Montfort and Hugh of Burgundy were his friends. That they are prisoners of the Muslims weighs heavily upon him. I will give him your news and I, too, will pray for your father."

Around the castle hung an air of despondency and despair. It was not only the Earl of Fife who had taken ship for home. Some of those whose lords had been captured either sought another master or, in most cases, cut their losses and headed for more familiar and less dangerous pastures. The reason for the depression in my camp was the worry about my father. However, I was now the leader of this conroi and I sought out the five men whose knights had died. Sir Walter, Sir Henry and Sir Robert had joined Sir Hubert of Lewes in a grave in the Holy Land.

"You have served your lords well and if you wish to take ship home then I will pay your passage. If you wish to stay then I can offer you employment with my retinue."

Tom of Rydal said, "Lord, I can speak for all of us as we have discussed this in your absence. All of us are happy to serve with you and the other lords for we wish vengeance on our foes. We are doing God's work and our souls will be saved. We will stay."

I was relieved. It meant we could still function as a conroi. I wondered if Richard of Cornwall and the other English barons promised by the King would reach us soon. The crusade had begun in August and it was now almost December. If they did not leave England soon then they would have to wait until the spring and more favourable weather. I wondered if that was the real reason for the delay. It would not surprise me for Richard and Henry were King John's sons and whilst they were not as bad as their father, they must have inherited some of his blood, and when news of the defeat at Gaza reached England it would give them pause for thought.

I slept badly that night because I worried about my father. I spent an hour praying for him and I know that the rest of the men of Stockton did the same. When I woke, I went directly to my father, even though it was dark. One of our three priests was with him. I gave a questioning look to Father Paul who shook his head, "He has not moved, lord. That is a good sign. His breathing is regular and he has not brought forth the water and broth we fed him. Do not worry. This doctor knows his business and we are all anxious to help him that we might learn."

Baron's Crusade

I just wanted my father whole. As I left, I saw Conrad. He was dressed in a simple white shift. He had a piece of cloth which he unwrapped. I saw within it a curved piece of gold a little larger than a golden crown. "This may save your father's life. There is enough skin left that when we have cleaned the wound and examined the problem, we should be able to stitch this in place so that none will know that your father wears a golden crown." My doubt must have shown for Conrad went on, "This is the first time I have done this but I have read of such an operation being carried out many times. The method is tried and tested. When it goes wrong it is down to the lack of skill in the doctor." I looked him in the eye, "So you see, William, if this fails and your father dies then you can blame me and that may help. I will do my best but I am just a man."

I nodded, "I know for the alternative is that he dies and I do not wish that. As you say it is in God's hands and your honesty speaks well of you. Good luck!"

He left. Padraig and Peter of York arrived. They had followed the Teutonic Knight into the hospital. "You two stay and guard the door. Send to me immediately if you know anything. I will try to keep my nephew occupied."

"Do not worry, lord. I have followed Sir Thomas since well before you were born. He will survive."

The Duke of Brittany was not happy to sit back and do nothing. He had his men patrolling the major roads to keep the pilgrims there safe. The military orders all did the same but we were crusaders and it was better than sitting, as King Thibaut did in Acre's Great Hall. If my father had not been so close to death, I would have had my men doing the same. As it was, I just tried to keep myself occupied.

Mark and his brother sought me out. In a way I was pleased for conversation would keep my mind off the knife that was delving into my father's skull. "Lord, can we speak?"

"Of course, Matthew."

The two squires were twins but Matthew always seemed the elder and I knew not why. He was always sensitive and thoughtful. He showed that now, "It is my brother. He has not slept since the battle."

"Bad dreams, Mark?"

He shook his head, "No, lord, I let the Earl down. I should have saved him and I did not. What kind of squire am I?"

"Like your brother a good one. What do you think you could have done?"

"I could have done what he did at Arsuf!"

That was the trouble with the legend. My father had often spoken of his frustration at what people perceived he had done. "You did more than he did, Mark, for his knight, my grandfather, died. You helped to prevent the Earl from suffering more wounds."

"But he was wounded twice!"

I said, quietly, "What you are saying, Mark, is that Sir Stephen and myself failed my father for we flanked him!"

He looked shocked at the thought, "No, lord, you both fought bravely,"

"And yet he had one wound on Sir Stephen's side and one on mine. What other conclusion can I draw?"

He shook his head in frustration. He was not able to make himself clear, "I am saying that I should have been there."

"Mark, one day, you will be a knight as will your brother. When you go into battle there is no certainty that you will survive. My father and I confess our sins before we go into battle for we know that we may not survive. We hope that we will but there are no certainties. All of us can fall in battle and there is no blame attached to any other knight or squire, except those who flee. You did not flee. You stood your ground and were willing to die for my father. For that I thank you. There is no greater accolade to give a dead warrior than to say he died saving the lives of others. Now go and get some sleep. When my father recovers, and I pray that he will, he will need as much attention as we can give him."

They left and I was glad that they had asked the question. If they had not then it would have eaten away at their insides and, in the next battle, they might have done something foolish. It was after noon when Padraig came for me.

"Sir William, the doctor has finished." He saw my look and shrugged. "He did not die under the Teuton's knife, lord. He said he would speak with you, first."

I went with a heavy heart for I feared the worst. I would be the one to have to return home and tell my family that I had failed to protect my father and he was either dead or the shell of the man who had left England to do the bidding of an ungrateful king. When the door opened, I was taken aback for the white tunic worn by the doctor now looked as though he had been butchering animals. The three priests were cleaning the floor and they, too, bore the blood of my father.

Conrad smiled as he washed his hands, "It looks far worse than it was. The operation went well."

"Then he will fully recover?" My heart soared.

Shaking his head, Conrad said, "I did not say that. I removed some embedded bone from the brain and some clotted blood. That is why we are so messy. I placed the plate in place and sewed up the skin around it. We had to shave your father's head first and so he will look strange to you."

"Can I see him?"

"He is there."

I saw that my father's head was swathed in bandages so that only his nose, mouth and eyes were visible. If the bandages had been made of metal then he would have looked as though he was mailed. His hands still clutched the cross.

"Will he recover?"

Conrad smiled, "He will wake but it is too early to say what effects the wound and the operation will have in the long term. As I told you, I am uncertain what parts of the brain control the body. There was damage. I just do not know what the effects will be. He breathes easier and he will open his eyes when he recovers from the opiates we gave him."

"Opiates?"

"They have potions here, in the east, which come from much further east than any I know have travelled. They numb pain and ease sleep. Used in quantity then they can kill but, in small doses, they can help a healer. He will sleep and hopefully start to recover. The three of us are weary. Have your men watch him for the next twelve hours. If he wakes then send for me. Other than that, you pray to God."

In the time we had been talking the three priests had cleaned the room and there was just my father and me there with the doctor.

"Thank you, Conrad. I am in your debt."

"I fought in the Baltic Crusade and know the reputation your father had. It was an honour to try to save him. I have only made a down payment on the Sword Brethren debt. And now I will pray and then eat."

I sat in the seat next to my father and held his hand. Padraig opened the door, "Well, my lord?"

"He lives and we wait. Send for Mark and Henry Samuel. They will wish to be here. As for the rest, you can stand down. This is now my watch."

"Aye, lord, but we will not be far away."

Baron's Crusade

Sir Thomas

I was floating. I knew not where I was except that I could hear voices but they seemed to be in the next room. I thought I recognised Mark and his brother but I could not be sure. I was just fascinated by this feeling of lightness and floating. I felt no pain and yet I should have for I had been cut about my leg. I looked down and saw nothing save white. It was not the white of Baltic snow. It looked like clouds. Was I dead? That would explain why I did not feel pain. I tried to think back to the battle. Was it yesterday or last week? I had been hit in the head! I heard more voices and they were ones I did not recognise. I forced myself to think back to the battle. We had been winning and then I was struck from behind. I was getting old for there would have been a time when my reactions would have saved me. Perhaps we had won. That was an illusion. We could not have won. Winning would have meant defying the greatest odds I had ever fought and I knew that our enemies were good. I had to be dead. Was this purgatory? Crusaders were said to be able to miss out on purgatory and go straight to heaven. This did not feel like heaven for I was alone and heaven should be filled with others who had died well. Where were my son, Alfred, and my father? Where were my grandfather and the Warlord? Where was Aunt Ruth? Then a chilling thought came to me. Despite Bishop Albert's words and the promise of Pope Gregory perhaps my murder of the Bishop of Durham was so great a sin that St Peter and St Michael would not let me enter heaven. Or perhaps I was not dead and this was some dream. I had had bad dreams before and forced myself to wake up. I would try to do so again! Suddenly I felt a great heat as though I had been plunged into a fire; I tried to scream but no words came forth. Had I gone to hell? Was this the fire of hell which burned me? Then I saw a cross before me and I reached for it. My fingers wrapped around it and I felt the smoothed wood. I felt easier. The heat disappeared and I saw the face of my son, William. He looked pained. Was he with me? Had he been wounded? I gripped the cross and tried, once more, to rouse myself from this dream.

No matter how much I tried I could not wake myself and then I felt the blackness return. The white clouds disappeared and I felt pain again. Did this mean I was not dead? If I could feel pain then I had to be alive. I felt as though I had a great weight upon my head. My skull felt as though it was being crushed. Then there was a blinding light and both the pain and weight went. Once more I was in a white world and I began to hear voices again. This time I did not recognise any. Then the voices disappeared and silence enveloped me once more; I was not used to silence. Even in my solar at my castle in Stockton, there were sounds: the guards on the fighting platform, the laughter of women at St. John's well, birds singing, my wife commanding the servants, horses neighing in the bailey. This was total silence. Even the voices disappeared and then, when they came back again, I recognised my son and grandson. They were close and I had to wake to find them. This was a dream and this time I would free myself from its tentacles. I would wake myself. I forced myself to remember the faces of my family. I began with the hardest, my grandfather, and worked through all the others until I came to my newest grandson, Richard. I could not make out his features for he was just a baby but I felt better for having remembered him. The white began to thin. It became less cloud-like and more like fog.

Chapter 8

Henry Samuel sat on the other side of the bed and Mark at the foot. I think he still felt some sort of responsibility for the wounds my father had received. Silence filled the room and Henry Samuel broke it. "Will we go home now, uncle?"

"Why? Our work is not done."

"We lost the battle."

"A battle was lost but not by us. We still hold Jerusalem and our enemies are divided. We must stay strong and we will prevail but my father may well travel home if he is well enough. You should go with him."

I saw the dilemma written all over my nephew's face. He would wish to travel home with my father yet not miss out on potential glory. My father had been knighted after Arsuf. It was the sort of dream every young squire and page dreamed of. There would be no test, no vigil, no song composed and sung before an audience, no sergeant at arms to test you with lance and sword. One moment a squire and the next a knight. My father had shown that it could happen.

I smiled at Sam; he was still young, "All of this is in the future. The doctor says that he will not know my father's condition until he wakes and he can be examined. We just sit and we watch. If he wakes, we tell the doctor; that is all." Twelve hours can seem endless and just watching this mummified man who was as still as a corpse was hard to bear. We knew the passage of time when candles spluttered and died and we relit a fresh one. Twelve hours had passed and still, he had not woken.

The doctor returned and frowned, "He has not woken?"

"He has barely stirred, Conrad. I listened at his mouth and he breathes but that is all."

The doctor leaned over and listened. He put his hand under the bedsheets and felt his heart. "His signs are all good. This may mean that the operation has failed. A man can only survive for so long on broth, beer and wine." He turned and spoke to Father Paul, "Fetch sal ammoniac. Let us see if it can rouse him."

"Is that wise?" I had heard of this liquid whose smell was so powerful that it was said, it could wake the dead!

"There is much we do not know about the medicine we practise. I know not if it is wise but it is something that I will try."

Father Paul returned with the vial and, after opening the waxed top and looking for the nod from Conrad, held the pungent potion under my father's nose. There was a momentary pause and then my father coughed; suddenly his eyes popped wide open. It was the first time I had seen his eyes since the Battle of Gaza and I took it to be a good sign.

"Praise God!"

His eyes darted to me as I spoke!

Conrad nodded, "He can hear and, I am guessing, he can see for he looked at you. We know that he can smell. Let us see if he can speak. Sir Thomas, who am I?"

His eyes narrowed as though he was concentrating. "I know I should know you but your name... you are next to my son and so you must be a friend!"

"Praise be to God; he knows you are his son! I am Conrad von Schweistein your physician and this is wondrous. Father Paul, have some soft eggs and bread prepared. Fetch a bowl of soft fruit."

"He is healed, doctor?" My hopes began to rise.

Conrad laughed at my question. "Let us say we have taken a couple of tentative steps. We have more to learn but for now, this is enough. While he eats why do you not tell him what has happened since he was wounded?"

I stood, "Aye, I will but first, Mark, go and tell our men the good news." I threw him a purse. "The ale and wine are on me. If they drink that purse dry there is another!"

"Aye lord." He caught the purse and then ran to my father. He grabbed his hands and kissed them. They still clutched the cross, "I am sorry I failed you, lord. If you will give me another chance, I will do much better." Before my father could respond he ran out.

"He seems like a thoughtful boy; do I know him? I seem to recognise him but I could not put a name to him."

I looked at the doctor who shrugged, "It is early days. He knows you and that is important. Ask him if he knows Henry Samuel."

"Sam, speak."

I saw tears welling up in my nephew's eyes. What if his grandfather did not recognise him? "Do you know me, grandfather?"

My father turned his head and smiled, "Of course for you are the image of my son, Alfred. You are his boy."

We all breathed a sigh of relief. He knew his family and that was a start.

Conrad said, "Do you think that you could move up the bed to sit upright? If not, we will help you."

"I am not a child nor an invalid, doctor. Of course, I can!" Although he managed it, I saw trouble in his eyes.

The doctor did too. "What is wrong, Earl?"

"It is probably nothing but I could not feel the covers when I pushed."

Conrad went to the bottom of the bed and lifted the sheet. "But you can smell?"

"I smelled the stink which woke me and I can smell the perfume you wear doctor. I can smell my son's sweat. Aye, I can smell."

The doctor lowered the sheet. "But you cannot feel me stroking the bottom of your feet. Like your memory that may return but…"

My father nodded, "Then again it may not." He gripped his cross tightly and then frowned. "I have much to thank God for. I have a son and grandson who live and I am not yet dead. Yet I cannot feel the wood on this cross."

"I will leave you. The Master of the Hospitallers has some writing about this type of wound. I will read. Your father is correct, Sir William. This is a time for celebration for he lives and we know not what the future holds."

He left us and I saw my father had laid the cross next to him and was looking at his hands as though they were not his own. "So, father, we fought a battle, or rather a battle was fought at Gaza and you bravely led our men to try to save the remnants of the army which was being slaughtered."

"I had forgotten that." He folded his hands together and smiled, "Tell me all and perhaps it may stir some memories in my head which I confess feels as though I am in a fog."

I told him of the battle and Henry Samuel added other details. Although I saw sadness when I told him of the deaths it was clear he knew not who they were. The Earl of Fife, Amaury de Montfort, all these were unknown. Yet, as we spoke, he recalled the names of all of our family and the landmarks around Stockton. He commented on the women laughing around St. John's well as they collected their water. I knew there was hope but I was confused. My father would take time to heal and until the day came when he was whole again, I would still be the leader of the conroi.

The next day Conrad allowed the men of Stockton to visit in twos and threes. My father remembered some, like Cedric, Padraig and Richard Red Leg, but the ones who had served less than a year he did not. The Duke of Brittany came and my father did not recognise him. The King did not come.

At the end of the week, Conrad met with me and Henry Samuel. "This has been a most interesting case, Sir William." He saw the frown on my face. "I am sorry, I know this is distressing for you as I talk of your father as though he is inanimate but you must understand I delved inside a brain and a brain which was damaged. I can now see the damage." I almost held my breath. It was like waiting for a sentence. "Firstly, the memory; he has lost the most recent memories yet he can remember his latest grandson being born. He can relearn the memories he needs to. He still recalls events from long ago. I believe you spoke of Arsuf?"

I nodded, "It was close to Arsuf where we found him when Peter of York lit the fire. He said it was wyrd."

Henry Samuel said, "I did not understand the word."

Conrad smiled, "It is from the Baltic. All this is good. What is less good is the lack of feeling. It is as though the senses on his skin have been taken from him."

"So, he cannot feel, where is the problem?"

Conrad took a candle and held it to me. "Put your hand close to the flame." I did so until the heat made me pull it away. "Your father would not pull it away. He will need to be watched. Tomorrow I will return to Montfort for I have been away for long enough and I am needed there. Before I do, we will take your father to walk around the castle. Let him see his horse. If we can I would like him to try to ride. Riding is a skill which is learned. Does he still have that skill? I do this not because I wish him to go to war again but I have spoken at length with your father and believe I know him a little. He will not wish to ride in a car or a wagon. When I have watched him attempt these things, I will be able to give a more accurate assessment of the effects of the wound and the operation I conducted. I have examined the surgery and there is no bad smell. Brother Paul and the other priests will continue to keep the wound clean. He has eaten well and just needs to walk. We will see if he can walk unaided. He may be unsteady but that is to be expected."

Mark and Henry Samuel helped to dress my father. Padraig had saddled Willow and our knights and men waited in the bailey. When he stood, my father swayed a little. Conrad said, "That is not unusual. Older people do not have the same balance as someone who is young. Earl, can you walk?"

My father said, irritably, "Of course, I can walk." I noticed that he constantly rubbed his fingers together as though trying to get feeling back into them. He stepped forward and reminded me of my nephew Geoffrey when he had first learned to walk. My father reached the door and smiled, "There, I told you."

"Now the stairs. There is a rail and I would use it to keep yourself steady. Mark, walk before him to stop him from falling."

This seemed inordinately cruel of the doctor. The spiral staircase was not easy to navigate but my father nodded and, stepping through the door took the rail and began to make his way down the stairs. That he made it, surprised all of us save Conrad and my father. I carried my father's sword. Conrad had asked me to bring it. As we stepped out into the bright and chilly December morning my father raised his eyes to shade them from the sun. For some reason that delighted Conrad. He saw my look and said, "I feared that some other of his natural instincts would have gone but this bodes well."

As we stepped into the bailey and Mark moved to the side our men saw him and cheered. My father smiled and walked toward Padraig and Willow. He stroked Willow's muzzle but the frown told me that he had hoped he would feel the soft hair. Willow snorted and seemed to nod.

Conrad said, "Sir William."

I stepped forward. "Father, your sword." He looked quizzically at me. "You do not need it here for you are safe but you are a knight."

"Quite so. Mark." He held his hands up so that Mark could fit it.

Conrad said, quietly, "Earl, could you draw the weapon?"

Mark said, "My lord, he will not have the strength!"

"No, Mark, the doctor is quite right. I am a knight and I should be able to hold a sword." He took a deep breath and drew the sword from the scabbard. Mark had cleaned and oiled it and it slid out easily.

As he raised it up Padraig shouted, "Sir Thomas, Earl of Stockton!"

Our men took up the chant. I saw my father smile and then swing the blade back and forth in the exercises he had taught Alfred and me. He had not forgotten how to wield a sword. He slid it back in the scabbard and nodded.

"And now, Earl, try to mount your horse."

Willow was the gentlest of horses and she stood stock still as Mark helped to place my father's foot in the stirrup. Henry Samuel was on hand in case he could not swing his leg over Willow's rump but he managed it and even succeeded in slipping his foot into the other stirrup.

Padraig handed him the reins and nodded to him, "It is good to see you in the saddle, my lord."

In answer, my father touched his heels into Willow's flanks and the palfrey began to trot around the bailey. At first, my father used two hands but then changed first to his right and then his left. He stopped next to Padraig, "So I am not completely useless. I can walk, wield a sword and ride. There is hope."

Conrad took me by the arm as Padraig and Mark helped him down. "I have done all that I can. I believe that there is nothing more your father can do in this land and should return home to England. He came as close to death as any man I have ever treated. God has given him a reprieve. He should exercise regularly and within a month or more he should be able to travel."

"But the winter storms mean that he will not be able to do so until April or May, but I thank you. I will retain command of the retinue until he goes home."

"You know that he will wish to stay but you must be strong and make him return to England. I have written a letter to give to the doctors he will see when he is home."

"Of course, he will try to stay and I have my arguments ready. Take care, Conrad von Schweistein and go with God."

I never saw him again but my family, England and the King had much to thank him for. He gave us back the warlord's heir.

The first thing my father demanded was to leave the hospital and move back to our camp. Despite the conditions, it seemed to make him happy and, indeed, except for the memory losses, which continued, and the constant rubbing of fingers, he looked to be back to himself. The bandage would remain wrapped around his head for another two weeks. I spent as much time with him as I could. All of the men knew to watch for danger. He was like a small child who knew no fear. Hot things were a danger as were sharp objects. He managed to badly slice his hand on his sword the second day after Conrad left. It was so deep that it needed stitches and I knew that he was annoyed with himself. It meant he could not practise with his sword.

A week after Conrad had departed a rider galloped in with the most unwelcome of news. Jerusalem had fallen! An-Nasir Dawud, the emir whose caravan we had raided, had captured it after a short siege. He allowed the garrison to march out and they brought us the news. It caused much consternation and conflict in our camp. The King of Navarre was held responsible for he had made no attempt to strengthen the paltry garrison and the arguments, to which my father and I were a party, almost did the Muslim's work for them. It nearly came to the point of Christian fighting Christian but good sense prevailed. That good sense came, ironically, from my father. He was the one who had had a serious head wound and yet he seemed to think clearer than any. Perhaps it was the wound which afforded him more consideration for while others were shouted down, when my father stood, silence fell upon the gathering of barons.

"It seems to me that we are making more of this incident than we should." I saw knights look at each other wondering how he could make light of such a disaster. "The enemy is still a loose confederation of men who do not like each other." He smiled and waved a hand around the assembled warriors, "A little like we are becoming." I saw Duke Peter smile as some knights flushed with embarrassment. "Emir An-Nasir Dawud is neither popular nor powerful. He has allies in Egypt but As-Salih Ismail, Emir of Damascus is his sworn enemy. What of the Emir of Homs and the Emir of Hama? Let us use our enemies to defeat our enemies."

He paused and drank some wine. Each day he had had me tell him about the politics of the Holy Land for he knew his faulty memory had too many gaps in it. It seemed to me that his memory improved each day. It was as though it was a muscle he had ceased to use and it needed to be active to help it to recover. Although his fingers could still not feel, his memory gradually improved. However, I was by his side all of the time and when he hesitated with names, as he had done with Al-Adil, I had been able to prompt him quietly.

"And then there are the knights who live in this region; men like Bohemond of Antioch. Let us use them. I say we use this time to visit our allies and those who might be allies to build up a confederation which can defeat the Egyptians and retake Jerusalem from this Turk!"

It was a masterful demonstration from a man who was still an invalid. He had shown me his skill on the battlefield many times but that day he showed me another skill, the skill of strategy; he had said that which the King should have done and it united the knights. King Thibaut thanked my father and it was decided to ride north to visit with Bohemond of Antioch and seek an alliance with Emir Al-Muzaffar Mahmud of Hama. At the same time, other parts of the army were asked to raid the lands around Jerusalem to probe for weaknesses. My father wished to travel to Hama but it was decided he still needed to recover and was left at Acre. That meant that my knights were amongst those sent east to probe for weaknesses. The English contingent was going to war once more. Richard Red Leg and Mark were left with my father's page, John, while the rest of us left the safety of Acre for the dangers of the Jordan!

Chapter 9

This time we were riding to war and that meant a different approach than the last time we had headed for Jerusalem. The Duke of Brittany who had gone north with the King had also left ten conroi to do as we were doing and raid the land held by An-Nasir Dawud. Men who had been at Gaza and whose lords were still in captivity volunteered to join the conroi for they wished to fight back. Our intention was to conduct what was, to all intents and purposes, a chevauchée. We would kill soldiers, capture animals and destroy, where we could, enemy strongholds. It was my father's strategy and a clever one as it would focus the attention of the man who had captured Jerusalem on us while the King and the Duke tried to negotiate alliances with other Muslim leaders. It was also well-thought-out as the weather was more conducive to warfare. This was winter. There was rain but neither snow nor frost. Grazing was always a problem in the Holy Land no matter what the season.

The planning was meticulous. Each of the conroi leaders was shown the map of the area and each of us told the others when we would be leaving and how we would raid. The land we had been allocated was towards Nazareth. Others were heading for Nablus and Galilee. This was the heartland of Emir Dawud. My father helped me to plan it. In many ways, it aided his recovery for he had to use his mind and recall battles fought long ago. Richard, Padraig and Cedric sat in with us and they proved a boon for they were able to jog his memory and fill in the blanks and holes.

"Nazareth is twenty-five miles from here. That is too far to get there and back in one day. Better to take two days and scout out the enemy. Recklessly riding into enemy strongholds is never a good idea. That way you have plenty of time to collect animals and drive them back to Acre."

"What of the defences in this land? Will they be forts?"

Padraig and the others could not help my father here and I saw him frown. I prompted him, "When I was young you spoke of Aqua Bella?"

He suddenly smiled, "Aqua Bella! Of course! That belonged to my grandfather for a while but that was built by Christians and is different from the way the Muslims build." He suddenly smiled at me, "Thank you, William, your words have been the key to opening another undiscovered memory. The Muslims like to use mud walls and a single tower. There will, probably, be just one gate in and out. If there is a ditch, and it is unlikely, then it will be a dry one. If you can avoid trying to take these defences for it will cost men. You know that from when the enemy attacked you at Elsdon. If their soldiers are inside their forts then they cannot stop you from taking their animals. When you take their animals, it will draw their men to you." He suddenly glared at us all, "Wear mail!" He fixed his gaze upon Matthew, "Get yourself a full-face helmet or one with a visor and a good head protector! I am living testament to the need for that."

I saw our knights and squires taking in the import of my father's words. All of them now wore mail but I knew that some still had an open helmet. "Thank you for this advice and while we are gone you can continue to recover."

"While you raid, I will continue to ask questions and find the best targets for you to raid. On this first chevauchée, you will not reach Nazareth. I wish to find out more about the men of the towns and villages that you need to attack. You can never have too much knowledge."

I took Flame, and we left before dawn the next day. Cedric was at the fore with a local Christian we had hired. Jean was not a Frank but his mother had married a sergeant from King Richard's Crusade and they had farmed close by Bethlehem of Galilee until the Muslims had killed him and taken their farm. The man was keen to help and Padraig, who had questioned him, trusted him. I knew that it would make our life much easier if we had a local. For one thing, it would enable us to interrogate any prisoners we took.

I rode just two hundred paces behind our archers and our scouts. The archers of the other knights were our rearguard. Our losses meant that we were all much closer in every way possible. Our trials had bound us together. Sir Stephen was my de facto lieutenant. We got on well and he had proved himself to be a doughty warrior. We spoke as we rode.

"From what I can gather, this Bethlehem of Galilee is not the Bethlehem where our lord was born but another with the same name. Jean, our local guide, told me that there is a single tower there and that the locals retire there when they are attacked."

"There is a garrison?"

"That he does not know. We use our archers to get close to the village and then they can signal us. When we are in position our knights and men at arms can charge into the village. Do not expect great numbers of animals or vast quantities of treasure. What we do has no glory but it is necessary. Every warrior we kill means one less to man the walls of Jerusalem should we have to assault it."

That was our other fear; the Emir would gain allies who might join him in Jerusalem. We could not afford an alliance of all the emirs. We needed the discord which kept them at each other's throats. The King's mission to Hama was vital.

This was the first time that Matthew had gone to war without his brother since we had reached this land. Padraig understood him better than most and he kept him close to him. He acted as a mentor to him. The rest of my men were mindful of the losses we had incurred and watched constantly; I do not think that I had ever seen such vigilance. There was neither chatter nor banter. The usual songs my men sang when we first set off were missing. As we passed each jumble of huts, houses and farms, arrows were nocked and men stared intently at every rock and bush watching for an ambush. I knew that Jean or Cedric would have scented any danger but it did no harm for the men to scrutinise everything.

As we rode, I pulled back the mail mitten on my right hand and looked at my palm and fingers. The sense of touch was something we all took for granted. I knew that when I held my sword I preferred to do so without metal between my hand and the hilt. I had wanted to ask my father what it felt like and then realised the ridiculousness of such a question He did not feel. If he went to war again then he would not have the control over his sword that he needed. I knew that I should be grateful that he was alive but what else had he lost that we had yet to discover? His memories would come back, or so Conrad had said, but there were some memories only my father held. We could not stir those memories. What would happen if they never came back?

Padraig was just behind me and he said, quietly, "My lord, the skyline."

I realised that my concentration had lapsed. I turned to see where Padraig pointed. To the south of us was a ridge which followed the road. I forced myself to concentrate and to put my father's ailments from my head.

"There, lord."

I saw what Padraig had seen, a flash of light from metal. The ones who worked on the ridge were shepherds and they needed no metal. The only ones who used metal were warriors. There were soldiers there and they were following us. If they followed us then they had known we would be raiding. Were we riding into a trap?

"Thank you, Padraig! That was remiss of me."

"You have had much on your mind, my lord. The top of the ridge is more than a mile away and the slopes are steep. Whoever it is cannot attack us."

"Yet!" I nodded, "They will wait until we are committed to attacking and then attack us."

Sir Stephen was confused, "Who, Sir William?"

"Do not turn your head but there are warriors on the ridge and they are paralleling our course. Bethlehem of Galilee is just two miles ahead. When I studied the maps, I saw that the village was in a bowl surrounded by high ground. In most parts, the high ground is more than three miles away but in places, it is less than a mile. Matthew, ride to Cedric and tell him that I have seen warriors to the south of us. When we reach Bethlehem of Galilee, he is to surround the village so that no one can escape and then listen for your horn."

"Aye, lord."

"Sir Stephen, now is the chance for you and the other knights to operate by yourselves. When we reach the village and I sound the charge you will lead the knights and your men at arms to attack the town. You will kill as many warriors as you can and capture as many animals. My men at arms and the rest of the archers will stay by me. We will rescue you."

He turned to me, "We are bait?"

"You are bait but the kind of bait which is hard to swallow for you are mailed! We need as many animals collecting as we can get for that will feed us and starve the enemy. If the men who are not warriors fight then slay them, if not try to take them prisoner. They may come in handy when we bargain with the Emir for the return of Jerusalem." He nodded. "Now keep moving while I drop back to speak with my men at arms and the archers."

The conversation I had with my men at arms was easier than that with the ten archers who served the other lords but once I had explained what they had to do they seemed happy enough. I spurred Flame to ride back to Sir Stephen. As I reached him, I sniffed the air and a few paces later I held up my hand. "The village is close."

"How do you know, Sir William? I cannot see the houses nor the huts."

"Nor will you for, as I said, this is in a natural bowl but I can smell animal and human dung. More than that I smell woodsmoke. That means habitation. Have your men move into position."

"But I can see nothing!"

"Good! When you do see anything then stop. Listen for Matthew when he sounds the horn. You will not be facing many warriors. You do not need to ride boot to boot. Cover as much ground as you can. They will run and that will be to the east. There Cedric and my archers wait for them."

"And you, Sir William?"

Baron's Crusade

I pointed to the south, "We will be dealing with the warriors who are already filtering down to attack your rear."

The plan seemed simple but I knew there were many things which could go wrong. The warriors on the ridge had seen our numbers but they had not seen me stop for there was a stand of trees to our right. It was an olive grove underplanted with vines and it had been allowed to grow wild. The Muslims frowned upon wine. In the twenty years since the village had been taken this part had been lost to farming. I pointed my spear to the right and led my tiny band of men into the undergrowth. The vines plucked at our chausses and I took that to be a good sign. The enemy would not expect any warriors to use it.

"Matthew, sound the horn!"

Matthew sounded it three times and I dug my spurs into Flame's sides. I was gambling but I knew that any attack on my men would have to come from the south and the ridge. We would be unseen but, if they did attack Sir Stephen and the others then I would be able to strike at them and take them from their left. I counted on the ten archers I had with me being able to send fifty arrows into the enemy within a short time.

Towards the town, I heard shouts and then screams. There was the clash of metal on metal. We were nearing the edge of the abandoned vineyard and olive grove and I saw, ahead of me, Khwarzamians; the emir had hired mercenaries. Their version of men at arms would have padded garments and a helmet with an aventail and would be called askari. Their horse archers would have neither helmet nor mail. All of this I had learned in Acre; I had spent my time wisely. I said not a word but turned and waved my spear in an arc. It was a signal for the archers to get as close to us as they could and to dismount. They would discomfit the enemy while I led my men at arms and my squire in a ridiculous charge. We would be totally outnumbered but I hoped that the surprise would carry the day for us for they would expect all of our knights to be attacking the town.

I could now concentrate on the enemy. I pulled my shield a little tighter to my body and rested my spear across my cantle. I could now see the enemy through the undergrowth; there appeared to be almost a hundred of them. A daunting number to be attacked by so few but we would be aided by the fact that their horse archers would ride ahead of the men with lances and spears. Their job would be to make our knights and men at arms waste their energy in fruitless attacks on men who could turn and release over the backs of their horses. They would hope to infuriate our men and draw them, weary, onto the spears of their askari. As was normal in such armies they had a higher proportion of archers to askari. I had told Matthew to ride directly behind me. It was partly to protect him and also to give him a better opportunity to strike at someone who was trying to kill Padraig and me! Our silent approach and the noise of the battle in the village meant that we closed with them almost silently despite the coursers we rode. My men at arms all rode a horse which was the equal to any knight's. I turned Flame slightly to the right for I wanted to hit towards the rear of the Khwarzamian askari warriors. That way we would allow our archers more targets and, when we turned, we would be charging into the rear of the enemy. It was neither honourable nor glorious but, then again, honour and glory were highly overrated.

I waved my lance and spurred Flame. With Peter and Padraig flanking me we hit the five askari on the extreme left of the enemy line. I struck first and I was able to bring my lance into the rear of my enemy. He tumbled from the saddle and his falling body helped my lance to slide, bloodily free. Padraig, Rafe and Peter had their own battles to fight. I concentrated on my next target who, obligingly, turned his head to face me and I punched my spear beneath the edge of his mail aventail. He too fell from his horse. The archers who had now dismounted were sending arrow after arrow into the flanks of the askari and heads turned to see where lay the threat. I began my turn and pulled my arm back to strike again with my wooden lance. I saw the broad back of an askari and he was riding a much smaller horse than mine. He heard Flame for my horse had the joy of battle in his nostrils and was snorting loudly. The Khwarzamian saw my lance as it tore into his back. He was a big man and he must have had a mail vest beneath his flowing cloak for the head of my lance broke as it smashed into his back. I threw the now useless weapon away and drew my sword.

The Khwarzamian askari were turning to see who attacked them but there were just five of us, our paucity of numbers merely confused them. I brought my sword across the back and spine of another. It was then I heard another horn and it was not Matthew's; it was Khwarzamian. I began to rein in for I knew that the signal was to turn his men and face the new threat. He knew our numbers!

I shouted, "Matthew, between Padraig and me and prepare your spear!"

As he nudged his horse between us, I saw that he still held his spear and it was bloody. He had killed a man. Now I depended upon Cedric and my archers to defeat the Khwarzamian horse archers. I estimated that the handful of us had killed at least ten men. That was a quarter of their askari. Of course, we were still seriously outnumbered but, to the left of us, were ten archers who could still whittle down the enemy numbers.

"We go for the standard! If that falls then they flee. These are mercenaries! Close up!"

Whereas in our initial attack the open nature of our charge maximised casualties now we needed to be close and make it harder for the enemy to hurt us. Peter and Matthew were the ones still with spears and it was their spears which knocked two askari from their saddles and allowed me to shatter a third spear. Their smaller horses parted to allow our bigger warhorses through. There was no cowardly intent on the part of these brave warriors. Their horses simply would not face the snapping teeth of four Frankish horses. I saw men, to my left, plucked from their saddles by arrows. My archers were doing their part and soon we would have parity with the enemy. Their leader was mailed as was his standard-bearer. The standard-bearer had no weapon except for the standard. The leader's face could not be seen for he had a full-face coif; it was intimidating and his conical helmet had a spike on the top and a horsehair plume. It was an affectation. The advantage I had was in the shield I had for it covered more of my body than the round one held by the amir.

The amir would have an advantage when we clashed for his lance would strike me before I would be able to get my own blow in. I braced myself. I could not see his eyes and I had to use his body language to determine where he would strike at me. If he was experienced then he would not go for my shield as that would shatter his spear. The way I held my shield meant that left only one target, my helmet. If he struck close to the eyepiece then I risked losing one or two eyes for splinters from a shattered spear were deadly. However, I would need to keep my eyes open. It was a risk no matter what I did. To give me as good a chance of survival as I could I forced Flame to get closer to him. Timing was all when a warrior used a lance and the sudden burst of speed from my courser might be just enough to put him off. I began to draw my sword back when I saw him pull back the lance. Had he been going for my middle he would have stood. He would strike upwards and go for my helmet. Knowing that I tipped my head forward slightly. If he mistimed the blow at all then the top of my helmet would make the spearhead slide over it.

His horse must have stumbled slightly for the lance dipped down and struck my shield before springing up and over my helmet. Had his animal not stumbled he would have hit me square on. I stood and swung my sword from on high. He was almost past me when it bit down into his aventail. All of my anger at the wound my father had suffered was

Baron's Crusade

in that blow and I must have broken his neck for his head lolled to the side and he fell. As I had expected that tore the heart of the Khwarzamians. I turned and saw that Matthew had lost his helmet but he held the Khwarzamian standard and his shattered lance had impaled the standard-bearer. I watched as Peter and Padraig slew two more askari. Rafe War Axe was laying about him with his favourite weapon and none could come near to him. Few of the askari who were not killed escaped unwounded. My archers rained arrows into the flanks and then the Khwarzamian horse archers burst forth. They looked to have lost the battle of the bow. Padraig hacked at one as he passed him but they all avoided their dead leader and his standard.

When the last horseman had passed us, I raised my visor. When I had ascertained that the enemy had fled, I said, "Well done, Matthew. How did you lose your helmet?"

"He used the standard as a lance, lord, and he struck my helmet with the end; my strap did not hold."

Padraig had taken off his helmet, "And there is a lesson, Master Matthew. You are responsible for Sir William's war gear. What if that had been his? Check everything; not just the sharpness of the blade. Leather straps should be perfect too."

I nodded, "But you did well. Now sound the recall!" I did not think that any would have charged off after the enemy but it was good to get men into the right habits. The strident notes echoed off the walls of rock to the south and east of us. As our archers mounted and joined me, I shouted, "Collect any treasure you can find and mail. We need their horses. If any are lamed then butcher them and we shall eat well!"

Matthew pointed to the dead, "And the enemy warriors who lie dead?"

"Can be buried by those we leave alive after we leave. It will be a good lesson for them. If they oppose us then this is what they can expect. Padraig, I leave you in command. Matthew, let us see how our knights fared."

We picked our way through twenty or so dead men. Some were archers and some askari; half had arrows in them. When we neared the village, I saw some dead men from the village. All had a weapon in their hand. My knights had dismounted and were drinking from a wineskin. I frowned.

"What is this? Carousing?"

"We won, lord!"

"Aye, Sir Stephen, but we did not come here for the wine! We came for animals. Get off your backsides and collect animals. We drink when that is done and the village secured!"

He and the other knights looked shamefaced, "Sorry, Sir William!" They still had much to learn!

I sought out Jean and Cedric. "Well done, Captain Cedric. You stopped many from leaving?"

He nodded, "Aye and they had a milk cow, goats and sheep with them. The four warriors who guarded the village fled to the tower but we slew them easily for they wasted arrows trying to hit Sir Stephen and his knights."

"Good. Did the knights have much to do?"

He shook his head, "As soon as they were spied then the ones with weapons dropped them. A knight is like a supernatural being to these people for our horses are so much bigger than theirs."

I turned to Jean. "Is there a different way we can return to Acre tomorrow? One, perhaps, that might also pass some village or town?"

"There are a couple but the road we would have to take is not as good as the one we used. In places, it is little more than a track and the villages are so small that they barely have a name."

"But they have animals and a well?"

"Yes, my lord."

Cedric asked, "What is amiss, lord?"

"A hundred mercenaries, Khwarzamian at that is the problem. They followed us along the ridge. Either they were waiting on the off chance that they might find us or they were warned. Some of them escaped. They will return to their Turkish overlord and I do not wish to make life easy for them by retracing our steps. I think that someone told them what we had planned. We go back a different way and avoid another trap."

Padraig smiled, "Your father taught you well, Sir William. It is what he would have done!"

"We will use the same strategy tomorrow. If the villages and settlements are smaller then it should be easier. The other archers can drive the animals."

I felt weary. It was not the battle or the journey it was, quite simply, having to think of everything myself. I now understood the burden my father had borne for so many years.

The huts were crudely made and my men thought they smelled strange. We lit good fires and slept outside. We had guards on the animals and the prisoners as well as sentries to watch for the enemy. None came and we left before dawn. We would be far slower returning to Acre as we had thirty horses not to mention thirty sheep, a cow and twenty goats. We had found treasure and Padraig had shared it evenly. That had been a lesson taught to me by my father. We also had wheat, olive oil, beans and chickens. We would eat well back in Acre but carrying it would slow us down.

This time Padraig, Rafe, Peter and I almost damaged our necks by craning them around to see if we were followed. After five miles I decided that we had evaded them and we concentrated on taking as much as we could. The next two settlements did not even offer a fight. We took their animals for there were no wagons and our captured horses were laden with the weapons and food we had taken. We reached Acre after dark.

One of the sentries smiled and shook his head, "You were the smallest conroi which left lord but you have returned with greater prizes and fewer losses."

"The others had trouble?"

"One returned yesterday for they were ambushed south of Acre."

It was as I suspected, there was a spy in our camp and he had told them of our destinations. The two leaders and the three masters of the military orders were all in the north of the land. Who was there to take charge and come up with a better strategy? There was but one person, Sir Thomas, my father!

Chapter 10

When I told my father what I had learned he concurred with my findings. "You must call a council of war of the lords who lead the raids."

"It may be that none wish to raid if they have all had a disastrous day!"

"Nonetheless they must be informed. Your intelligence might well save lives and we have too few men to waste. You call them together and I will speak to them."

"You are well enough?"

"The alternative is for me to sit and count the stones in the wall of my chamber. This keeps my mind active; I believe I am strong enough." He smiled and I saw that he looked healthier already. There was colour in his cheeks and his eyes were brighter than they had been. If it was not for the heavily bandaged head then a stranger would struggle to know that he was wounded.

I asked the Master of the Knights of St. John to convene the meeting for they were the most powerful order in Acre and my father always spoke well of them. The most important lord, outside of my father, who remained in the castle was Balian of Sidon. His family had been in the Holy Land for many years and I could see, from his face, that he objected to being summoned by a young English knight; I cared not. It was not just the knights who would lead the chevauchée who packed into the hall. There were others. Many knights had lost their feudal lord in the battle of Gaza and had not wished to go home while others had escaped from the disaster. Many came to the hall in an attempt to secure another place in a retinue; it would be a crowded hall. It took my father some time to reach the meeting and so I first faced the knights alone while he was escorted by Henry Samuel and Mark who were his ever-present shadows.

Balian of Sidon had been drinking, "Why have we been summoned here by a whey-faced boy who has barely started shaving?"

Many of the knights who had been rescued by my father and I objected and began shouting at him, fists, as well as voices, were raised. This could degenerate into a drunken brawl unless I did something. I raised my hand for silence, "Because, my lord, I have reason to believe that our enemies know all of our plans." That brought silence. "When we began our chevauchée, two days since, it should have come as a complete surprise to our enemies yet I was attacked by a hundred mercenaries serving An-Nasir Dawud and they were waiting for me close to Bethlehem. Others did not even manage to raid and many men were lost."

Balian of Sidon bellowed, "What foolishness is this? Of course, there are spies in Acre but the Muslims do not have a leadership which can plan attacks on such a wide front. It is just a coincidence."

My father's voice came from the doorway, "In my experience, Balian of Sidon, such accidents and coincidences always show the hand of man."

"I heard that you were wounded, Earl!" It was one thing to insult me but Balian of Sidon knew better than to disparage my father.

"And I was but luckily that whey-faced boy you mocked had the wit, the courage and the ability to save me and most of not only our men but many who followed the Duke of Burgundy. Today while others brought back wounded men, Sir William of Elsdon brought back horses, goats, sheep, cows, chickens, wheat and weapons so I would suggest, my lords, that when my son speaks, you heed his words."

I saw him sway a little and I said, "Mark, Henry Samuel, take my father back to our chambers." I was angry now and my words showed it. "Balian of Sidon, I care not if you and every other foolish knight dies except that it means I will be here longer than I need to be and I want to go home. Keep to the same plan you had and you will find the same result. I agree there are spies and to find them would be almost impossible. We cannot find them so be unpredictable. I will take my conroi raiding tomorrow but I will not even tell my men the direction until we are outside Acre's walls. I will tell no one how long I will raid. Until the King and the Duke return, we must do all that we can to upset the plans of An-Nasir Dawud." I stared at him, "And that is the only reason I convened this council, to save lives. Do what you will! I have a great warrior to tend to. Unlike you, he is worth my time and attention."

As I left Jean de Joinville, one of the knights of Bar we had rescued took my arm, "Sir William, ignore the blowhard. There are many of us who agree with you."

I nodded, "Then adopt my plan and lives will be saved."

"We will, Sir William. We will."

When I reached our chambers, my father was being tended to by Father Paul. He saw my face and waved an irritated hand at me, "I had not eaten that is all. It is my own fault."

"Would you have me confine you to this chamber?"

"You are my son and I am the Earl of Stockton!"

"Your doctor left me in charge of you and I will continue to determine how you live. Father Paul will advise me and I will consult with him on every action which you take. You were close to death and I realise how much we need you but we need a well man and not one who staggers after a few steps. Get well and then I will return your power!"

He glared at me and then burst out laughing, "The cub is a lion grown! I will heed your words until I am well and then watch out, Young William!"

Despite my words to the council I fully intended to consult with Padraig, Cedric and Jean, our guide. I trusted them. After my father had retired, I sought them out. "We will not leave in the morning as I said but the day after. Instead, Jean, I will ride with my squire and Padraig here and you. We will ride some nearby little-used trails and see if we are followed, for I would have you follow us at some distance and identify those who are curious about our destination. Can you do that?"

He grinned, "Aye, lord."

Padraig persuaded me to take Peter and two archers too. "The thing is, lord, just a couple of us would not arouse interest but four or five would make a spy think we were scouting or perhaps even raiding somewhere small."

He was right and I heeded his advice.

Balian of Sidon had not listened or perhaps he was making a statement. He and his conroi were already saddled and preparing for their chevauchée as my small group of horsemen saddled. Everyone knew where he was going and I feared that few would return alive. I knew, from words I had spoken the night before that some conroi had been so badly handled that they were not ready to ride again while there were others who would heed my advice and spend the day deciding upon a better course of action. The only two groups to leave would be my handful and the one hundred and ten men who rode with Balian of Sidon.

The knight of Outremer jeeringly called out as we headed towards the stable, "You see I do not fear these heathens! I will fetch back more than the paltry offering you did!"

Padraig growled, "He brought back less than we did yesterday! Everyone knows that!"

"Peace, Padraig. He is full of sound and fury; it means nothing. His words are for his men. I would not ride with him this day for all know that he heads towards Nablus and that is a strongly defended place." I turned to Jean as we mounted. "If no one leaves within an hour then ride after us and fetch us back. There is little point in putting our head above the parapet if our spy is too careful to fall into our trap."

"Aye, lord. I will watch." Jean would remain in the stable where he would groom his horse. His presence would go unnoticed for there were many such servants and grooms in Acre. It was one of the reasons we adopted this strategy. The spy might not be someone important. It could be a groom. The fortress of Acre was so strong that it felt like a bastion against the Muslim world and men spoke openly as though it was a safe environment. It was not.

Jean had told us of some meandering trails which led due east into the high ground which lay there. The Turkish-held enclaves were more than fifteen miles from Acre and we would be safe enough from attack as the farms and small settlements were settled by ex-crusaders. My father had spoken of men he had served alongside who had not returned to England and he had wondered if their children lived here still. It would be unlikely for any of the warriors my father had known to be alive still as he had been a young man when he had gained his fame. When he had spoken of them, he had grown teary-eyed. Apart from those who now lived in Stockton my father was the last of his generation for the rest had died.

The twisting and climbing nature of the ride made it hard to see if we were being followed. When we stopped for water, we studied the land. Alf Fletcher, one of our archers, rubbed the back of his neck. There was little sun and so the action was not initiated by its heat. He shook his head, "There is little evidence, lord, but I know that there is someone behind, following us and I do not like it!"

I shaded my hand against the sky to try to find where the sun was hidden, "Aye, you may be right. It is almost noon and Jean would have joined us if there was no one behind. We are being followed."

Matthew suddenly lifted his head and said, "Then, Sir William, why not turn and ride back to Jean? The follower will not be expecting that and we can find him out!"

"A good idea, Matthew, except that would not tell us who he was working with."

Padraig said, "Sir William, I have a sharp knife and an hour alone with him will tell us all that we need to know."

They were both right. If we had the spy in hand then he might tell us his confederates if any, and as much as I might abhor torture, sometimes it was necessary and if any followed us then that was a sign of his guilt. I looked around the small huddle of houses. I spied a tiny trail which wound up from them through the rocks towards the ridge. I called over a young shepherd boy, "You there. Where does that trail lead?"

"Why back down the track you follow, lord. Our sheep sometimes wander up into the rocks and using the trail helps us to gather them."

I flicked him a copper coin, "Thank you! Alf and Godfrey, take the trail and try to get behind him. The rest of us will ride hard down the trail."

My two archers were all happier to be doing something positive rather than being the bait and we quickly mounted. As soon as Alf and Godfrey had disappeared, I turned Hart and pricked him with my spurs and he leapt down the trail back towards where I hoped that Jean would be waiting. Our spy had to be close and our sudden appearance startled him. It was like a game bird when dogs approach. I saw a cloaked figure mount a horse some two hundred paces from us and gallop down the trail. Jean, of course, was watching and I saw him emerge from the rocks two hundred paces from the spy. Jean had a bow and, as he nocked an arrow, the spy veered left to begin to climb through the scrubby rock-covered slope. It would be hard for us to follow but there would be no need for Alf and Godfrey were already above him. He had nowhere to go. When we reached the place he had begun his climb I lifted my hand to halt us.

"We have him surrounded. Unless he is a better horseman than us, he cannot escape."

He was already a hundred and fifty paces up the slope but his horse was clearly struggling. The rider was leaning forward to try to help it but the slippery and crumbling stones beneath its hooves did not help and the inevitable happened, it slipped and threw the rider from its back. The horse did not fall far but the rider did. He was not wearing a helmet nor was he wearing mail. He struck a rock and rolled from it. Beneath the large rock, he had struck were scrubby bushes and smaller rocks. He rolled and tumbled down the slope until he landed just ten paces from us on the track. We galloped up to him. He lay on his back. His baldric, sword and dagger had been torn off on the descent and his cloak was torn and shredded. His face was bloody but his eyes were closed.

I dismounted and handed my reins to Matthew as Jean rode up. I recognised the spy. He had been one of the Duke of Burgundy's knights and had arrived at Acre five days after the battle having avoided the Egyptian patrols. I struggled to remember his name but I had spoken to him for he had thanked me for our intervention and had asked after my father. And he was the spy? This made little sense.

Jean spoke as he dismounted, "He left within moments of you, my lord. He had been waiting in the shadows by the stable. He let Lord Balian leave and then headed out after you. He was very good. He kept far enough back so that had you turned you would not have seen him. Once he was on the trail he would know where it went." He pointed to a wax tablet which had been attached to his belt but had broken free during his fall and it now lay on the ground. The wax had been smudged and was indecipherable. "Each time you turned from one track to another he made a mark on the tablet."

"And now he is dead."

Matthew shook his head, "No, lord, I see his chest moving."

I knelt down and spoke, I used French, "Can you hear me? Do you live?"

The eyes opened and he croaked, "I do but I can feel nothing."

Padraig said, "Look at the angle of his feet. His back is broken. He is as good as dead."

I saw the terror in the young knight's eyes. "Then I beg you to hear my confession, then kill me lord and send me to heaven."

I saw the cross around his neck. I took it and, using my dagger, cut the thong. I prised open his fingers, "Can you feel that?" He shook his head. I placed the cross in the knight's hand. "The cross is in your hand."

He tried to smile and then said, "My horse, Star?"

I looked up the slope. The horse, a courser, had risen to its feet and was standing forlornly lost halfway up the slope. "Matthew, fetch the knight's horse and his sword."

"Thank you, lord. He is a good mount and deserves a better rider than me."

"I am no priest, knight. I cannot give absolution."

"I know."

"What is your name?"

"Raymond of Lyon." He took a breath, "I confess that I am a traitor and a renegade for I have aided our enemies. I beg forgiveness for my sin."

I looked down at him, "That is your confession?"

"Yes, lord, now kill me with your dagger."

I shook my head. "That confession might satisfy God, although I doubt it. I need to know all." Already there were two carrion above our heads. "If I leave now then you will have our friends from above for company. When darkness falls the rats will join them and feast on your flesh while you live." I heard the clatter of Matthew fetching the horse. "Give us all and I promise you a swift end and a burial in the church at Acre."

He closed his eyes and then opened them again. "I was captured at Gaza. My young brother was my squire and captured with me. Many of those who looked to be poor and not worth ransom were slain except for me and my brother. I was told that if I kept them informed of the

Baron's Crusade

actions of the crusaders then my brother would live and when the prisoners were ransomed then he would be freed. He and the other poorer captives were taken by the Emir of Kerak."

"And whom did you tell about our raids?"

"A mile south of Acre there is a farm. The man is half Muslim and half Frank. He serves An-Nasir Dawud. I told him when the King left for the north, and I was able to tell him of the chevauchée."

I shook my head, "Christians died! Was one life worth that?"

"There is just my brother and me left for my family were all killed by Cathars. Surely you would do all that you could for your family."

"I might but I could never do that. What is the name of your brother?"

"Geoffrey. He looks like me. Lord, I pray he lives but I beg you to try to help him. He had nothing to do with this. My actions are all mine."

I nodded. He was right and his brother was innocent of all treachery, "If I have the chance, I will try to help him. None of this is his fault."

"Thank you, Sir William, you are a good man, I am ready." I had learned all that I was likely to learn and I said, "Go to God and receive your judgement." I slit his throat. "Matthew put this knight's sword on his horse. The least we can do is to keep it for his brother."

As we headed back Matthew said, "You know, lord, as much as I hated what the French knight did, I can understand his actions. If Mark had been captured then I might be tempted to become a traitor to keep him alive. I would not like myself but I would give anything to save my brother's life."

Padraig said, "Better, Master Matthew, to try to rescue the brother. As soon as they released the knight, he should have followed the prisoners and made an effort to rescue his brother. The longer a man is with these heathens the less likely it is that they will survive. They are a cruel people."

I do not know what I would have done. What if Henry Samuel had been a prisoner? I suppose I would have done what Padraig suggested for it would be better to die trying something than becoming a traitor.

By the time we returned home, it was dark. In my heart, I knew I ought to ride to the farm and find the other traitor but I was anxious to speak with my father and events conspired against me. In addition, there had been another disaster. Balian of Sidon had been ambushed two miles from Acre. It was a bold attack but the audacity had paid off as Balian and his men were not expecting it. Twenty knights perished and Balian himself was wounded.

I was summoned by the Master of the Hospitallers to the hall where Balian was being tended. The Master was a kindly man. "Sir William, I understand you returned to the castle with the body of one of the knights of Burgundy." It was simply stated and allowed me to explain what I had done.

Balian glared at me and then, as the ramifications of my words sank in, he subsided. "You and your father were right then."

One of his knights shouted, "Let us ride and capture this spy!"

Before I could counsel caution, a dozen knights had left the hall. The Master and my father, who were also in the hall realised the futility of such an action. The spy would hear them coming and, under night's cloak, flee. Even Balian realised this and shook his head. They did not arrive back until after midnight and I learned, the next day, that the man had fled. The knights had burned his farm. It was a petty and vindictive act for it served no purpose at all.

When I dined with my father and told him every word which had been spoken by the dying knight, we did not know that the raid on the spy's house would be a failure. It was the next day we discovered that. What we did speak of was the shame on the name of Raymond of Lyon. His brother, although innocent, would be tarnished by that shame. He would never be able to return to France. Our squires and pages looked at each other when they realised what the knight's actions had begun. It was nothing to do with Geoffrey of Lyon and yet his life was now, forever changed. My father showed that his mind was improving day by day. As we spoke, he recalled events in the past which had been as cataclysmic. I was pleased that his memory was almost back to normal and he remembered more and was able to concentrate for longer periods. His touch remained a problem and he would often look at the palms of his hands as though he could see what the problem was and solve it. That was his way. He was always positive.

Matthew said, "If this spy is caught then that might be an end to this problem, my lords!"

"It will not matter if we find this spy and torture him. What more can he tell us? We know who he serves. The bigger problem is that we do not know who we can trust. Before you brought us the news, I would have been certain that the spy could not be a knight but what you told me makes it clear that any knight could be thus suborned. There were many stragglers from the battle. There are many farms close to Acre whose owners have no love for Franks. We must accept, as a fact of life, that the enemy will know what we are about. The surprise will have to come from doing the unexpected on the battlefield and I am not sure that Thibaut of Navarre is the man to do that. He strikes me as a very unimaginative man."

I drank deeply from the goblet. The wine in this land was always good. Perhaps God had blessed it. "And will you not reconsider returning to England, father?"

I saw Henry Samuel listening intently. My father also drank deeply and smacked his lips appreciatively, "I am tempted but the answer is no. I am no longer close to death and it is unlikely that I will have to raise my sword in anger. As much as I wish to see how much your new son has grown, I must remain here until the English element of this crusade arrives. I am the senior lord and if I departed, even with this wound, it would incur the wrath of the King. He has too much of his father in his veins for me to risk the retribution which might follow. "We have half a year to wait here for I expect whoever leads this crusade to be here by May or June at the earliest. Then we can hand over the responsibility and sail home."

We spent three months awaiting the return of King Thibaut. We raided and we did not go hungry but the King and his attempts to negotiate back Jerusalem failed and they returned to Acre just as the weather improved. By then my father, except for his lack of feeling in his skin, was healed. His memory had fully returned and he had his strength back. He was able to practise with Padraig where it soon became obvious that his lack of feeling affected his swordplay. He would never be the warrior he once was. He was philosophical about it for he knew he had his life and that was much to be grateful for. My father's bandages were removed and his hair had begun to cover his scar. It would be barely noticeable within a month.

More crusaders arrived; this time overland. None were English. Walter of Brienne was a powerful lord from Sicily. He had lost lands to the Emperor Frederik and came to gain power. Guiges of Forez's brother, Alan, was another French lord who had lost land in France and Italy. He too sought power. Odo of Montbéliard came from Cyprus where his family had land and power. He sought to gain Muslim lands now that they were in apparent disharmony. Then there were the young lords of Outremer, the brothers Balian of Beirut and John of Arsuf. Nether had taken part in the battle of Gaza but now saw an opportunity to take land for when Thibaut of Navarre returned from his fruitless sojourn in Antioch he was, finally, ready for action.

For the English contingent, the politics and posturing were irrelevant. We were here to ensure that Jerusalem remained Christian. I believe that the King and the Duke had similar intentions. The plotting and the coalitions which abounded in Acre did nothing to further the crusade.

So it was, in the middle of May, that my father and I were delighted when we were summoned to the presence of the King. Duke Peter and Raoul de Soissons were also there.

"We have heard that the Emir of Damascus may be able to end this impasse in which we find ourselves. He has let it be known that he is willing to talk but he does not wish an army camped outside Damascus. Duke Peter has agreed to go with some of his knights and the English brotherhood." The King smiled. "You seem above the plotting with which Acre is riddled. Are you well enough to travel, Earl?"

I saw my father nod, "I am more than well enough I am desperate for the air in Acre is more poisonous than it was. I would be honoured."

And so, we left Acre to ride beyond the land controlled by the crusaders to meet with As-Salih Ismail. He was not a politician like the Emir of Homs he was a warrior who had defeated the Christians at every turn.

Chapter 11

The Emir had been quite clear in his instructions. We had to bring no more than one hundred men in total and that included servants. It was why the King had chosen not to travel to Damascus. He would have needed a larger entourage. It suited me for I enjoyed the company of Duke Peter. He was like my father in so many ways. The men he took were all knights and their squires. We were the ones with the men at arms and archers. There were few of them but they could be used as scouts. As my father said, once we had left the Sea of Galilee and headed through the Muslim-controlled land, "If the enemy wish to ambush us then no number of scouts will help us. We have to trust to God and the word of our enemy but I feel more comfortable with our archers ahead of us." He smiled at Duke Peter, "Perhaps this is a test set by God to see how determined we are to achieve peace."

The Duke laughed, "Then I am happy to be travelling in your company, my lords, for there are many in the Holy Land who care not about our convictions. I know that the King and I chose to heed the Pope's call for we wish to serve God. Many of those in Acre serve themselves and seek land. They wish to be King of Jerusalem!" He shook his head, "There was only one King of Jerusalem and he was crucified by the Romans!"

I asked, "What do you know of this Emir of Damascus, As-Salih Ismail?"

"That he is a warrior a little older than your father and that may explain why he is held in such high regard by the other leaders. Even the Egyptians heed his words and deeds. If he says something then it is so. He served with Saladin and is said to be a fine warrior and general. I have hopes for this meeting but they are not high. This is a man who believes in his religion as fervently as any Archbishop. He does not want us here." He shrugged, "He asked for the meeting and as the alternative is a battle, we will try this first."

My father had told him about the spy and the prisoners held by the Egyptians. I continued to press the Duke, "But if we cannot get a negotiated peace then where does that leave the captives?"

"That is a most interesting question and one I would love the answer to. The Egyptians do not care for coins. They are fanatical. If we achieve a negotiated peace, they could take it out on the prisoners and slaughter all of them."

That was not the news I wished to hear. The spy I had killed had been a traitor but I had made a promise, however vague, to try to do something about his brother. One did not break the word given to a dying man.

We were passing through the land upon which Jesus had walked. I was seeing names that the priests in Stockton Church had told us about. The fishermen of Galilee and the wedding at Canaan. They had been names until now and here I was riding the same land and yet it seemed unreal. I did not think that any of those who lived in Stockton would ever manage to make a pilgrimage here to this land. There had been a pilgrimage of peasants but it had ended in disaster with most of them ending up their lives as slaves. Perhaps it was better just to read the story and not witness the reality.

Damascus was and always had been, a Muslim stronghold. No Crusader had even come close to holding it for longer than a week or so. That might have explained our invitation. We could spy all we liked but, as we rode through the gates and the immensely thick walls, I knew that Franks could never take this city without an incredible loss of life. We were viewed with suspicion rather than hostility as we rode through the streets. I guessed that this draconian leader, this Muslim warlord, had let the people know that we were not to be dishonoured in any way. A column of horsemen had escorted us to the palace. These were not the Khwarzamians we had fought. These were the real Turkish askari. They were mailed from head to toe and rode horses which were almost as large as ours. Around their heads, the horses wore mail hoods. I doubted that the horses, mailed as they were, could carry the warriors on their backs for great distances. The warrior in me worked out that they probably rode to battle on a different horse and then charged to fight on these mighty beasts. Even Dragon, the warhorse I had brought, could not compare with these. They had to be the Emir's bodyguard and he was making a statement.

When we reached the palace, it was a Frank who emerged. He had grey hair and a beard. He smiled, "I am Rufus of Tyre and I am the Emir's slave. Would you ask your knights to retire to the hall which has been prepared for them? The four senior lords and their squires and pages will be housed in the palace."

I looked at my father; I did not wish to be separated.

Rufus of Tyre saw my look and smiled, "I am sorry, lord, I should have used your names and titles: The Duke of Brittany, Raoul of Soissons, the Earl of Stockton and Baron William of Elsdon, will be accommodated in the palace."

I felt like a fool but I was also suspicious. How did they know so much? The spies in our camps had to be more numerous than we thought. Our men took our horses. I saw Padraig and Cedric cast looks which would have turned many men to stone, at Rufus of Tyre.

"We have some way to walk, Sir Thomas. I can have a litter fetched for you if your wound troubles you."

My father waved a hand, "I can walk but, Rufus of Tyre, you interest me. How did you come to serve this emir?"

"Like you, Sir Thomas, I was at Arsuf and, like you, my knight was slain." He shrugged, "I was younger than you and I was taken as a slave. The Emir found me when he was just the lord of a hundred serving Saladin. He was interested in me for I worked hard and he bought me from the man who had taken me and was... let us say the Emir of Damascus saved my life. It proved to be my salvation. I have risen with the Emir and I am happy."

"But you live amongst the Muslims!"

He stopped and turned to address the Duke of Brittany, "I am now a Muslim, Duke, and I find the life to be better than when I was a Christian."

Raoul of Soissons could not hide his horror, "You have rejected Christ!"

Rufus smiled, "But his father is still the same God we worship. He is the God of Abraham. I sleep well at night."

The palace was cool after the heat of the city and the road. It was clean and I felt dirty as I laid a trail of dust along the stone floors. It was almost as if he was reading our minds for he said, as we neared a large pair of double doors made of cedarwood, "You will need to refresh yourselves before you meet the Emir." He pointed to a second set of double doors to our right. "Those are your quarters. There are eight rooms and there is a bath with slaves who wait to tend you. They were chosen for their ability to speak French and English." He smiled. "They have learned the language from the many prisoners we have taken. There are cooler clothes for you to wear. You will not need your mail this night. Here you are as safe as in any fortress in Brittany or England. I will fetch you in two hours."

He opened the door and we entered. Closing it behind us we stared at the half-naked slaves who awaited us and the enormous bath which we could see.

My father broke the silence, "This is a clever man. Already we are intimidated by all of this; the preparations have been made to make us in awe of him before we meet him. He intends to make demands which will be unacceptable to us and this is a way of striking the first blow. Let us enjoy the pampering."

He was right of course but I now feared meeting this emir.

The four of us bathed first and then my father said, "It would be churlish not to let our squires and pages enjoy this. I am certain the emir will comment if we do not allow them to bathe and be attended by these slaves."

While our squires and pages enjoyed the bath we were taken to marble slabs where the slaves worked on our naked bodies with strigils and then oiled our bodies and hair. I felt uncomfortable but my father took it all in his stride. I felt better when I realised that our squires and pages would have to endure this and they would be even more uncomfortable than I was.

As we were being dressed Raoul began, "I wonder what this emir…"

My father wagged a finger, "These slaves speak English, French and Breton. Let us keep our thoughts to ourselves, eh? This is not the place to let the Emir know of our position."

The clothes that the slaves dressed us in were incredibly light. It was almost like a lady's dress but it felt cool. I was almost afraid to go to the feast in case I spilled food upon it. Rufus nodded approvingly and said, "Now you smell and look civilised."

My smile turned to a frown. I did not like this turncoat.

He led us to the double doors we had seen and they were opened. We walked down a long corridor which had a fresco painted on the wall. It was of Muslim warriors slaughtering Christians. I recognised the shields of the Knights Templar and worked out it was Hattin. There were two guards at the end and when they opened them, I saw the room in which we would dine. It took my breath away. The table was laden with food and there were enough slaves around the side to guarantee one slave for each guest. I knew this because there were just eight people in the huge room. This would be a relatively intimate meal. As I had expected there were no women. This was a Muslim country.

When one grey-bearded but lean warrior walked toward us, I knew that he was the Emir of Damascus. He had a scar down one cheek which told me that he was a warrior. He smiled and spoke to us in French. "I know your names but as I have never met you before, I cannot put a face to a name. I am As-Salih Ismail, Emir of Damascus." He looked at the Duke, "I am guessing that you are the Duke of Brittany."

The Duke bowed, "It is an honour."

"Which would make you his lieutenant, Raoul de Soissons."

Raoul also bowed, "I am, my lord."

He turned to look at my father and I saw his mouth opening to speak and then he stopped and stared. I looked at my father and he too had a strange look. I might have thought he had had a relapse except for the smile which appeared. My father said, "I know you, Emir! I recognise you! How is that possible?"

"And I recognise you. You must be Sir Thomas and suddenly all that I have heard about you makes sense. When I heard that you were coming, I was looking forward to speaking to you of the Battle of Gaza and also the Battle of Arsuf but now I see that we have been bound by longer silken threads than that!"

My father shook his head, "Now I remember! You have grown older."

"As have you but when you spoke it took me back thirty years."

My father nodded and took the Emir's proffered hand. He had not offered the handclasp to the Duke or Raoul. I could not contain myself, "Father, I do not understand! How do you know this warrior?"

The Emir said, "And you must be Sir Thomas' son, Sir William. Now that I see you, I am truly transported back thirty years for you and your father have the same look. I will explain all but let us do so seated. Your father and I no longer have young legs." He turned and whispered in Rufus' ear.

I noticed that Rufus hurried ahead. The seating arrangements were about to be changed. Instead of the Duke sitting on the Emir's right-hand side, it was my father and I was seated next to him. Our squires and pages were at the very end of the table. I might have been worried about such an arrangement if it was not for the strange conversation I had just heard.

The Emir clapped his hands as we sat and said, "We do not drink wine, as you know, but in honour of this meeting and, especially in light of the twist of fate which has bound Sir Thomas to me there will be wine for you this night. I see the hand of God in all of this. Allah be praised."

As desperate as I was to hear the connection, I knew that I would have to be patient. It was like being a squire again. The Emir waited until we had all had a sweet and chilled lemon drink. He told me its name but I did not hear it. Then, as the first course was brought, he began to speak.

"When I was young, I led a hundred warriors and served Lord Saladin. I fought at Arsuf and killed many Franks. Sir Thomas, then a young squire, slew many Seljuk Turks. It was war. I was given a valley to watch and one day some Franks came through who butchered villagers for no reason. I caught up with them and ended their miserable lives. I did so painfully. Then I met Sir Thomas who appeared to be from the same retinue. I captured him and his companions and I was angry enough to have slain him except that, when I looked in his eyes, I saw no fear. He was not afraid to die and he was honest. He told me that the Franks I had killed were enemies of his and I believed him, more than that, some of the survivors of the attack told me how Sir Thomas and his companions had saved their lives. I freed Sir Thomas and never saw him again until this night but it changed me. Until then I had believed that every Christian knight was evil and without honour. I saw in Sir Thomas someone I could admire. It was like Saladin and King Richard." He looked up at Rufus, "You owe Sir Thomas your life, Rufus of Tyre. I bought you because I thought to do a kind act such as that which Sir Thomas had done. That meeting made me realise that not all Christians are evil and not all Muslims are to be trusted."

My father nodded, "And it taught me the same lesson."

The two of them began to chatter away. I caught parts of their conversation. They were telling each other what had happened to them in the intervening years. I was just stunned as I had never heard the story before.

Rufus appeared at my shoulder, "I am sorry, my lord, that I was so condescending towards you. I had heard the story of your father before but neither the Emir nor myself knew his name. His and your actions at Gaza speak well of you. I am sorry. Please accept my apologies."

"You have no reason to apologise. You have treated us well."

He looked relieved. The feast passed in a blur. I could not have foreseen this outcome when we rode north. When the food and wine had finished the Emir addressed all of us. "I had planned to speak of other things this night. Allah has shown me that I was wrong. Tomorrow will be the time to speak of politics and, besides, I have to think deeply about the significance of this meeting. Until the morrow, I bid you all a good night. Know that your men have been fed well although they had neither wine nor beer. Tomorrow we will convene here again but then we will talk about other matters. Sir Thomas." My father stood and the two men embraced. "Goodnight."

My father still had some Arabic and he said, in Arabic, "Goodnight and may Allah watch over you!"

The Emir burst out laughing, "Think of all that we could have said to each other. The years we have been apart might have made us different men."

My father shook his head, "No, Emir, for we are still, in our hearts, the same men we were all those years ago. It is weaker men who change!"

There were no slaves in our chambers and as soon as we entered and the doors were closed the Duke said, "Sir Thomas! What just happened?"

My father just smiled and tapped the side of his head where he had been wounded. "I was spared for a reason. This is God's will and you all saw that. I met the Emir when I was a young knight and the evil Frank he executed was Robert of Blois and the Emir, although he was no emir then, spared my life. I had forgotten it and that was a mistake for nothing happens in our lives without a purpose. I now have hope, Duke Peter. The Emir may be a Muslim but I believe that he is a Muslim we can trust. I know that you are senior to me but I also know that if you let me speak then we may get more from these negotiations than if I do not."

The Duke nodded, "You are right and I will play the vassal for you."

I knew that my father was distracted yet I wished to know more. I knew about the knight from Blois who had been so treacherous but why had my father failed to mention the Muslim who had spared his life? I would save the questions for our journey back to Acre. None of us were under any illusions. The Emir of Damascus would strike a hard bargain. The coincidence allowed my father's foot in the door but no more than that.

Henry Samuel woke me early, "Uncle, grandfather has risen and left the chamber. What should I do?"

I smiled, "If he did not wake you then he does not need you nor does he need me. I think he will be safe enough."

Henry Samuel nodded, "Last night was a revelation was it not?"

"Aye, I was surprised for certain."

"How many other secrets does grandfather hold?"

"This was not a secret. It was a memory hidden deep. Compared with my father we have not yet lived. We will meet people who will change our lives although we do not know it at the time." I was thinking about the knight whose life I had ended. Although I had been preoccupied with my father, my dreams had also been about the squire I did not know, Geoffrey of Lyon.

As I was awake, I dressed and headed outside. The imposing and intimidating-looking guards made it clear which route I could take and which I could not. It was almost like a maze and the mailed men were markers for my passage. I found myself in a courtyard surrounded by pots of lemon trees. There was a bubbling fountain in the centre of some seats and a table. The pots had been cleverly arranged so that a visitor could always find a shaded seat. I found a shady spot and sat beneath a tree covered in yellow and green fruit. It was a powerful smell and, so I had been told, kept away flying insects. Certainly, it was pleasant.

"I like to come here too, Sir William, at this time of the day. It helps me to focus my mind."

I looked up and saw Rufus. He had a tray upon which was a jug and some goblets. "Refreshment?" I nodded and he poured me a sweet lemon drink. He put the tray on the table and gestured to the seat next to me. "May I, my lord?"

He had obviously been a slave for so long that he could not help himself, "Of course."

We sipped our drinks and both looked east for the sun was just peering over the wall which surrounded the palace. "The morning rays of the sun are welcome but they are also a chilling reminder of the danger from the east."

"The east? I know we, in the west, fear danger from the east but that is the threat of the Turk and the Egyptian. Sorry, that was rude of me."

"I know it is hard for I look as you do yet I am a Muslim but I am not offended. I understand your words. No, we have always feared the east. The Khwarzamians were a threat but the danger from their warriors ended when fierce warriors from far to the east appeared. The Mongols are a threat to the whole world, Christian and Muslim. They have no religion save rape and slaughter. They have conquered the land from so far to the east that a man could ride all day and all night and still take half a year or more to reach the farthest side. They are knocking at our door and even the mighty Egyptians fear them. It is why the Khwarzamians now hire themselves out as mercenaries for they have lost their land." He had finished his drink and he stood. "I will leave the jug for you. I have duties to perform. It has been good to speak to a fellow Frank. I have missed their…" he smiled, "honesty!"

I sat, after he had gone, and finished my drink. I had much to think about for Rufus had told me secrets and I had to work out if that was deliberate or an accident. Certainly, it explained why we had been invited and why the Emir was so keen to talk. He and his people were on the eastern side of Outremer. A threat from Mongols would affect them first. Perhaps that was why the King had been invited to Homs and Hama; the emirs there would fear the Mongols too.

Our squires and pages found me. Sam's eyes were wide with wonder, "This is an enormous palace, uncle. This is a powerful people."

Mark nodded, "Aye, lord, it makes even York look mean and shabby and as for Stockton…"

"You are right, it has much to commend it but do not disparage our home." I pointed to the lemon trees. "This land is blessed with plants we cannot grow. God has given us our land and we make the best of it. When we came here the journey was hard because we had to travel through a parched and dry land. We had to seek water all along the way. When my father and the first crusaders came here it was the land which defeated them and not a force of arms. The Emir would pay much gold for the water which flows past our home in England. Do not yearn for other grass. A wise man makes the best use of the grass he has been given."

I stood and looked at them. We were alone and I could speak freely. "You four have a great opportunity today. You will not be required to serve us but you will be present at a meeting which is normally only accorded to kings and great lords. One day you will be knights. Remember this day for if you watch and listen then you will learn a great deal."

A slave found us as we were preparing to leave. We were taken to the hall where food had been prepared. My father was there and was talking with the Emir. The Duke and his party followed us in. He nodded towards my father, "He never stops, does he? You would not think that he was at death's door months ago."

"It is his way. His whole life was shaped by Arsuf. When my grandfather was slain and my father was all alone, he knew he wanted to live and if a man wants to live, he must fight for life. When he was between life and death, I was not afraid for I knew that he would choose life and do everything in his power to return to life."

"And I can see that trait in you."

I nodded, "Before we go in, I have learned something which might have a bearing on today's meeting." I told him what I had learned.

He smiled, "I can now see God's hand in all of this. Had the King come with me then this meeting might have gone very differently. You are right. We now have something to bargain with but how do we tell your father this news? He will be the one who will be leading the discussion."

"Do not worry, I will find a way."

After we had eaten the tables were cleared. This time there were more people present than when we had eaten the night before. The seating arrangement was also different. The four of us were seated at one table with our squires and pages standing behind us while the Emir was flanked by warriors and mullahs. It was as though we were outnumbered. Had we not spoken the night before I would have been worried but I saw the Emir smiling and my father also seemed relaxed.

As the ones with the Emir were taking their seats, I said, in my father's ear, "I have news to impart which might change this meeting's outcome."

He turned and smiled, "You mean the Mongols?" My drooping jaw was his answer. "I know already."

"But how?"

"The Emir. Fear not, my son, I know what I am doing and I now know why I was sent back to the Holy Land. It was not King Henry's will it was God's will."

The Emir spoke. Knowing that the Emir had told my father all I watched the others who were seated with him. Their faces were a mixture of expressions but most of them were hostile. The Emir had his own battles to fight and we were about to be used to win that battle. "It is good that the Christians and the Muslims come together to speak for we have common enemies." He gestured to his right. "The Emir of Homs and the Emir of Hama are here to show that we can all speak with one voice; the voice of reason." A couple of the mullahs flashed angry looks at him. He continued as though he had not noticed them but he had. "An-Nasir Dawud, Lord of Kerak, is such an enemy. He conspires with the Ayyubid in Egypt and brings the Khwarzamians into our lands. He says it is to fight the Franks but how long before he turns those dogs of war loose on the rest of us? He seeks power and we all know that Al-Adil is not the warrior that was his uncle." He turned to the mullahs, "I do not wish to rule this land as Saladin did. I wish to make that quite clear. I am happy to be Emir of Damascus and for my children to rule after me but the danger from the Mongols in the east is quite clear." He turned his gaze to us. "What do you propose to end this conflict and to bring peace to this land?"

I saw the smile in his eyes.

The Duke stood and said, "I will ask my friend, Sir Thomas, the Earl of Stockton to give our position."

My father stood and spoke in French. The ones who did not have enough French each had a translator next to them. They were slaves. I saw that some, like Rufus, were Franks, "I am a simple man and I will speak simply." My father's wits had returned totally. By speaking simple words and sentences, he would make it easier for those who did not speak French to understand his meaning. "We wish the return of Jerusalem and the land which surrounds it. We have no desire for any land which is to the east of the Jordan River. We are happy to keep open the roads and allow free movement of all peoples. We are happy for those who worship Allah to continue to do so in the holy places. We are happy to join the Emir of Damascus and fight against any incursion from the Mongols. All that we wish is the return of Jerusalem, Bethlehem, Nazareth and Galilee." I hid my smile for those were the places which were controlled by An-Nasir Dawud. Although they were not his to give the Emir of Damascus could give his support to us without any loss to himself. "That is all we ask." He sat down and said, quietly to me, "I hope that eases the fears of the mullahs. They are terrified of the Mongol horde. The lands to the east of Damascus are no longer Muslim!"

The Emir stood, "Eloquently put, Sir Thomas. We will now debate your words. We will, perforce, use Arabic. For that discourtesy, I apologise."

The Duke was beaming when he turned to speak to us, "Will they agree, do you think?"

My father nodded, "An-Nasir Dawud is seen as something of a mad dog. He seeks power. Kerak is a shadow of Homs, Hama and Damascus. The other emirs support each other. None of them wants the power Saladin had and they do not want An-Nasir Dawud to take that title with Egypt and the Khwarzamians behind him. They will debate but I am hopeful that they will agree. Of course, that is just the beginning of our problems for he gives away that which is controlled by others! The Emir of Kerak! We will still have to fight."

The Duke asked, "And what of the Duke of Burgundy and the captives?"

My father shook his head, "One battle at a time. The Emir is not yet ready to take on the Ayyubid of Egypt. We have not yet gained Jerusalem. When we have that we can set our sights further afield and by the time we return, who knows, the rest of the knights promised by King Henry might be here and that would give us great power to force the Egyptian Ayyubid to come to terms for the captives."

The Emir and his people spoke all morning. There were, of course, interruptions for prayers but by early afternoon agreement had been reached.

"We have decided to return to you those places you regard as necessary for peace: Jerusalem, Bethlehem, Nazareth and Galilee. However, any attempt to colonise or take land east of that will negate this treaty."

The Duke stood, "Of course."

"Then we will send word to the Emir of Kerak. We cannot promise compliance but, if you have to use force, then know that we will not interfere. You have the word of the three emirs here present."

My father walked around the table as did the Emir of Damascus. They clasped hands and then embraced. Thus, was the truce and treaty settled; not with pen and parchment but with the handclasp of two warriors. That the treaty was eventually broken was nought to do with the two veterans who bade farewell to each other. That was the work of other men, on both sides, who had ulterior and selfish motives which had nothing to do with the Holy Land.

Chapter 12

While the King was delighted with our news there were many who were not. They were the ones who had hoped that they would have been the ones to bring the crusade to a happy conclusion while others had hoped that the war could continue. To our faces, they were all smiles but my father and I knew that they were false smiles. My father cared not what other lords thought. He had done his duty and served his king, the Pope and the King of Navarre. We prepared to take the castles and lands promised by the Emir. Of course, An-Nasir Dawud would not hand them over without some threat and the Egyptians were still his allies. We gathered our army. We had news that Richard of Cornwall and Simon de Montfort had finally left England. That disappointed my father. They would arrive in Acre too late to have any effect. By the time they reached us then we would have retaken the major towns.

One concession which the Emir of Damascus had made was that he turned over the Templar castle of Beaufort to Balian of Sidon. We were still gathering our armies and so the Emir took his forces and besieged the men of An-Nasir Dawud who refused to hand it over. It was a momentous event. For the first time, crusaders and Turks were acting in concert and it put heart into our whole army. The King divided the army into two. He led one half with the Duke of Brittany and my father's contingent to Jerusalem, while the rest attacked Nablus, the stronghold of An-Nasir Dawud. It was high summer and the relatively short journey to Jerusalem took its toll. My father was not one who suffered particularly badly but some of the other lords who had spent the last months sitting in Acre found the heat, the roads and the constant attacks by the Turkish horse archers of An-Nasir Dawud something they were so ill-prepared for, that I wondered at their ability to fight at all.

When we reached Jerusalem, envoys were sent to ask for the peaceful surrender of the city. We knew, of course, that it would be rejected. If An-Nasir Dawud was to have any credibility with the Egyptians then he had to show that he could attempt to fight the Christians.

The city walls were daunting and beyond them rose the keep-like building known as the Tower of David. It was as high as any keep I had seen in England except, perhaps, the White Tower. One advantage we had was that it had been damaged when the Emir of Kerak had captured it and it was not as high as it had been and the buildings which had surrounded it had been destroyed. Even so, it would be hard to take for in places the city wall was less than forty paces from it. The most successful strategy would be to take the city first and cut off the tower.

We closed off all traffic from the city and then used the knowledge of the Knights Templar to our advantage. They had spent longer in Jerusalem than any of the other orders and knew the city well. It was they who managed to find a side gate which was unguarded and they slipped in with the Teutonic Knights and the Knights of St. John. The gates were taken with barely a lost man while we captured some one hundred Turkish guards. We would have fewer men to fight once we attacked the tower. When the main gate to Jerusalem was open, we had the city but not the Tower of David and that was where the Turks and their Khwarzamian allies were gathered.

When the city had been taken the Emir of Kerak had cleared buildings around the sides of the tower and that was where we would begin our attack. The uneven nature of the ground precluded the use of a ram. This would need men to scale its walls using either ladders or a siege engine. We had brought wood from Acre and engineers began to build towers and ladders. The Tower of David was a huge edifice and the defenders had not only spears, darts and arrows but also Greek Fire. This weapon was seen as the devil's own for it burned, even on water and was far more dangerous than burning oil or boiling water. They had, on each wall, a projectile thrower for the fire was hurled in a clay pot which would shatter on impact and spread its deadly flames.

In honour of success in Damascus, our contingent was not the first to attack. Nor was it the Bretons. Instead, Walter of Brienne, desperate to garner some glory led his men. Our men attacked before dawn for then it was cooler and their archers would struggle to target our men. Protected by shields his dismounted knights and men at arms marched steadfastly towards the walls carrying their ladders. The arrows and darts were ineffective for every one of those who attacked had a full-face helmet and wore mail. The King of Navarre became quite hopeful when they closed to within twenty paces of the walls and had lost only eight men. It was as they began to raise their ladders that more men died for the defenders hurled, first stones, and then unleashed Greek Fire. It was truly horrible and terrible to behold: the tail of fire that trailed behind it was as big as a great spear; and it made such a noise as it came, that it sounded like the thunder of heaven.

Henry Samuel said, "It looks like a dragon flying through the air."

He was right and it was such a bright light it cast, that one could see all over the attack camp as though it was the noonday sun which shone. However, the effect was even more dramatic. One pot hit a line of knights and men at arms who were hurrying to the walls with ladders. It ignited when it struck and set alight not only the ladders but the surcoats and very metal of their mail. Their screams were almost unbearable to hear. Even as men who were nearby turned to flee, I watched the second thrower hurl another pot at a second group of knights. These had dropped their ladders and were running. They did not have shields to afford some protection for faces. The sound of the fire hitting them was like thunder and even two hundred paces from the impact we felt the wave of incredibly hot air which followed the impact. The sun was now up and their archers and ours had a better chance to use arrows.

"Cedric, can you hit those operating the machine?"

"We can try, lord, for that is no way for a man to die." He turned to his archers, "Nock!" The attack had failed and the knights were fleeing. For that reason, I suppose, the defenders did not waste more of the valuable and deadly weapon.

Cedric shook his head, "Stand down lads!" He turned to me. "We could hit them, lord, but there is little point unless they are using the weapon. It looks like two men lift the pot onto the thrower. They appear to be wearing gloves of some kind. If we hit them before they loaded the fire it could set fire to the machine."

"Is it possible?"

"It would be a difficult hit, lord, for the parapet offers protection but we can try."

It was decided to launch another attack but after dark. Cedric, when he was told, shook his head, "Sorry, Sir William, we can do nothing for we would not be able to see well enough."

I nodded, gloomily, for I knew he was right. The night attack was not the complete disaster which had been the attacks at dawn but twenty men at arms died needlessly. We held a council of war that night. Some, especially Walter de Brienne, were keen for a siege rather than an assault. King Thibaut shook his head. "We would look foolish. Much of this is about face. The Emir of Damascus has given us an opportunity here. The Turks captured this quickly with fewer men. We must take it or risk losing all the gains we were given thanks to the Duke of Brittany and the Earl of Stockton."

Duke Peter said, "To be fair, Your Majesty, when the Muslims attacked, they did not have to contend with Greek Fire."

"Find a way! Tomorrow we attack again and this time it will be the Bretons and the English who attack."

I did not point out that the Navarrese had yet to make any kind of assault. There would be little point; they were the King's own men. My father appeared to be unconcerned as the four of us sat in the house we had commandeered. It had a good cellar of wine and we were enjoying the bounty while planning the attack.

My father nodded appreciatively as he sipped the wine, "My own preference is for the wines of La Flèche but the wines from this region are acceptable."

"Never mind the wine, Earl Thomas, how do we avoid losing all of our men tomorrow when we attack?"

"We attack in daylight and so we have the archers of Cedric with us. Your crossbows are of no use at all because they have a flat trajectory. Secondly, they will have a limited number of pots of this infernal weapon of the devil. They will not use it until they are certain they can kill a large number of men. I noticed that we had captured many cattle when we took the city."

Raoul nodded, "Aye, my lord. They were to feed the garrison but the Templars captured the walls so quickly that they fell into our hands."

"Good, then slaughter eight of them. Feed the meat to our men and have the hides soaked in water. You will advance beneath the wetted, fresh hides. It will slow down the effect of the fire. Also, we do not advance with ladders. They encumber the knights and they burn. We send them over with the squires and pages once our knights make the walls."

The Duke asked, "Make the walls?"

"Have you not noticed that they have to load the projectile in a thrower? It is too risky to lift it and drop it. If we make the walls then the squires can carry the ladders without fear of fire. They will not waste Greek Fire on squires and pages. They wish to hit large numbers of mailed warriors. It is a risk to our squires and pages but an acceptable one for I am certain they will relish the opportunity to contribute to the assault."

I looked at my father and the shock was clearly written all over my face, "Henry Samuel?"

He looked me in the eye and said, "He will not be hurt. That I believe with all my heart for if I thought the fire would even come close to him then I would not allow it to happen."

I wondered at his belief. He was my nephew and I would have kept him safe. What did my father know that I did not?

We had much to do. The cattle were slaughtered and skinned. The animals were put on to cook so that the men chosen as the attackers would have a hearty meal before they began. The skins were soaked in water. The squires and pages, as my father had predicted, were honoured to have been chosen to take part in the assault and although they were given the chance to withdraw none did. I saw the fear on the face of my nephew and I admired him more than ever. He was petrified yet he would still risk all.

Baron's Crusade

Before I retired, I went to Cedric and told him the full plan. "If the Earl thinks they will be safe then it will be so but we will do all that we can to slaughter those working the machines, lord. You worry about the squires but it is you who will be making the attack!"

I was concerned but my father's confidence had transmitted itself to me and I had to believe that we would prevail. We had done so much already that it seemed a small step to climb the walls and defeat the garrison. Before I slept, I prayed as hard as I had ever prayed before. I had a wife I had barely seen and a son whose face I could barely remember. I had to get back to England!

We rose well before dawn and my knights and I met to prepare for the attack. Padraig led my men at arms over to the start line. He seemed the most philosophical of all of us but then he was the oldest and had been doing this for many years. Even my knights listened when he spoke. "Keep your shield before you and hold it high for that way it will cover most of your body and if a stone hits it hard then you might have a broken arm but it will not be a coxcomb! Keep moving and do not run in a straight line. You may still be hit but that will be fortune and if you are virtuous and God wishes you to live then you will. Do not stop until you reach the wall for there, with your shield above you and your helmet on your head, you will be fine."

"And the climb?"

If Sir Stephen expected similar reassurance he was in for a disappointment. "Why, lord, that is the hardest task of all for you must climb while holding a shield and the ladder. They will use darts, arrows, spears and stones to dislodge you. If you do make the parapet then you will have to draw your sword and fight two or even three men alone! It matters not if they are mailed for they will have the protection of the stone walls. When you make the fighting platform you will, in all likelihood, have to fight three or four men."

Sir Stephen shook his head, "You do not give us much hope, Sergeant!"

"Hope is for fools. Skill and God are my best allies and before I leave for the assault, I will say my prayers and beg God's forgiveness."

We had learned the lesson of an attack in the dark and we would attack at dawn when the first rays of the new day shone in the eyes of the attackers. Cedric and the archers had prepared well and each had twenty perfect arrows selected. Half were bodkins in case the men on the thrower wore mail. My father was there to bid us farewell. His son and grandson were risking all and I saw in his eyes the concern that was belied by his parting words, "Men of Stockton, today you go with the Bretons to take this mighty castle. I have no doubt that you will acquit yourselves with honour. If I thought I would be of any use in the battle then I would attack with you!"

Padraig shouted, "No, lord! You watch us and that will make us fight all the harder!" I had never heard Padraig shout at my father but he did then and showed me how highly he was regarded by my men who were facing death but could not bear the thought of losing the Earl. Would I ever have that sort of loyalty?

The Duke of Brittany would not be leading his men. That honour would go to Raoul de Soissons. We formed up our men with shields above our heads and then the squires draped the dripping hides over them. It was imperative that we all begin to march at the same time for it would split the targets. The wall we attacked had just one machine capable of hurling the Greek Fire projectiles at us. They would have to choose which men to kill, us or the Bretons. A horn sounded three times. I was at the fore between Sir Stephen and Padraig; it should have been another of my knights but Padraig would have none of it. I peered under my shield which was held high and I saw arrows flying toward us. They thudded into our shields but we had shields which were well made and the arrows did not penetrate for we had a thick animal hide above them. I watched men topple from the walls as Cedric and his archers, not to mention the Breton crossbows, killed the men on the walls. The projectile throwers hurled stones. They were aiming at us. I heard one hit the shields at the back and someone groaned.

"Is anyone hurt?"

"They cracked my arm, my lord, but I shall live." I recognised the voice as one of Sir Stephen's men. We were now closing with the charred bodies from the previous day's attack. They had not been removed and the smell turned my stomach. When I saw smoke rising and knew that meant they were fetching the pitcher of Greek Fire, it also told me that we were now within range of the fire. If they loaded and sent it towards us then more than half of us, even with the wet hide, would die.

Even though we were a hundred paces from them I heard Cedric shout, "Loose!"

I glanced up and saw a shower of arrows strike the top of the parapet. Suddenly there was an unearthly scream and then a sound of thunder. I watched a column of flame leap into the sky. Our archers had slain the men working the machine and destroyed it by hitting the men loading the projectile thrower. Its contents would have spilt and the fire destroyed the Turks instead of its intended target, us. Behind us, I heard a cheer. It spurred us on and all that we had to endure were arrows, darts and spears. The wet hide stopped all of them from getting close to hurting us. The stones were the danger and our archers slew those who tried to drop them. We reached the wall and all pressed our backs into the stone. Still holding my shield above my head, I lifted the visor on my helmet and looked along the wall. Apart from Gurt, the man at arms with the injured arm, all appeared to be intact. Above us, I could hear the cries and screams as the enemy's weapon was turned against them.

I took out my sword and waved it. That was the signal for our squires and pages to make the perilous journey. "Keep your shields in place! Once they have their fire under control then they will turn their attention to us again!" I sheathed my sword.

Padraig nodded, "Aye, lord, but it will take them some time to manage to do so. The sooner our ladders are here the better."

I watched as the three ladders were picked up to be carried by the six squires and two pages. While it was true that most of those above us were trying to quell the fire there were archers who were not near to the fire and they would be able to send arrows at the three targets which hurried across the ground towards us. My father must have organised them for they carried the ladders so that there was mutual protection. Half of the squires carried their shields on their right sides. When they reached the charred bodies, I saw hesitation for they did not want to cross the dead who had been burned.

I shouted, "Run or you die!"

Already there were arrows sticking from the shields and the ladders. I heard arrows ping off the well-made helmets. I had seen war arrows penetrate mail. It did not happen often but often enough for me to worry. It was the sheer number of arrows which made it possible. They were just thirty paces from us when disaster struck. Sir James' squire, Brian, was hit in the knee by an arrow. It did not penetrate but the power of the arrow, sent from a composite, horn bow made his leg buckle and he fell to his other knee. As he did so Henry Samuel pitched forward and he must have struck his head on some object embedded in the ground. I knew not what it was but he did not move.

Padraig shouted, "Pick up the ladder and run!"

They obeyed my Captain's commanding voice but Henry Samuel lay there. The archers on the walls saw their chance and arrows flew. I left the safety of the wall and with my shield held behind me, I ran to my nephew. Even as I was nearing him four arrows hit his back but, thankfully, none stuck although they would have bruised him. I knelt next to him. I saw that his head had hit a discarded helmet. It was the wide-brimmed type and the edge had caught him in the temple. He was stunned.

"Sam, rise."

I heard him groan and I tried to lift him. He was not yet a man grown but he was wearing mail and it was hard to raise him to his feet. He must have begun to come to for it suddenly became easier as he pushed with his legs. He had his shield on his right side and so I supported him with my right arm and I held my shield over our heads. Arrows rained down. Some hit me and I understood the pain Brian had felt. Sam could not move quickly but I did not want us to fall and we plodded on to the encouraging arms of the knights, men at arms and squires who awaited us. Already two ladders were placed against the wall and they were just waiting for the last ladder to be raised. A final stone was hurled at us and it hit my shield. I had it slightly angled and the stone slipped down to the ground. Nonetheless, it numbed my arm. I could not worry about that for I was the one to climb this last ladder first.

The squires had done their job and I shouted, "John, see to Henry Samuel."

I walked to the ladder. Padraig said, "Lord, your arm was hit. I will ascend first."

"Padraig, that is my place."

"And I am second. I would like to live beyond this battle lord and if you cannot protect me with your shield then I will die." He was right and I nodded. He turned to Matthew and Mark who would hold the ladder for us. "Brace your feet and lean against it. You are big lads and it will stop the ladder from moving. For England and Sir Thomas!" He began to climb. Despite his age, he almost scurried up the ladder.

As I began to climb, I saw that the other ladders, further along the wall, also had climbers upon them. We had not had the losses Walter de Brienne's men had suffered and we now had a chance. I saw a spear come towards me. With my shield above my head and my right hand on the ladder, I could do nothing about it. It caught my upper right leg and broke mail. The head broke the skin but did not lodge there. As it fell, I felt blood begin to seep from the wound. Experience had told me that it would not impair me, not for a while at least. The plan was for us to secure the parapet and then the knights and men of Navarre would follow us. In theory, I would only have to fight for a short time but, first, we had to gain the parapet.

I was stopped by Padraig who had reached the top. I heard blows striking his shield and I heard his curses, "Away you murdering heathen bastards!"

I could feel the heat from the fire and the stones also appeared to be hot. As Padraig slowly climbed the last few rungs on the ladder, I followed him closely. If he began to fall my job was to hold him in place. I heard his sword ring against metal and stone which told me that he had reached the top and was fighting the defenders. Suddenly he was no longer above me and I hurried up the last steps. As I stood on the parapet and before I could draw my sword a Khwarzamian ran at me with a spear. I began to draw my sword and started to jump. The spear did not reach me for an arrow smacked into the side of his head. It struck so hard that the head and shaft came out of the other side. The red fletch told me that it was Cedric's arrow. I looked around and saw that Padraig was fighting two men. Three men ran at me. Padraig and I had to buy time for the rest of our men to ascend. Our own little battlefield was a corner of the tower five paces by six. The fire on the projectile thrower had been so fierce that it was hard to see if the charred lumps had been wood or the men serving it.

The three men who ran at me were not mailed but they held spears and had small, buckler-type shields. We had practised this back in Elsdon with my men. My men were better than the three who came at me for one was too eager, thinking that odds of three to one meant that they would win. Instead of awaiting the attack, I stepped forward and that made him lunge prematurely with his spear. As I deflected it with my shield, I brought my sword across his neck and body diagonally. I tore through flesh and bright blood spurted the warrior to his left. I back slashed with my sword and as the next man was temporarily blinded, he did not see the edge coming towards his head. The blow knocked him from his feet and stunned him. The last man had a free strike with his spear and the head rammed at my side. I was already turning when the blow struck. It ripped through my mail but, unlike my chausses, I had a padded gambeson beneath the mail and it was that garment which took the damage intended for my side. His charge had unbalanced him so that when I swung my sword it was at his unprotected back and my sword sliced through to his spine. I ran at the man I had stunned and rammed my sword down into his neck. Padraig had killed the two men he had been fighting although I saw that he had been wounded.

Peter of York and Rafe War Axe had joined us and I shouted, "England! Shield wall!"

Sir Stephen and my knights heard me. They turned and joined up with Padraig and my men. Raoul de Soissons and the Bretons were attacking the other side of the tower. We simply had to hold the fighting platform until we could be reinforced by fresh men who would not have done as we had done and fought to gain a toe hold on the tower.

"Are you badly hurt, Padraig?"

"It is not the slightest wound I have ever had but do not fear, lord, I will protect your side."

More of the enemy emerged from below and this time we did not advance. We would let them charge at us. Some of the men we faced were mailed and there were at least three who were askari with mail from head to toe. They advanced toward us and I saw that they were not using spears but had fine swords. Three of the mailed askari came towards Padraig, Sir Stephen and myself.

I could feel the blood slipping down my leg. Already the leg was stiffening and movement would soon be difficult. I raised my sword and pointed the tip at the askari. He was a skilled man and his blow came down towards my head. I raised my shield and the blow made my arm shiver. Already numbed by the stone thrown from the tower it would not afford me as much protection as I might have wished. I would be slow to raise it. There was little point in using the tip of my sword. I would have to break bones beneath the mailed man I fought. I knew from experience that the bone which protected the shoulder was not the strongest and so I swung at it. He raised his shield but my strike was so hard that it cracked his buckler and made him recoil a little. That gave me encouragement and so I lifted my sword to hit at his right shoulder. He could not move his shield quickly enough and I heard him grunt as my sword connected. It was not as hard as the first blow but he was hurt. As I pulled back my arm, he swung again at me and this time my numbed arm was slow to rise. Although I caught his sword, I merely deflected it into the side of my helmet and my ears rang. My father's wound told me the danger of such a blow. Had I had the use of my shield arm I would have punched him. If my head was not hurting, I would have butted him. I had few options left but the weapons which remained to me were my spurs. I had forgotten to take them off when we had begun our attack and I had been lucky not to trip whilst climbing the ladder. Now they came to my aid. The askari did not wear chausses for their mail hauberks came to below their knees. I hooked my right leg behind the askari and dragged it back towards me. The rowel was sharp and I tore through his tendons. He screamed and dropped to his other knee. Raising my sword, I fell upon him driving the tip of the sword through his eyehole. The point embedded itself in the fighting platform.

Standing I picked up the dead askari's sword and hacked into the back of the head of the askari fighting Sir Stephen. It was a well-struck blow and I must have broken something for he stiffened and then fell back as though poleaxed.

Behind me, I heard the cry, "Navarre! Let us through England for you have done your duty!"

I raised my visor and shouted, "Let them through! Break ranks!"

This was a practised manoeuvre and turning our shields as one we stepped back and the knights of Navarre stepped through the gaps we left. I knew then, as blood dripped down my leg and my left arm hung uselessly that we had won and we had taken Jerusalem. Our crusade had achieved its objective.

Chapter 13

I went directly to Padraig. He had been hit in the side by an axe. It had broken his mail and sliced through to his gambeson. It was a long cut and a deep one. He already looked pale. I turned to Peter of York, "Shout down to Mark and ask him to fetch a healer."

"Aye, lord."

"Rafe, take one of those turbans and try to staunch the bleeding." I looked around, desperately seeking some alcohol but there was none. I found a waterskin and handed it to him. "Lie back and rest."

He nodded to my leg, "And you, too, are wounded, lord. Heal yourself."

"It is a cut only and as I will have to remove my chausses I will wait."

He drank deeply and then sank back, "This is a poor country, lord, for it is full of disease, contagion and," he waved an irritated hand at the creatures which flew around, "these damned insects. If a wound does not kill you then these little bastards will!"

Rafe and Peter began to take the mail and gambeson from Padraig. Peter shook his head, "It would have to be a tough insect to bite your thick skin!"

Padraig put down the waterskin and rubbed his head, "They seem attracted to this red hair. Perhaps I should shave it off!"

Rafe laughed as he unrolled a turban, "You have got so little hair any way I do not see why you bother!"

I knew what they were doing. They were bantering because the blood was still flowing and all three were trying to make light of it; this was their way. I went to the parapet and looked over. Below me, I could hear fighting as the Navarrese cleared each floor of the defenders. I saw Father Paul hurrying across to the tower, Mark carried his bag. The other two priests laboured behind them.

"Hurry, Father!"

When I turned back, I saw that they had finished bandaging Padraig. Other warriors had been hurt and they were being tended to by their fellows. It was what we did and we looked after our own. Padraig's eyes were closed and I looked at Peter of York. He stood and said, quietly, "He lives but it is a deep wound, lord. I fear that he will not fight again in this crusade."

Sir Stephen had joined us and had overheard our words, "Is this not over, Sir William? We have Jerusalem and we have a truce."

"There are still Christians held in the south and remember, we have yet to rebuild Ascalon but you may be right. When Richard of Cornwall brings the English barons then our work here is done and we can go home, but they have yet to reach us. Until then we must maintain our vigilance."

Henry Samuel appeared at the top of the ladder. He was grinning and lithely jumped over and then held out a hand to help Father Paul. Mark and John followed and then Matthew who carried some of the other priests' bags. I saw that Padraig had passed out; it was probably the blood he had lost.

As soon as Father Paul took off the bloody turban, he shook his head. "This is a deep wound and stitching will not do it." He pointed to the burning embers of the projectile thrower. "Rekindle the fire and heat up a spearhead. I will cauterize the wound once it is cleansed." He turned to the other priests. "I will tend to Padraig, see to the others." He glanced at my leg. "And I will tend to Sir William too!" My men and squires formed a protective circle around the priest as he probed in the wound for any foreign objects or cloth which might infect the wound. The blood flowed as he did so. I knew that Father Paul knew his business but it seemed to me that this cure was worse than the ailment. John had tended his father's forge before he became a page and he soon had the flames glowing. He cleaned a spearhead and washed it before plunging it, to hiss, in the flames. He kept adding unburned wood and fanning the flames to make the fire as hot as he could. There was skill in what he did for he had to ensure that the shaft of the spear did not burn.

Father Paul nodded, happy that the wound was clean, "Right, John, fetch the spear. Rafe and Peter, hold his arms, Mark and Matthew, his legs."

Although Padraig looked insensible, I knew that a body will often react to pain even though the patient is unconscious. It proved to be a wise precaution for even though he was held when the spearhead was applied his back arced. There was a hissing as the metal touched the flesh and then a smell of burning hair and flesh. Then the priest handed the spear back to John, "Put it back in the flames in case we have need of it again." He bent over Padraig to see if any blood continued to seep and when he rose, he nodded, seemingly satisfied.

I said, "Rafe and Peter, watch over him. When this tower is secured have him carried to the hospital. Mark and Matthew can help you."

Father Paul said, "First, my lord, your squires can remove your chausses. I will tend to you." His voice was firm and I knew he would not brook a refusal. My squire and his brother were well used to removing chausses and this time they only needed to remove one. I saw that there was more blood than I had expected and the wound was deep. "John, fan the flames. My lord, sit!"

This time, when he poked, it was my leg and I was awake. It hurt and I had to force myself to ignore the lancing pain of the sharpened knife he used to remove pieces of wood and metal. He shook his head. "Had we left the metal inside the wound you might have lost the leg." He took the skin of vinegar from his bag and said, "Mark, Matthew, hold his arms. Rafe and Peter keep his legs still." I knew what was coming and I braced myself but I was still not ready for the shock of the vinegar cleansing the open cut. I did not shout out but I know not how I did not. When the priest said, "John!" then I knew that the pain to come would be even worse.

Father Paul was clever and the vinegar had numbed the leg just enough so that when the white-hot spearhead sizzled against my leg the pain was not as bad as it might have been. This time, however, I could not control my voice and I yelled so loudly that those being tended stared at me.

Henry Samuel said, "Well, uncle, you have a reminder of the battle of Jerusalem and it will stay with you forever!"

I shook my head, "Thank you, nephew, that is a great solace to me!"

It took until evening to eliminate the last of the defenders. The Emir was not amongst the few prisoners we took nor the bodies we searched. It was as we had thought before the attack, he was at Nablus. My father was anxiously waiting for us when we emerged from the captured tower.

He saw that I limped and that Matthew was carrying my weapons, "You are hurt?"

"A cut and Father Paul has sealed the wound. It is not as bad as your wound father so fret not." I pointed behind where our other men carried Padraig who still slept. "Padraig's wound is worse. He and Richard Red Leg can now be your fellows!"

The King had given us a large house for us to use while the men who had not fought scoured the city for any sympathisers of the Emir. Groups of warriors were discovered and dealt with. The use of Greek Fire had eliminated any sympathy we might have felt for the men who were summarily executed; they had been asked to surrender and refused the offer. He then told us of his plans. He would divide the army into two. Half would go to Nablus where the Emir held out while Jerusalem was repaired and made stronger. We remained in Jerusalem until June when King Thibaut took the bulk of his army and the three military orders to Nablus. There An-Nasir Dawud still held out against the crusaders who were besieging him. It was when we reached Nablus that victory came within our grasp and, at the same time, perhaps inevitably, the crusade began to fall apart! The discord began in Jerusalem when the other leaders arrived from the siege at Nablus. There was no reason that they should have left the siege except for the fact that they wanted to say that they were there the day that Jerusalem fell. Over time the fact that they did not raise a weapon to take it would be forgotten and the chroniclers would just note that so and so of wherever was there when Jerusalem fell into Christian hands.

As we headed south, to Nablus, the bickering and the plotting for power had begun. It seemed that all wished to be given more than they had with the exception of the King, the Duke, and, of course, my father. The three of them rode alone for they had made it quite clear that their sole purpose was the crusade. Behind us, we could hear men arguing about which towns they wanted when Nablus was taken. I thought their words were unnecessary and premature for all the towns which the Emir of Damascus had given us had been apportioned to those lords of Outremer who had lost land. Having secured Jerusalem and more land than they had held for more than fifty years they should have been content but they were not for they were greedy men. There was a secure border with Muslims who were no longer enemies. That was seen as my father's contribution although, of course, it was King Thibaut who was given the accolades. All that remained was to rebuild Ascalon and recover the captured knights. I was given the task of guarding the three men for they wished to speak without being overheard.

"Do you think, Sir Thomas, that we will have to fight at Nablus?"

For some reason, even the King deferred to my father. My father shook his head, "The Emir must know that he is isolated. His allies, the Ayyubid Egyptians, are too far away to aid him and there is still a power struggle in Cairo. We took Jerusalem with relatively low losses and the Emir of Damascus took Beaufort easily enough. The Emir of Kerak will negotiate. There may be threats but he will have to agree to peace or risk losing all. He still has great fortresses to the east and he knows, as did As-Salih Ismail, that the Mongols are a far more dangerous threat than we are." He gestured behind him with his thumb, "As the plotters behind us so ably demonstrate, I fear, King Thibaut, that they will lose Jerusalem before my grandson is knighted!"

"Surely not, Sir Thomas!"

"You are a good man, Duke Peter. Not all knights are as noble as you are. There will be one, perhaps two, who seek to take total power. Once the alliance is fractured it will crumble."

Baron's Crusade

We reached Nablus not long after noon and saw that the siege was not being prosecuted as forcefully as it might have been. Guiges of Forez had been in command and he had merely dug a ditch around the town. There were no siege engines to be seen. The King just gave him a look of disdain when he saw the lack of effort. He turned to Duke Peter and my father, "I think that the two of you should ride to the gates under a flag of truce and ask for its surrender. You were the ones who attacked his caravan and took Jerusalem. I think he will fear you."

The King was an astute man and I went with the two knights to stand before the gates. As-Salih Ismail had given us a translator, Al-Shama, and we would be able to speak to this emir in his own language with no misunderstandings!

I was pleased that they observed the truce and we were not riddled with arrows for we halted less than a hundred paces from the gates. Part of me wondered if this was a plot and that the King of Navarre sought to end our lives so that he could claim the glory of the war. I was wrong and I had misjudged the Navarrese king. We did not have to endure a wall of arrows and the Emir was summoned.

When he arrived, he glared at us. "You are the men who began this war."

My father spoke and the translator translated, "If we begin with blame then we will get nowhere. I have a grandson I wish to see grow and I do not need to be here, Emir!"

Even though the words were translated I could see the effect of the words and my father's calm yet authoritative tone on the Emir. "What is it that you wish?"

My father deferred to the Duke who spoke, "The Emir of Damascus has granted us lands: Nazareth, Bethlehem and Galilee."

"But they were not his to give! They are my towns."

The Duke was a wise man, "Nablus is a strong town but Bethlehem, Nazareth and the towns of Galilee are not. Do you think that your people could hold against us if we chose to take them?" He allowed that to sink in and then said, "The Mongols are close to your eastern border. Where would you rather have your men? Defending against the Mongols in the east or here where you know we just seek the holy places of our lord?"

The threat of the Mongols had an effect, as the Duke had known. "We will not give a decision this day for it is almost time for prayers. Return at noon tomorrow and we will give you an answer."

The Duke said, "We will return at the sixth hour of the day for we will not sit here and burn."

The Emir nodded and I knew that we had won.

When we went, the next morning we had the King with us and within a short time, we were admitted to the town. The negotiations lasted all day but, in the end, we had confirmation that we could keep that which we had been given so long as we helped the Emir to defend against the Mongols. The King agreed and I thought that was disingenuous of him for he would not be in the Holy Land when the Mongols attacked. King Thibaut insisted that everything be written down in Arabic and French so that none could complain after. A week after we arrived in Nablus, we headed down the coast to Ascalon. I knew that the harder task lay ahead; we had to negotiate the prisoners from the Ayyubid Egyptians who were not as threatened as the Ayyubid Turks. My father seemed philosophical about it all.

"William, what will be will be. Richard of Cornwall will be here soon and then we can return home."

I did not mention Geoffrey of Lyon. My impulsive promise to a dying man could not be undone and I was committed. My father could go home and my knights could return to England but I would stay with my men and we would keep the promise to a dying man.

We spent a week at Ascalon organising the repairs to the castle. Emissaries were sent to Gaza and to Cairo to arrange for peace talks. We had enough money to pay for the return of the captives for we had taken it from the captured cities. I did not think that it would be a question of money; there would be other demands that they would make. The Ayyubid Egyptians had had a great victory but, thanks to my father, it was the Christians who had won the war. We spent a month waiting for them to give us an answer. All the while the King and the Duke were becoming increasingly frustrated by the attitude of the other lords. It became quite obvious that none of them cared about the captives. They were arguing about who would rule the largest castles and who would control the trade. The Crusade was an afterthought. My father, more than anyone was unhappy and it was he who went to the King.

"King Thibaut, let me go to the Egyptians. I will take my son and our men and the translator to discuss terms. We will not be a threat to the lords of Egypt and a face-to-face talk might well reap a reward. It is certainly better than waiting here. Besides, our men do not wish to rebuild Ascalon!" He said it with a smile so the King knew he was joking. Over the last months, my father's standing with the King had risen.

King Thibaut nodded, "I grow weary of this crusade. It is not the war I thought it would be. Whatever you do will be a step forward." He leaned forward, "I pray you take care. There are many lords I would be happy to fall into Muslim hands but you are not one of them!"

Our men were happy to follow my father even though they knew it was like putting their heads into the mouth of a lion! The three priests also showed their courage by volunteering to come. As Christians entered the most fanatical of Muslim worlds, they were at the greatest risk but they had seen our men face death and this was their chance to do so.

My father and I tried to persuade Henry Samuel to remain in Ascalon with our wounded men but he would have none of it. He shook his head, "Your son, Sir Thomas, would not have stayed behind and I have my father's blood in my veins. I will live or die at your side and that of my uncle!"

We took just one horse each and we headed south. We passed the battlefield where my father had suffered his wound. He did not seem upset; in fact, he seemed more concerned about the men we would meet. Our translator, Al-Shama, knew much about the men who held the captives. The stronger of the brothers was As-Salih Ayyub and our translator showed us that he was a lord of some importance when he told us that he believed that As-Salih Ayyub had managed to oust his cousin and take total control. He had knowledge of the politics of Egypt which someone who was just a translator would not.

"I believe this is a good time to speak to him for he has but a tenuous grip on the land. Crusader gold would strengthen his position."

My father nodded, "And his cousin, what of him?"

"He lost his chance for total control when he tried to play one emir off against another. He is Saladin's eldest but he is not a well man and will die soon. When he does there will be a struggle to see who can claim his title. I believe it will be my master."

I asked, "Then you do not like the man we meet?"

"No, lord, but I will be honest in my translation for the Emir made me promise I would do so. As-Salih Ismail is an honourable man, perhaps too honourable. He is a man of his word and has surrounded himself with others who feel the same way."

With such knowledge in our heads, we were able to prepare far more effectively for this most momentous of meetings. Al-Shama listened as my father and I spoke on the long road south.

"We do not yet know if this Al-Salih Ayyub has managed to wrest power from his brother so we must show ourselves to be above their politics, important though it is. Another reason I wished just the men from Stockton is that we do not wear the cross of Jerusalem. We are knights from England. My connection with Amaury de Montfort will make us less of a threat. Whoever rules in Egypt he will be wary of spies."

"And the money we can promise?"

"Let us be vague about the amount we have. The Egyptians are rich but a new leader can never have too much money."

Al-Shama chuckled, "You have an eastern mind, Sir Thomas!"

Just then Cedric rode back from the front of our ridiculously small column, "Sir Thomas, we have been followed for the last five miles. There are riders to the west of us."

To the west lay the coast and I looked. There was a haze of dust slightly behind us. My father nodded, "It is to be expected. This way they can cut off our retreat if we turn and run. They are assessing our threat." None of us wore helmets and our shields, although we had brought them, were hung on our sumpters. My father's wisdom in bringing so few men now reaped the reward. We were too small to be a threat and, if we were scouts, then we were not being very good ones.

We halted for the night at a small nameless village east of the city of Gaza. We would not ride directly to Gaza but wait for an invitation. We paid for food and water from the villagers and camped in tents. My father smiled when he heard a horse leave the village and head west towards the city. "Better than sending one of our men. This way they will come to us."

Henry Samuel had been taking a keen interest in all that had been said on the way south and he frowned, "But the riders who follow us know where we are."

My father nodded. He could be very patient with Henry Samuel and he explained the reasons in detail, "But the men following do not know our purpose. When we came and asked for shelter Al-Shama told the headman that we were heading for Cairo to negotiate the return of the captives. The rider will tell whoever rules in Gaza. If no one comes then we continue south. Whatever happens, it will show the Egyptians that we come in peace." He smiled, "Of course, they could ignore the niceties and protocols of negotiation and take us prisoner." Sam's mouth dropped open. "But I do not think that will happen. The riders who followed us know that King Thibaut has an enormous army to the north of Gaza. Whoever rules in Cairo has not yet a strong hold on the reins of power."

We had our answer the next day when a column of Khwarzamian askari, led by an Egyptian amir, appeared as we rose. Our men impressed me for none showed any fear despite the fact that the horsemen pointed their lances at us as they formed a half-circle around our camp. Al-Shama, my father and myself walked towards the amir's horse. My father said nothing and Al-Shama began to translate the amir's words when he spoke. I guessed that the amir had been sent to confirm what they had heard. He rattled off his own answer and Al-Shama turned to my father and smiled, "We are to be escorted to El-Arish. The governor of Gaza does not have the captives. They are being held close to the coast, sixty miles south of here."

"And does this mean that Al-Salih Ayyub will be there?"

Al-Shama shrugged, "That I do not know nor, I suspect, does this lord who takes us there. I am not worried about this and it does make sense. El-Arish is close enough to your crusader lands for their return and yet Gaza stands in the way of any rescue attempt."

We left. Half of the Khwarzamians rode ahead of us and the other half behind. We were outnumbered by four to one. Padraig had been left in Acre with Richard Red Leg and so we just had Peter of York and Rafe War Axe as sergeants with us. Rafe sniffed and said, "Very nice of them to take us all the way to the lion's den, eh Sir Thomas? It saves our lads from having to scout."

"Aye, Rafe, but if the lion opens his mouth do not be tempted to try to count his teeth! He may bite!"

"Sir Thomas, a lion would not enjoy the taste of Rafe for he eats a raw onion each day!" Peter was Rafe's best friend.

"It keeps my blood pure and you may not have noticed, Peter of York, but the insects do not bite me!"

Peter laughed, "That is because you stink!"

It was good-natured banter but it must have made our guards wonder at us for we were like men who were just out for a pleasant ride with friends rather than enemies being escorted to what amounted to a prison.

Al-Shama explained what we would find at El-Arish, "The place was known, in the past, as Rhinocorura, the place where noses were cut off. It has always been a place of punishment. It is a third of the way to Cairo and is used as a stopping-off place. The sea is not far away and the Romans used the port there which lies on the edge of the Sinai desert and Bedouin caravans travel from the south. I can see why they keep the captives there. The Duke of Burgundy and the others would have nowhere to run to should they choose to escape."

We camped at an oasis on the road. There were mean huts there, no more than a dozen and that was all. The next day we reached the muddy sprawl that was El-Arish. The captives were held in tents. We saw those from afar as we approached. My father shook his head, "Hugh of Burgundy and Amaury de Montfort will not be happy that they have had to languish here since the battle."

"But the King could do nothing about it."

"Do you think that Hugh of Burgundy will see it that way? Would you?"

"But it was these knights who disobeyed the King and rode off to raid."

"Which is what the Duke of Brittany did. Do not expect them to be reasonable, rational men. They are rich lords who are used to living in castles and not in a fly-ridden tent on the edge of a desert. It may have chastened them but I doubt it."

We were not taken to the tents of the captives which, we saw, were guarded by many warriors. I suspected that the large number was there to prevent a rescue attempt. There was a fort and we were taken there. It had all the feel of a prison to me. Our numbers meant that we could be held there. It also meant that we would not be sleeping in a tent but in a mud building. Al-Shama explained that we would have to await the arrival of someone from Cairo. After Al-Shama spoke with the governor of the town he said, "This will be whichever brother has wrested power from the other."

"Can we speak with the prisoners?"

Al-Shama translated and then said, "Not today. Tomorrow, after morning prayers, you will be allowed to speak with them, briefly."

The next day, it was just my father, me and the interpreter who were allowed into the camp. The smell hit me as we approached. There were more than two hundred and fifty knights and, as far as I could see the toilets were hastily dug latrines and there was no means of bathing. Had they surrendered in the west then they would have been treated well and housed in a lord's castle for it would be in his interest to keep them in good condition and obtain a healthy ransom. It was like keeping a prize bull in a good condition ready for when you took him to market. Here the Egyptians wanted payment for a herd! I had an interest in the squires and sergeants. I saw some squires but, from their livery, they were the squires of the most senior lords. There were no sergeants and few other squires. Both Hugh of Burgundy and Amaury de Montfort looked unwell. The joy on their faces when we approached told me that there would be relief and not acrimony.

"Earl, Sir William, you have come to fetch us?"

My father shook his head, "That is to be decided. We have come to negotiate for your freedom and we have funds to buy you all back!"

"God be praised! Come sit under the awning of my tent. I fear they will not allow us inside for fear that you give us weapons."

Baron's Crusade

The guards were Mamelukes and they were renowned for both their cruelty and their vigilance. The Duke's squire fetched boxes for us to sit upon. Amaury asked, "Has my brother come yet?"

"They are on their way but not yet arrived, my lord."

He sounded disappointed, "Thank you, Sir Thomas."

"And how goes the crusade?"

My father lowered his voice for although the Mameluke guards were thirty paces away, he was not certain if they could speak French. "We have Jerusalem, Galilee and all of the land between the Jordan and the sea. We have an ally in the Emir of Damascus!"

"God be praised! Then our captivity has not been in vain!"

I did not contradict the Duke but had they not recklessly charged towards Gaza then we might have achieved the same ends without the losses.

"However, we await someone to negotiate and if they are successful then we have to arrange an exchange."

"I know, Sir Thomas, but you bring the hope of dawn after a long journey into night."

We spoke in more detail about which castles and towns we now held and then I ventured, "The squires and sergeants, what happened to them, Duke?"

"They were taken away from here a week after the battle by an emir from the north."

I was guessing but I ventured, "An-Nasir Dawud, the Emir of Kerak?"

Amaury de Montfort said, "I believe that was the man. He had a hawk-like nose and a cruel disposition. He had two squires executed for nothing at all. Why do you ask?"

I would not speak ill of the dead and so I did not give the true details but I said, "I found one of your knights, Duke, Raymond of Lyon. He was dying and he asked me to try to find his brother Geoffrey." I was dreading that he would tell me that Geoffrey had been one of the two executed squires.

He nodded, "He was one of the men taken. I am sorry that Sir Raymond died. I knew his father and I swore I would look after him. I thought he had escaped when he was not here. I let him down." He looked across the camp at the huddles of despondent knights who squatted in the sand. "I have let so many people down."

The Captain of the Mamelukes came over and spoke to Al-Shama. "We have to go."

The look of despair and desperation on the two men's faces was pitiable. They had barely noticed my father and me in Acre and now they needed us as much as bread and water. "You will return?"

"As soon as we can. Do not worry, Duke Hugh. The Egyptians cannot want to keep you any longer than they have to. You will be released. It is all a question of price."

As we walked back, I said, "That means the prisoners must be in the lair of An-Nasir Dawud. Where will that be, Al-Shama?"

"You do not want to know, Sir William, for if they are there then they are dead men already."

"Where is it?"

"Al-Karak, the place you westerners call Kerak Castle."

"The Templar castle?"

My father said, "It was never Templar. It was built by King Baldwin and was only in our hands for less than fifty years! Al Shama is right. I have seen it and it is impregnable."

"I do not want to storm it, father! I want to rescue some men."

"It amounts to the same thing. Let us complete one labour before we begin another, eh, my son?"

He was right, of course, for our minds had to be focused.

As-Salih Ayyub arrived the next day and he came at the head of a small army. That meant that he had won the struggle. We learned that his brother had died although the circumstances of the death were a little vague. We did not know it then but this young warrior, for he would have been of an age with my dead brother Alfred, was the stone which begins an avalanche. He was the one who united the Turks and the Egyptians and wrested all of our gains back. Of course, that was all in the future. We just saw the army and assumed the worst. We were summoned into his presence the following day. As far as I was aware, he had not bothered to visit with the captives. He had his own interpreter but Al-Shama was allowed to stay with us when we spoke with him and we would know if our words were mistranslated.

He stared at my father, studying him. "You are the warrior who saved half of the Christian army are you not? You are Sir Thomas of Stockton."

He was remarkably well informed, "I am."

"And you recovered from a wound which would have laid low most men?" My father nodded. "Then Allah must favour you. I shall bear that in mind."

I watched his eyes as he took a breath to continue. He had sharp eyes and he was constantly watching our faces. This was a clever man and not one to be underestimated.

"You wish to buy back these prisoners?"

My father was equal to this Emir. He shook his head, "In a perfect world we would not pay for them but take them off your hands so that you did not have to feed them."

As-Salih Ayyub laughed, "You have much nerve. If the situation was reversed would you simply let your captives go?"

"When we took Nablus not a man was killed."

He glared at Al-Shama, "And that was because a traitor helped you!"

Al-Shama kept his face impassive. I realised then that he was in as dangerous a position as any of us; probably more dangerous as his lord was considered to be a threat to As-Salih Ayyub.

"Nonetheless, it shows that we can be merciful."

"And I will be merciful too. I will take one chest of gold. The chest will be a cubit by a cubit."

My father asked, "A Roman cubit or an Egyptian one?"

The Emir smiled, "You are a knowledgeable man. An Egyptian one, of course."

I learned later that a Roman one was a third as big again as an Egyptian cubit. The Emir valued his own culture more than profits. It showed that money was unimportant to him. I knew then that this Egyptian had a network of spies for we had four such chests back in Ascalon but only one had gold. The other three were silver. He knew how much to ask for.

"That is acceptable."

"Then return to Ascalon and we will bring your captives there for I would speak with your King Thibaut."

Now I understood the presence of his army. With the Mameluke guards and the Khwarzamians, he had enough to force a battle if things turned ugly, yet it was not enough to invade Outremer. I saw in that meeting that this was another Saladin.

Chapter 14

After speaking with the Duke to tell him of the arrangements, we left the next day to return to Ascalon. We had no escort this time and I took that as a measure of the faith they had in my father. He spoke the truth and they liked that. It was not true of all crusaders. Al-Shama confirmed as we rode north, of the personal danger he had been in when we were in the camp. My father turned to look at him and said, "Then you showed great courage by coming with us."

"It was what my master wished."

We stopped overnight at the muddy oasis and while Al-Shama negotiated with the headman my father said, quietly, "My friend, the Emir, was not quite as honest as he might have been. Al-Shama was also sent to spy on As-Salih Ayyub. I saw him assessing the forces with the new leader. I wondered why he sent a lord and not a slave and it is as I feared, this is a struggle between the two halves of the Muslim world. If the Mongols were not a threat then I think that our captives would have stayed in Egypt."

The King had taken over the house of a merchant in Ascalon and, when we arrived, we were ushered into a cool courtyard. The people of this land knew how to build so that the rich were cool and comfortable. King Thibaut was happy that the captives were being returned and that it had only cost us half of the treasure we had accumulated.

My father was suspicious and said, "That begs the question of why? What concessions will he seek when he speaks with you, King Thibaut? Do not underestimate this man, he has rid himself of his brother and I think our ally, the Emir of Damascus, is the next threat to his power."

King Thibaut nodded, "And An-Nasir Dawud?"

"In chess terms, he is the bishop to the King that is As-Salih Ayyub. He serves Egypt and hopes for crumbs from their table. He knows his own limitations and now we can see that the caravan which the Duke Peter and I took was of more significance than we thought. It was there to weaken Damascus."

The King looked weary. "When the captives are safely within our walls then Duke Peter and I will take our ships and return home. I came here on a holy crusade and now see that, apart from those present, the rest are self-serving, power-hungry knights. They would carve up the lands we have negotiated. From what you say this new ruler of Egypt will become a second Saladin and I have seen little amongst the knights here to see any who can counter him." He smiled, "Of course if you stayed and took command…"

My father shook his head. "As soon as the King's brother arrives then my son and I return to England. We have done all that was asked of us and more."

I shifted uncomfortably on the seat I had been given and the King, an astute man said, "You wish to stay, Sir William?"

"No, King Thibaut, but I cannot go back to England without attempting to rescue a squire from Kerak. He is held there as a slave by An-Nasir Dawud."

The King shook his head, "Then that quest is doomed to failure. It would take an army to rescue one man and is not worth the effort."

My father smiled, "He is my son and I know that he will try. It is in his blood."

The Duke said, "I have one of my knights who wishes to stay and take part in some quest which brings honour with it for he feels he has yet to achieve that which he hoped. I will send him to you, Sir William, for it may well be that this quest may give him peace. Sir Philip is a troubled man."

When we reached our camp the English knights were also pleased to see us. They did not enjoy the talk of power. "We all hope to return home with you, Sir Thomas."

"You do not wish to stay and serve the King's brother?"

Sir Stephen said, "I speak for all of us when I say we have made enough sacrifices and lost enough men already. Besides, we have achieved that which we set out to do. Those who go home now will be seen as heroes. Those who stay will be tarnished with the lust for land and power."

Padraig was healing well but I knew that neither he nor Richard Red Leg would be able to come with me, as much as they might wish to. When I told them my decision they were both less than happy. "But Padraig, there may not be a happy outcome to this. I will only take those men who wish to come!"

"All the more reason to take me, lord. Richard has a bad leg but my wound is almost healed."

His face looked drawn and I knew it was a lie. "And you and I know that almost is not good enough." His face told me that he understood that I was right.

The rest of the men were all happy to come. Henry Samuel also asked to come but I refused. "I will not take John. Instead, I will take my father's squire, Mark, for Matthew has told me that his brother wishes to serve. This is dangerous and not a quest for any other than warriors who are fit and skilled. You two pages have heart but that will not be enough. In any case, we have to wait until the prisoners arrive."

It took three more days for the captives to be marched north. They were in a piteous state when they arrived. Duke Hugh and Amaury de Montfort were broken men. They had fought their last battle; of that, I was certain although both stayed in the Holy Land after the King had departed for they felt they owed the Pope service.

My father and I were present at the negotiations. Not all of the lords of Outremer were there and some took offence at that but King Thibaut had tired of them all. Al Shama was not present and I think that was deliberate on the part of Al-Shama for As-Salih Ayyub was no fool and he would recognise him as a spy. I do not know if Al-Shama knew that or simply feared for his life but when we emerged from the meeting he had gone back to Damascus.

As-Salih Ayyub made it quite clear that he would brook no further territorial concessions. He was forthright when he spoke. "Ascalon, Acre, those you can have. For the moment you can retain Jerusalem, Galilee and the lands conceded to you already but they are contingent upon your lords leading peaceful lives and not attempting to take any more land!"

King Thibaut nodded, "I agree and when the captives are well enough to travel then I will return home to Navarre."

It was clear that the information was not a surprise and I wondered who the spy was for he had to be privy to the private meetings we had held.

The gold was brought and handed over. The Egyptian looked unconcerned. It was a symbol only. His translator asked, "Sir Thomas, do you return home also?"

"No, my lord. I await the rest of the English crusaders."

"There are more who are coming? I thought that your Pope just wanted Jerusalem. You have that. What else do they want?"

I saw my father's face. He was trying to give an acceptable answer and one which would not pose a threat to the Egyptian. "Crusade is not only about war, lord. Knights hope to see the holy places which were part of Our Lord's life. It is a pilgrimage."

"Yet you wait until they arrive before you leave?"

My father nodded, "I obey the commands of my King."

"And that is the difference between us, Sir Thomas, for I obey the orders of Allah and I bow the knee to no king!"

At that moment I saw the danger to Outremer. He bowed no knee for he would be King!

The most powerful man in the Holy Land left with his army and his gold. For him, the gold was unimportant as what he sought was a world ruled by the followers of Islam. I now understood why my father had been so reluctant to return to this land. We could both do far more good in England than here; this was a war which could never be won. It took a week for the army to return to Acre. For my men and me it was a stopping-off place only We would be returning to Jerusalem and then head into the highlands around Kerak. We needed a guide and Jerusalem seemed the best place to find one.

On the way back to Acre Henry Samuel tried to dissuade me from this quest. Part of it was envy as he wished to be with me and the other part was a genuine fear that I would not return. I told him that I had no intention of dying or wasting the lives of the men who followed me. "I made a promise, Sam, and I will try but if it is impossible then I will return, empty handed."

We stayed long enough in Acre just to say goodbye to the Duke, and the King to introduce me to the knight and his men at arms who wished to serve God in battle. The knight had only taken part in the last assault on the Tower of David and he had not felt as though he had put his life at risk. There was more to his decision than that but he did not know us well enough, then, to confide in me. After the King had departed my father and I questioned the knight for I did not want a reckless fool who wanted a glorious death at the hands of the heathens. His evasiveness made me concerned.

Sir Philip of Arras was a serious knight as were his squire and ten men at arms. I wondered why he had not joined a military order and rather than beat around the bush I broached the question as soon as we were alone. "It seems to me, Sir Philip, that you have already done enough in this crusade to merit a return to France. Answer me, honestly, why you wish to go on this quest with me."

He smiled and suddenly looked younger, "Lord, I am to be wed to Eloise of Fontainebleau as soon as I return from Holy Crusade. Her father died in the Fifth Crusade. I cannot return to her without having taken some risk for her father was a great man, and if I am to be her husband then I need to achieve something more than just emptying a tower of a handful of Turks."

"Then if you come with me you take the greatest risk of all for we go deep behind the lines of the most implacable enemy of Christendom to attempt to rescue half-starved and beaten men from an impregnable fortress."

He smiled again, "Then I am even more convinced that I wish to go for that is truly a noble endeavour and, lord, I have no fear that we will be lost for your family has a reputation for courage and facing impossible odds. The story of the Warlord who won back a country for the Empress is one I grew up with; I grew up close to La Flèche. We will prevail." The dour young man had a backbone of steel, I could see that, and optimism which bordered on the ridiculous.

I said farewell to the English knights. They had wished to come with me but I had declined their offer. "You have all served my father well and this is a task best undertaken by a small number of men. It has been an honour to fight alongside you."

"And we have learned much from your father and from you. It seems like a lifetime since Sir Hubert charged off wildly after those archers."

"Aye, Sir Stephen, and you have all changed for the better I think, and that is down to my father. If trouble came, I would be happy to have all of you at my back."

My father would arrange their passage while he waited for Richard of Cornwall.

We gathered what we would need. I took Thorn as my horse and the Turkish horses we had captured would go with us. We could use them for any captives which we rescued or we could trade them. My plans were flexible as I had no idea what we would find when we travelled east to this prison in the mountains. We took only the equipment we would need; water, food, arrows and weapons. We had a day or two to get to Jerusalem and find a man, someone who might know a way into Kerak. We had been given a few names of men in Jerusalem who might fit the bill. Then it was two or three days to Kerak. We would not need to take much with us as Kerak was a day or two from Jerusalem on the other side of the Dead Sea. I bade farewell to my father.

"I hope that Richard of Cornwall arrives soon but I shall put in place the plans to take us home. We have taken chests of silver and I would spend some on gifts for your mother, wife and your sisters." He looked at me and his eyes bored into me, "This is right what you do for you promised a dying man, but heed my words, he would not wish you to die in a vain attempt. If it is impossible then come home. That is my command."

"And I will obey for I wish to see my own son. He will be walking when I return. I have missed so much."

We slipped out on the morning that the King left so that all of the attention was on the harbour and not the road to Jerusalem. I knew that there were spies everywhere. Our archers had become skilled at scouting in this land. They had had much experience and were now more familiar with the land. Cedric assured me that we were not followed and I believed him. We had been given names, whilst in Acre, of some men who might help us. The names came from the Knights of St. John and I trusted both the veracity of the information and the discretion they would employ about our mission. He had told us that there was one man, in particular, who would be useful, Jean of Rheims and advised us to seek him first. The man worked in a stable in Jerusalem and he had been a prisoner in Kerak. When he had been ransomed, he had stayed in Jerusalem. He had lost the full use of one leg and, apparently, hated the Muslims with a passion. He was one of a number of names I had been given. The Hospitaller who had given me the names thought he was the one who would be able to give us the greatest aid. I was sceptical for he sounded like a bitter and twisted man.

The King had ensured that having taken Jerusalem, we did not lose it easily, and it was well guarded. We stayed in an inn close to the city wall. We chose it because it had a stable. The Christian who ran it was philosophical about the recent reversal of fortunes in the city. "Christian or Muslim, lord, there are always men who wish to visit the city. Caravans still bring goods here and we serve them. Most of the Muslim rulers turn a blind eye to our selling of wine and so we make a living." From the prices he charged it was a good living!

I went with Sir Philip and our two squires and left our men to listen to the gossip about the region around Kerak. Jean of Rheims, when we found him, was almost as old as my father. I could see that although he had been lamed, he was a strong man. He thought we had come for horses to be shooed for he also did some farrier work.

"No, my friend, I bring silver for information."

His eyes narrowed, "Information? I do not know you. Is this some sort of trick?"

I now saw that he had survived as long as he had by being careful. "I am Sir William of Elsdon and my father is Sir Thomas of Stockton, the Earl of Cleveland."

He smiled, "The hero of Arsuf?" I nodded. "I have heard of him. That name and a coin mean that I will listen to your questions, Whether I answer them or not … well, we shall see."

I gave him a silver coin. He nodded and I began. I told him my story and my promise. He rubbed his chin, "It is a worthy cause but a foolish one. You go to save just one man?"

"I go to save as many as I can but rescuing Geoffrey of Lyon is my main aim."

He stared at the single coin I had given him and I wondered if I should offer him more. When he spoke, I knew that he was not planning on asking for more. "You were with the knights who raided An-Nasir Dawud's caravan?" I nodded. He chuckled. "It was his father who was responsible for my leg. I hate the whole family. There were forty of us who were captured. When the Knights of St. John ransomed us there

Baron's Crusade

were eight of us left. He had us working in the quarries close by to the castle. He and his people are making it stronger. If you wish to get inside then forget it; that will not happen, however, if you wish to rescue the squire that is a different matter and there is a way but it will not be easy and will need great planning."

My heart rose. He was willing to help and now that I had met the man, I was more confident that we had a chance. "Whatever you need. Name your price."

"Ten gold crowns and I go with you." I could not help but glance down at his leg. He laughed, "Do not worry, I can ride and no one walks close to Kerak. I will not slow you down but either I go with you or you can find another."

"Then tell us your idea for I am happy that you join this quest."

He shook his head, "Not here. Where are you staying?" I told him and he said, "Then I will join you there this evening. I have things to do." He saw the concern on my face. "Do not worry, lord, you can trust me for I have given you my word. I am your man now until we have succeeded or the carrion crows pick the flesh from my body!"

As we headed back Sir Philip observed, "He seems a strange character. I wonder why he did not return home?"

"Perhaps all of his friends were dead. I know not. I think this land gets under a man's skin. I know that my great grandfather, when he was a crusader here, left friends behind who chose this land. What I do know is that we now have a chance to do that which I promised. I do not know what Jean of Rheims has planned but whatever it is will be better than any idea I had."

My men told me the gossip that they had heard. The Emir of Kerak hated Christians. When he had held Jerusalem, he had imposed a Christ tax, as the locals called it. The inhabitants had to pay half of their earnings to be allowed to live in the city. It explained how the Templars had managed to gain entry to the walls so quickly for there was a resistance movement within the walls already. The inn had food although it was expensive. Now we understood why the Christian's prices were so high. He was trying to recoup some of the losses he had incurred during the misrule of An-Nasir Dawud.

Jean arrived just as we were finishing the meal. He seemed to know the owner and I saw a look of guilt on the innkeeper's face. He had brought us wine and I poured a goblet for Jean who had drawn a crude map on the back of an old document. As he described features, he jabbed a finger at them. "You cannot get into the castle; it was always hard but now, with the improvements they have made, it is impossible. It was only lost through treachery. The slaves are taken each morning before the sun has risen, and marched three miles from the castle here southwest to the quarry, here." He had marked the castle on the map. He jabbed a finger at a spot that he had marked with a cross. "This is where we can take the captives; it is close to the road which winds to the castle and the slaves carry the blocks from the quarry to the road and they are then loaded onto wagons. I know not why but they only have four wagons." He shrugged, "If I was them, I would have more wagons and complete the work faster. The slaves have their legs encumbered with ropes to stop them from fleeing. They only had twenty guards when I was there but that was all that they needed for they were archers and they surrounded the quarry. In addition, there is an overseer and they have four masons. To help him, the overseer has four men with whips to encourage the men to work. They stop work at midday but that is not out of kindness; the masons do not wish to work. The wagon drivers take the wagons back to the castle where they eat their midday meal in the shade and comfort of the castle. They return only after the men in the quarry have begun to work. In the middle of the afternoon, the captives are marched back to the castle. Those who die during the day are left in the quarry."

"Men die?"

He nodded, "Normally one every two days. There is a high turnover of slaves. The odds of finding this one squire alive are slim."

I nodded. "I am guessing that if we take out the guards then we could overcome the overseers easily and escape."

He turned and looked at our men, "How many men do you have?"

The ones you can see. Six of them are archers."

He brightened, "English archers?"

"Just so."

"Then there is a chance for you have archers the equal of these Turks." He pointed at his map, "As I said they just have four wagons. When they are loaded, they return together to the castle. It is when they eat their midday meal that we can strike. The wagons will not return until an hour after the rest period and the guards who watch will be as relaxed as they are going to be for the captives will not be moving around and will be easier to watch. If your archers could slay six guards with their first flight then we would have a chance. Six men killed quickly would cause confusion and a second flight might swing the odds in our favour."

"Our men are all mailed."

"Then there is a chance. However, taking them is only the first part. You would have to slay everyone. Then the prisoners would have to be freed."

Baron's Crusade

"We have some spare horses."

He nodded, "The overseer and his four guards ride horses. We would only have the time until the wagons return before the alarm is given. If we struck at the start of the midday break then, by the time the alarm was given we would have a three-hour start." He let that sink in. "But it is a hard and difficult journey between Kerak and Jerusalem."

"If we hide our men where the sentries watch then we could slay them. That would help us get the captives but you are right, the Emir would send horsemen after the captives." Jean nodded. "First, the enemy would go to the quarry and then they would head down the road to Jerusalem. The road, from your map, passes north along the Dead Sea."

"And that is where they would likely catch up with us. Even on horses, the captives will not be able to move quickly and there is a garrison in Kerak."

"And if we left the road and crossed the Jordan south of the Dead Sea?"

"Then they would catch us there instead."

"Unless we ambushed them. I take it the ground to the south is rough ground?"

"It is, Sir William, for there is no road just hunter and shepherd trails across the rocky ridge there."

"Then we place our archers on the high ground and my knights and men at arms hide there. The Turks will see the captives and hurry on to catch them."

Jean of Rheims smiled, "That is a plan ridden with risks but it has merit. We could scout out that route on the way there for that way we would avoid scrutiny. Once we pass the Jordan then we are in the country of the horse archer."

We spent the rest of the evening planning what we would need. Jean still had his mail hauberk from when he had been a sergeant. He had kept it in good condition and knew he would need it. He also had his own horse but he approved of the extra horses we would take. After he had gone, we spoke of the good fortune which had sent him into our path. Although he was right and the plan had risks, he had ensured that we had a chance of success, however slim.

Mark and Matthew sat and talked with me. Since my father had been wounded Mark had changed and was desperate to be the best squire that he could be, "I would be as Matthew, my brother, lord. He does not make mistakes as I do."

Matthew shook his head, "I do make mistakes and you are too hard on yourself. Did not Sir William tell you that the Earl's wound was not your fault?"

"He did but…"

"Your brother is right, Mark, you cannot let that incident colour or cloud your judgement. You will make mistakes; Matthew will too. I know that I did when I was a squire but you cannot live your life worrying about the mistakes that you might make. Often, in war, you have to react, almost without thinking. That heartbeat you spend debating if you should do something or hold back is the time that you die. Better to do something which is a mistake than do nothing and suffer the same end result."

He nodded, "I am glad that I have my brother to watch and to copy. We are twins but I know that he is the better squire and I will aspire to be like him." He smiled, "Believe me, brother, this quest will be the making of me."

When we left, we first headed east to take the road which headed down the western side of the Dead Sea. The busier road was to the east where the traffic between Damascus, Jericho and Jerusalem passed heading south. That we would be spotted was obvious as you could not hide so many warriors in mail and the string of horses. Another advantage of having Jean with us was that he spoke the language and that helped too. Whenever we stopped for food, water or shade he made a point of telling the locals that he was a horse merchant and we were his guards. If they noticed the two sets of spurs, they did not say anything. He even offered to sell our horses to them. I was worried when he told me what he intended as I knew we would need every horse we had and more. He had laughed and told me that he knew how to price it so that they were too expensive and the locals would think us fools. When we reached the southern end of the Dead Sea, we had to leave the road and turn east. There was no road here, it was a jumble of tiny trails which picked their way up and down the rocky ridge. It was dangerous for the horses and we took half a day to negotiate but it was half a day well spent.

I rode with Cedric, Philip and Jean. We had to picture the scene if we were successful and we returned with Turks in hot pursuit. We would have had a twenty-mile ride during the heat of the day. In England that would be as little as a one-and-a-half-hour ride. Here it was more likely to take us four hours or more. The men pursuing us would be more tired than we as they would have been trying to catch us. When we left the road, I hoped that they would think us fools for no horseman chose this track willingly.

It was Cedric Warbow who showed his experience and skill in setting ambushes. He spotted a high point just a mile from the eastern end of the ridge. He pointed to the rocks on both sides, "From here, lord, we could loose arrows with impunity." He pointed to a natural dell to the south of the ridge. "We could leave our horses there. You and the men at arms could wait below us." He pointed to two spurs which made a piece of dead ground where we could hide. "Our arrows fix their attention and then you and the men at arms flank them."

Jean looked sceptically at Cedric, "You can be that accurate that you will not stick an arrow into one of your own men?"

I laughed, "Jean of Rheims, I could be fighting An-Nasir Dawud himself and Cedric would be able to hit him and not risk me." I nodded, "That plan has merit. Mark and Matthew can help you, Jean, to get the captives to the road and you will not need to hurry for we will be there to hold up the pursuers. We will withdraw as soon as we have bloodied their noses and we can escape under the protective arrows of Cedric and his men."

We camped close by the road at the eastern end of the ridge. There we explained the whole plan to our men. "Tomorrow we have an eighteen-mile ride towards Kerak. It will be upon the road. For that reason, we split it into two rides. We ride the first half before dawn and find somewhere to take shelter during the heat of the day. When it is dark, we ride to the quarry. It is unguarded at night and that will allow us to get into position early and secrete ourselves. Mark, Matthew and Sir Philip's squire, Guillaume, will watch the horses. Jean thinks that the sentries watch from the same place each day and that should mean we can see where they will be. When we strike then it must be at the same time."

Sir Philip said, "That would be hard to coordinate."

Jean shook his head, "No, the Turks will provide the signal for they sound a horn at the midday break and another when it is over. After the first horn we each count to one hundred. When we reach one hundred then we begin to kill."

I nodded, "That sounds like it might just work. We take no prisoners; we are here to rescue the captives. If any captive is too ill to walk then we will have to carry them and we will not be able to bring our own dead. If you are killed, we have to leave you for this will be hard enough as it is. I know it goes against our grain but these are a cruel people and what we do will stop others suffering."

We sharpened our weapons that night. Cedric and his archers each chose the best twenty arrows they had for their arrow bags and we fed our horses grain and an apple. The animals would be hard pushed the next day. Having crossed the Jordan had meant we had full waterskins and they had water at the quarry; water, that most valuable of commodities in the Holy Land would not be a problem. If we had the chance, we could water our animals there. We rode, the next day, on a war footing for Kerak was truly enemy territory as it was the heart of the Emir's domain. We were lucky we saw no one and we later discovered why. An-Nasir Dawud was meeting with the new lord of Egypt in Cairo where the Egyptian was already planning his war. Now that King Thibaut had left there was no leader to unite the crusaders. I wondered if Richard of Cornwall would assume that mantle. Perhaps his brother had planned it this way so that the English knights had been instrumental in winning the war and with King Thibaut gone then Richard of Cornwall could garner the glory. I had become cynical!

Jean's knowledge of the region proved invaluable as he led us off the road to the castle at a place which was hidden in both directions. I had not noticed the trail but Jean took us unerringly along what must have been a hunter's path. When we stopped, in the shade of a huge slab of rock, he explained. "When I was one of the castle's garrison, we used to come here for there are small deer which forage in the scrub close by. They augmented the beans and broth we lived on. I was quite a good hunter in my younger days and I made silver from the practice."

I knew how close we were to the quarry when I heard the double horn sound. Jean nodded, "They now go back to work after their break. That is how close we are."

We unsaddled the horses and rubbed them down. More than anything we needed reliable horses if we were to escape the men who would be pursuing us. I spent time with Matthew and Mark. They had both come a long way since they had been taken from the tannery but what we were doing was beyond even their wildest dreams.

"Remember, when we ambush the enemy you two have one job and one job only, to get the captives to the road. It will be hard for I am uncertain about the condition of the men."

Matthew nodded, "Aye, lord, but we are your squires. What about you? I would not wish any harm to come to you."

"I am happy to be in danger for I am the leader and that responsibility weighs heavily upon my shoulders. What I would ask you to do is that, if you can, identify Geoffrey of Lyon; do that and I would be grateful."

"We will do our best, lord."

We did not leave our hiding place until it was getting late and we heard the triple horn which signified the end of the working day in the quarry. We followed Jean as he picked his way back to the road. This was the time of day when the road should have been empty but we took

Baron's Crusade

no chances. We had arrows nocked ready. When we were at a place where I saw wagon tracks in the sand, Jean held up his hand and then led us south, off the road. It was not yet dark for the sun was setting slowly to the west. The trail Jean took us down twisted and turned and we had to watch our footing. When he halted and said, "We are here." I saw that we were on flat ground. As I dismounted, he pointed to the skyline to the west of us. There, silhouetted against the setting sun were three crosses.

He came over to me, "When a man can work no more, they put him there to die. They think it is funny."

"Three crosses?"

"They know the story of Jesus, Sir William; it weighs upon a man when he works watching others die and knowing that if he slacks then that will be his fate."

Others heard Jean tell me and it was like a breeze blowing over wheat as the story was told from man to man. It cast a depressing air as we tethered our horses and made a camp beneath the three crosses which dominated the skyline, even in the dark. I left my shield and helmet close by Thorn. I would not need them. I would need my dull cloak for disguise. It had been white once but the dust of the land and the lack of water to wash it meant that it was now a dull cream colour. We knew what we had to do and followed Jean as he led us up to the quarry, which was less than half a mile away. The three crosses were on the high part and were to the east of the quarry. Jean had taken us past the quarry so that our horses were also to the east of the camp. There they were on dead ground and would not be seen. The only danger would be them making a noise and our men would have to keep them quiet. We had to walk along the ridge where the crosses and the corpses stood. As he neared there was a scurrying as carrion fled. It was dark by the time we passed the crosses and for that I was grateful; I did not wish to see the half-eaten bodies of warriors. We had arranged an order when we had rested earlier in the day. It would be an archer then a man at arms and so on until the archers were all allocated a place and then Jean, Sir Philip and myself would alternate. It was almost a complete circle. The crosses marked the gap between sentries. The plan was simple. We would all hide close to where a sentry normally watched. We would hide on the side away from the quarry. The sentries' attention would be on the quarry.

As each man took his post I said, "You can see where the guard sits. Find somewhere close where you can hide. You can move around all you like until the first hint of dawn and then you hide and remain motionless."

I was between Jean and Peter of York. I saw the flat ground and the discarded shells of the nuts were a clear indication of where the guard I would kill, spent his day. I saw his piles of dried dung where he emptied his bowels and I even guessed which rock he sat upon to watch the prisoners for there were two rocks and one made a backrest for the other. I found myself somewhere behind the stone seat. There were plenty of rocks in which to hide; this was a quarry. I laid my sword and scabbard between the two large rocks I had chosen as my hiding place and then walked, first to Jean and then to Peter. I needed to know where they would hide. This was the part of the plan I feared the most. It was one thing for Jean to say that the guards had a routine and only had eyes for the prisoners and quite another to hide in almost plain view.

Jean seemed to read my mind, "Lord I watched these guards every day when I worked in this quarry. Not once did they change their routine. Even when new guards came, they followed the same system."

He was right, men did follow patterns and we would be, in the main, swordsmen attacking archers. They would not have an arrow nocked nor even a bow strung. A good archer could perform both actions in a heartbeat and a strung bow was a weakened bow. All I had to do was, when the horn sounded, count to one hundred take four steps, swing my sword and end the man's life. I had managed to find my hiding place in a direct line to his toilet. Men were creatures of habit and he would use exactly the same spot each day. I was confident in my ability but what of the others? The majority of men were Sir Philip's and I did not know them. It was all in the hands of God now. I could do no more.

Chapter 15

As I sat and waited for dawn, for I could not sleep, I ran over what we would do. Even if we succeeded and escaped to the Dead Sea, I knew that the odds were that I would not find Geoffrey of Lyon. Would that torment me? Would I return home and fret that I had failed to keep a promise made to a dying man? My father was right; a man cannot change his nature nor his blood. My blood went back, so I was told, to one of King Alfred's housecarls, a Varangian Guard. Neither the housecarls nor the Varangians had ever broken a promise. The Warlord had been faithful even though it had cost him his wife. My father had been unwilling to endure the Bishop of Durham's treachery and risked his soul. This was my test and how I dealt with it would show what kind of man I was.

I knew that the castle was just a few miles away. When the evening breeze shifted, the smell of their fires drifted towards me. I knew that I would hear their mullahs calling the faithful to prayer. Jean had estimated that there could still be more than a hundred men inside the castle despite the fact that An-Nasir Dawud had taken the bulk of his warriors to Cairo. I was pessimistic enough to expect more than two hundred men. The Emir of Kerak had managed to capture a poorly held Tower of David and he would not risk the same happening to his stronghold. I stood, to stretch and face east. I would have to remain immobile for a couple of hours. I walked some distance away from the quarry side and made water. I heard others doing the same for the night was so silent it was eerie. The only sound we heard was the sound of the carrion feasting on the three corpses. I could have shifted them but they would return when we had gone. It was life.

I saw the thin line of dawn as I heard the distant trumpet awaking the castle. The men there would be rising and it would still take a couple of hours for them to reach us but we were now on the cusp of battle. I went back to my hiding place and took out my sword and scabbard. I would have to attach them now. It was unlikely I would make a noise in doing so but I dared not risk doing so when the guard was a few paces away. I attached it and slipped the sword in and out a couple of times. I watched the sun peer over the eastern horizon and I went into my hiding place. I pulled up my hood and covered my chausses with my cloak. The cloak would shade me a little and keep me hidden. I would look just like a rock although as I was below the eye line of any watching sentry I should be as near invisible as it was possible to get. I took my dagger from my belt. That would be in my left hand and if I was surprised then I could use it while drawing my sword.

The sun had been up for some time when I heard, from the road, the creak of wagons and the sound of men talking. The speakers would be the guards as Jean told us that whipping was the smallest punishment for talking! None of us was in a position to see the quarry. By the very nature of our plan, we were hidden and we would all have to wait for the horn and then count to one hundred. Of course, we would listen for the sound of discovery. That had been a real possibility and if that happened then I would shout, 'Arsuf!' as the signal to start our attack. If that eventuality occurred then we would, in all likelihood, lose. It was when the voices drew closer that my heart began to race. The guards were coming to their sentry posts and talking to each other. Until they turned to face the quarry, their guard posts circled, they would be looking in the direction my men had hidden. This would be the only time that they might accidentally see us. When the conversation stopped and all we heard was the crack of stone on chisel and the smack of whip on flesh we knew the work had begun.

The heat began to rise with the rising sun. It was bad enough for us but we were shaded and not moving. How much worse for the captives who were labouring under the blazing rays of the sun with minimal water and having been fed starvation rations; just enough food to eke out another day of work? Jean had told me that they had a constant source of slaves and dead prisoners did not worry them. I wondered what the time was. My secret place was between two rocks and while I could detect the movement of the sun, I could not ascribe a time to it. This was not my country. When I heard a shouted conversation between two sentries begin then I prepared myself. This had to be close to the time when the horn would sound and the sentries would be starting to relax. It became silent again and then I heard the horn sound. I counted to one hundred and then was out of my place so quickly that I had taken a step before I began to draw my sword. I turned to look at the guard. He was moving toward me. He must have been heading for his toilet. It meant I had a shorter distance to cover before we met and I swept my sword across his neck. I am not even sure that he actually saw me. It was a merciful killing for the spurting blood told me that he was dead before he hit the ground. I saw Rafe War Axe bury his axe in the back of his sentry. The arrows from our archers had killed their men and now they targeted the overseers. Cedric had an arrow already winging its way to the man with the horn even as he raised it to his lips to summon help from the castle. I trusted the others to kill their men and ran towards the quarry. I saw that there were about twenty-two or three captives. The overseers and guards who had not been slain were shouting. I hoped that the wagon drivers, who would already be heading back to the castle would not hear them and then I remembered the creaking, groaning wheels which had heralded their arrival. That sound would mask any shouts which reached them.

I think the huge overseer who ran at me must not have realised that his archer guards were all dead for he was bellowing for dead men to kill us. He had a long two-handed sword. Jean had told me that sometimes, the man known as Black Abdul, would show off his skill by beheading a prisoner who had annoyed him. He would be a strong swordsman. I did not slow as he swung the sword. Timing was everything and I used my sword to deflect the blade to one side as I carried on running, when his foul-smelling face was close to mine, I rammed my dagger up under his ribs. I twisted and turned it and, as I pulled it out, a snake-like mass of intestines came with it. He dropped his sword and tried to push them back inside. He sat on the ground. His wound would take many hours to kill him.

I saw Sir Philip and his men at arms slaying the last of the guards while Jean was gutting the last overseer. We had eliminated the guards. All that remained were the captives and the dying sentries. Peter and Rafe were close behind me. I shouted, first in French and then in English, "We are here to rescue you. We have horses. Follow us!"

These men had been abused on a daily basis and even though freedom was close by some could not but resist running to their guards and, after taking weapons, mutilating their bodies. I was wrong about the large overseer taking hours to die. Three men ran to him and, picking up his sword hacked his body into six pieces.

"Hurry!"

I looked around to make certain that all of our men had survived. There were five extra horses which my archers were already riding back to our camp. Cedric Warbow also had bundles of Turkish arrows. "You never know, my lord, these might come in handy."

"Did any get hurt?"

"Two of Sir Philip's men were a little slow. They have cuts but nothing serious, lord."

I nodded, we were still hurrying after the captives, "Let us see if the rest of the plan goes as well."

We were the last to reach the horses and Matthew and Mark had mounted the rescued captives first on the Turkish horses. I was thankful that we had captured so many from the Turks and now we had extra horses and they might prove invaluable. Cedric and the archers would lead off for they would, if all went well, set up their ambush. Next

Baron's Crusade

would come Jean, Mark and Matthew with the rescued men. Last would come, Sir Philip, his squire and our men at arms.

Matthew held my stirrup for me to clamber onto Thorn's back. He grinned, "That was a long night, lord!"

"You did well; now remember, get these men to the road! Leave the Turks to us."

"Do not worry lord. I will not let you down and one day you shall knight me and make my father proud."

We gave the men on the Turkish horses forty paces start. Then we followed at a steady pace. Our horses had been rested. They had been fed grain and they were well watered but they had twenty miles of heat to endure. I estimated we had no more than an hour before the Turks sent word back to the castle. The vengeful captives had wasted time taking out their vengeance on the dead and dying and I had not been expecting it. I had Peter and Rafe at the rear as they were the most experienced men, apart from our archers, and my handful of archers would be needed on the ridge. There were people on the road and they would be able to tell the Turks the direction we had taken. Had we so wished we could have slain the few that we met. That did not seem right. We let them live knowing it was a risk.

Sir Philip rode next to me. "Your archers are remarkable. Four of my men did not have to use their swords so quick were your archers."

"I know and my father and I have many more back in England."

"Then why did you not bring them? With an army of archers, this land could be ours."

"I came not for land and neither did you. Do you recall? You do this for a bride. Do not be drawn into the crusader trap. Too many knights came here thinking it was for the cross and then deciding it was for the land. I would rather live in England."

Sir Philip said, "You are right and I can see the trap I almost fell into. One little victory and I see myself as Charlemagne!"

"Besides, we are not out of danger yet. When I see the road and the captives smiling at me then I will begin to hope."

The fact that the road sloped down to the valley bottom and so our horses were having to work hard made the journey back quicker than the one we had taken the previous day. With my shield covering my left leg and my helmet hanging from my cantle, I was riding with just my head protector. It was cooler that way and I could use my ears. It was as we were approaching the Dead Sea and could see, ahead, the flatter part of the valley that Peter of York shouted, "I hear riders, lord."

"How far behind?"

"More than a mile and this twisting road means that they won't see us but once we reach the road, they will see us."

I turned to Sir Philip, "And now we gallop. We have four miles to go to the place of ambush and then we dismount. I know they will see where we have left the road but the rocks and scrub will hide us when we prepare our ambush."

We both touched spurs to the flanks of our horses. By galloping we would maintain the distance between ourselves and our pursuers. The difference was that they had been galloping for longer which would be more tiring and exhausting for their horses. The road twisted and turned. Even if they saw us briefly, we would soon disappear from view.

It did not take long for the effects of the harder riding to manifest themselves. Our horses became lathered and I knew that if our horses were like this then the ones chasing us would be even worse. The large number of horses which had left the road and galloped across the rough ground to the ridge would make it obvious to our pursuers that we had left the road but it could not be helped. Leaving the road we turned west and, looking ahead, although I could see the rescued captives, I could not see the archers. I knew that they would already be building their eyries. I was now looking for the small pile of white stones which marked the place we would split into two groups and await the enemy. They proved harder to see than I had expected.

I shouted, "Any sign of them, Peter?"

"Not yet, lord."

And then I saw the stones. As I trotted Thorn past them, I kicked them with my boot so that they scattered and would mix with the others. "We are here!" We had chosen two defiles which flanked the main path. The captives, with Mark and Matthew to the rear, would be clearly visible to the enemy but we would not. Two of Sir Philip's men came with me along with Peter and Rafe. The side trail led, eventually, to water. We had seen waterfowl there on our way east and had realised why the trail had been made. We found the small dip and dismounted. There was a little piece of grazing and our four horses would be able to eat. More importantly, they would rest. I poured some water into my hand and let Thorn drink. It would not do to let her drink heavily. I repeated it four times.

Peter said, "I hear them, lord."

"Then let us climb." This time I took off my spurs and left them with my horse before I began the scramble up the rocks to the trail where we would ambush the pursuers.

The fact that we could not see the Turks meant they could not see us but I could hear them. Their horses' hooves were clattering on the rocks and their leader was exhorting them, I assume, to catch us. The steep ridge had slowed the rescued captives. I could not see the Turks but Mark and Matthew were less than half a mile away as their horses laboured up the slope. The captives were in no condition for such a hard ride and they were slowing. It would give the Turks heart. I had left my shield and helmet with my horse and my cloak hid my coif. We reached the six rock slabs which rose like sentries along the side of the trail. Further west, on the other side of the trail, were four similar slabs. Sir Philip and his men would wait there. When they stepped out my men and I would be the first to attack the horsemen from our side, their left, while their attention would be on their right and the threat that was Sir Philip. As soon as we had seen these rock monoliths, we had seen the potential. We could wait, in their shelter and we would be hidden from the Turks. I was desperate to know how many men pursued us but it was too great a risk to try to view them. Cedric and his archers were in their lofty crags and they would see all. It would be Cedric Warbow who would launch the attack and we would add to the confusion.

I could hear the hooves drawing closer and even the laboured breath of the tired horses. I drew my sword and held it two handed. There were just five of us on our side of the trail and I knew this would be a hard fight. I had given us, however, a chance for this was not suicidal. All that we had to do was to hold them, however briefly and then descend to our horses. They could not pursue us on horseback but they could send arrows after us. We just had to shock and surprise them so that they halted long enough for Jean and the captives to reach the road. Once there he could, if it was needed, build a defensive camp. We had had one hard day's ride and we could not move again until men and horses were rested.

The first riders had already passed me when I saw the arrows arcing down. When the two scouts at the front fell, I heard an order shouted in Arabic. I knew enough to understand it. The order was to charge at the archers. One of the scout's bodies lay just two paces from me and I saw the bow slung around his back. It confirmed that they had sent horse archers after us. Another order was given and I guessed it was to nock arrows. Cedric and his seven men kept up a steady rain of missiles. Not all hit but they drew the line of Turks up the trail. I smiled when I saw one Turkish arrow, sent by our men, strike a horse archer who had just passed us. I liked the irony of that death.

Sir Philip and his men would step out first, he had more men than I did and he would draw their eyes to the right of the trail but my men and I would swing our swords first. The exhausted Turkish horses were struggling on the rocky slope as their riders forced them up. One slipped and tumbled down the slope taking a screaming Turk to his death. It was hard to see the effect of Cedric's arrows further down the trail but I had seen at least six Turks taken from the battle. Once we began our attack then Cedric would concentrate on the men coming along the trail. We had to hit the head of the snake so hard that it slithered back down the trail.

Sir Philip and his men roared as they stepped out to attack the Turkish horsemen who were next to them. I shouted, "Stockton!" as I stepped out. I was already swinging my sword to the right. I used an upward blow and I connected with the head of the horse which was next to me. The rider had a bow and nocked arrow in his left hand and was using his right to guide the horse. As he fell, he could not slow his descent and his head, even though enclosed in a helmet, smashed like an egg on a rock while the corpse of his horse tumbled down the slope. I turned to my left and ran after the next horseman who was pulling back his bow to send an arrow at one of Sir Philip's men. I am a tall man and the Turkish horse was little bigger than a pony. My sword hacked across the Turk's back and sliced halfway through him.

I felt something hit my back and even as I turned, I knew there was an arrow lodged there. I felt no blood and hoped that my repaired armour had held. The four men I led were hacking their way through the Turks. We had surprised them and were so close that they were struggling to bring their bows to bear. It did not help that their exhausted horses were terrified. Cedric's arrows still plucked men from their horses but I saw that some of those, further away, had their small shields out and were catching the arrows on them. One of Sir Philip's men, fighting next to Peter, was hit in the face by an arrow. He fell backwards, the barbed head sticking from the back. Even as he fell, I ran to stand next to Rafe whose war axe had hacked through the leg and into the side of a Turk and his horse. Another horseman had slung his bow and was riding at me with his sword already swinging to take my head. It was a narrow and congested trail. Rafe and I blocked it. Even as I swung my sword towards the scimitar which came at my head, I knew that we had done enough. By my estimate, we had held up the enemy for almost fifteen minutes. Jean would be descending the road. Our swords clashed and rang together with sparks flying. Rafe's war axe chopped into the middle of a horseman and I used a backslash to hack into the side of the man I was fighting. His horse could not get beyond Rafe and me, and it had reared. As my sword sliced into flesh the Turk fell backwards dragging his terrified horse with him; falling back down the trail made the following horses veer to the side. Peter of York's sword had taken the head of a horse and the dying horse and the terrified horse tumbled down the trail. The falling horses were like an equine avalanche and swept other horsemen from the trail, one careered down the slope. We had done all that I had hoped and I yelled, "Fall back!"

I saw the other of Sir Philip's men look at his dead friend and I said, "No, Pierre, he is dead. Save yourself."

He nodded. We quickly rushed behind the slabs and down the slope. It was as though we entered another world for we could not be seen and the sounds of battle seemed distant. To the Turks, it would appear as though the ground had swallowed us up and we had disappeared. As we headed towards the horses, I saw arrows still flying overhead although the rate was slowing. Cedric and his archers would continue to pin down the enemy. I took the time to don my spurs when I reached Thorn. Pierre took the reins of his friend's horse and I led us down the trail which would, eventually, begin to rise. Sir Philip had another trail to the north of the ridge. Neither of us would know the other's fate until we passed the crest and rejoined the main trail. Had my plan worked? We had saved the captives, of that I was sure, but I had also planned on saving Sir Philip's men and mine. One of Sir Philip's was already dead and Cedric and the archers' fate was out of my hands. How had my father endured the worries of leadership for so long? As I picked my way along the trail, I reflected that when he had been a sword for hire, he had just had to worry about himself. Once he had gone to the Baltic his world had changed. Now my world would change. My father would never be able to lead as he had done before. His mind could still plan and he could still watch a battle unfold but it would be me who would lead the men of Stockton and that was a frightening thought.

As I was picking my way up the slope Peter rode behind me and tugged at my back. I turned and saw that he had a Turkish arrow in his hand. "Your mail will need a link repairing, my lord!"

"If they ever learn to make bodkin arrows then the time of crusaders in the Holy Land will be over!"

Ahead of us, the sun was sinking into the west and I urged a weary Thorn towards the main trail. Cedric would not return with his archers until after dark which meant that the trail should be clear of our enemies. We reached the crest when there was still reasonable light and, in the distance, I saw that Jean and the others had reached the road. There was a mass of men and horses. As we turned around a rock I saw, as I neared the camp, Sir Philip and his men. They were approaching the camp having reached it quicker than we. There were two bodies draped over horses; he had lost men. The sun was a pink and orange haze in the west when we plodded into the camp. I saw the relief on the faces of Mark and Matthew. They took my horse and, as I dismounted, I nuzzled her muzzle, "You did well and when we reach Acre your travails will be over until we are home!"

I saw that Sir Philip and his men were digging graves where the trail met the road and that Pierre had gone to join them. He would tell Sir Philip the fate of his man. I would not impose upon them for I knew the bond between a lord and his men. I could talk to Sir Philip later. The captives were lying and sitting in friendship and national groups. They had been prisoners and were suddenly rescued. I did not expect euphoria. They would be in shock. Until they were in a Christian stronghold, they would fear the enemy. Those crosses at the quarry had served their purpose well. I walked over to Jean. "The plan worked! Well done!"

He shrugged, "You did the hard work, my lord, but I do not think these captives will be able to move until morning. They were already hungry and we took them away before they could eat their meal. We have cold fare for them but they need to rest here."

I nodded, "And the Turks will come."

"The fact that you and Sir Philip lost so few men tells me that you hurt the Turk. I counted more than a hundred and fifty of them, for I was at the crest of the hill and could count them. There looked to be more who were following. How many did you account for, Sir William?"

"That is hard to say but I would expect it to be two score or more and their horses will be weary. It was hard enough for us to pick our way here and we had an idea of the terrain."

Jean handed me an ale skin and, as he spoke, I drank, "Whoever was left in command of the castle has lost prisoners. For that, he is likely to lose his head. His only chance for redemption is if he brings the captives' bodies back and the heads of the men who took them. If you managed to kill him then this may be over. If not then, come the dawn, there will be a line of horsemen on the skyline and this time there is nowhere for us to ambush them."

The ale was warm but I was parched and I drank deeply. I handed it back. "This is your land. What do you suggest?"

He pointed north. "Ten miles from here is a half-deserted town, Ein Gedi. Emperor Justinian destroyed it for it was the centre of Jewish dissension. The mountain you cannot see to the west now is Masada which held out against the Romans. There is a spring at Ein Gedi and there are walls. If we have walls then we can defend ourselves against horsemen better than here."

"And are there people there?"

"We passed by it, lord, on the way here. There were a handful of shepherds and those who still try to extract the balsam resin."

I remembered then a ruined place which had been occupied by fearful people who had hidden when we had ridden through. We had not stopped for I had been anxious to get to the ridge. "It is a better plan than any I had. We wait for Cedric and discuss it with him. He may bring news that they have fled back to Kerak!"

Jean laughed, "Aye, lord, and that ale skin is half full!"

I nodded, "Then let us speak truly and say that the ale skin is almost empty. We leave before dawn. I would be in Ein Gedi when the sun rises. And now I will speak with the men. They need to know our plans."

Sir Philip and his sombre-looking men were returning from their sad duty and I waved them over along with my men. "I intend to speak with the captives. Jean and I have a plan for this is not over."

Sir Philip nodded, "Pierre told me. What we did was right but I find it hard to reconcile with the loss of three brave men."

"I know what you mean." We had reached the captives and I stood and spoke loudly, "I am Sir William of Elsdon and I was the one who chose to fetch you from captivity. You have all done well but this may not be over. Those who were your captors will want you back. You are weary and your horses are too. You cannot move yet and so I would have you sleep. We leave two hours before the sun rises and ride ten miles to some ruins where we will make it defensible. Some of you have weapons and we have spares. You will be able to defend yourselves." I spoke in French and then English.

One voice, English from the words which came from the dark, "I know not about these foreigners but I now have the chance to die with a sword in my hand. I have '*Black Abdul's beheader*' and I will use it until they hack it from my dead hands!"

I heard murmurings from the others. Then a French voice called out, "Whatever happens, Sir William, we are all grateful that someone came for us. I thought that after the disaster that was Gaza, King Thibaut would have come for us."

"How many of you were in Gaza?" It was almost completely dark but there were enough hands raised for me to see them. "Did any of you know Geoffrey of Lyon?"

The French voice which had just spoken said, "Aye, lord, for I am he!"

The raid had not been in vain. I had done that which I had intended and kept my word to a dying man.

Chapter 16

I walked over to Geoffrey of Lyon and said, "A word, if you please." Matthew followed me with a skin of water and a hunk of dried bread. While we spoke, he waited, discreetly.

As the French squire came towards me, I saw that he was the image of his brother but Geoffrey was just eighteen or so summer's old and his beard was not yet fully grown.

"My lord?" There was worry in his voice.

There was no easy way to say this and so I stated it as simply as I could, "I knew your brother, Raymond. He is dead."

I saw then that he had hoped his brother was alive for when he had last seen him it had been at Gaza and he had been with the lords waiting to be ransomed. "How did he die?"

That was the question I was dreading. You do not lie to a dying man nor do you lie to one whose life you have just saved. "I ended his pain for him."

He almost recoiled, "You killed him? The last time I saw him he was with the Duke of Burgundy before he was taken away by the Turkish lord who made me a prisoner and Raymond had not a wound on him. What pain did he have?"

"There is no easy way to tell you this, Geoffrey, but he was suborned by the Lord of Kerak. He was the Turk who took your brother away. He knew you were close and he was told that if he spied for him then your life would be spared and you would be returned to him."

"That is a lie! My brother would never do such a thing." His hands balled into fists and I thought his eyes would burst from his head such was his anger.

Matthew's voice was quiet and sympathetic, "I was there, Geoffrey of Lyon, Sir William speaks the truth. He confessed all to Sir William and then asked him to end his pain, my lord only did what your brother asked. I swear."

Matthew's voice oozed honesty and truth; it confused the French squire, "But my life was not safe! I was given no special treatment! I was whipped and starved!"

"I did not say that the Emir of Kerak spoke the truth just what a brother was forced to do for his only kin. Your brother was not proud of what he did but he had little alternative."

Geoffrey had been staring at the ground as though an answer would appear in the desert soil. Suddenly he looked up, "Why did you come for me? You could have let me rot and none would know of my brother's dishonour!"

I said, sadly, "Because he asked me to and in my experience where family is concerned then loyalties to kings and causes disappears."

I saw realisation sink in, "You risked all these men to save me?"

"You were the reason we came but we risked all to save every one of these men. I did not know if you were dead or alive."

"Yet you came to keep the promise that was made to a dying man. I am sorry, lord, when you said you had killed my brother, I wanted to end your life and I thought you a murderer. I apologise for I was wrong."

"There will be time for talk, I hope when we reach Acre. We have more dangers to face and battles to fight before then."

"Then I beg you, lord, give me a sword that I may fight alongside you."

"Matthew, go to my saddle and fetch his brother's sword and scabbard." As Matthew left, I said, "You shall have your brother's sword. It is meant to be."

Matthew had barely returned when we heard the sound of hooves on rocks. I drew my sword and Peter of York shouted, "Stand to!"

I heard Cedric's weary voice coming from the dark, "It is Cedric, lord!"

I hurried in the direction of his voice. I saw that one man had no horse but all my archers lived. "I was worried."

"Leofric's horse went lame, my lord."

"And the Turks?"

"They are camped on the ridge. We have hurt them, lord, and we slew their three scouts sent to follow you but they have not given up and they have been reinforced by more men who have fresh horses."

"It is as Jean said. We have a plan, Cedric." I explained it to him.

He nodded when I had spoken, "That is a good plan, lord, but we will need to rest. My shoulders and arms burn still. I am no longer a young man and I fear that this will be my last battle." He looked at the captives, "But it has been worth it. This piteous group of men is something worth fighting for."

I was desperate for sleep. It had been more than a day since I had slept but I could not, for now, I had the lives of all these men in my hands. When we reached Jerusalem, I would sleep. Jean and Sir Philip kept me company as did Rafe. I made Peter sleep for I wanted him to take some men ahead of us and to secure the ruins.

I roused Matthew and Mark first and told them to wake our men, then the captives and finally the archers. The animals had all been well watered and what little grazing there had been was now in their bellies. Cedric's horses would suffer but that could not be helped. We would have forty miles to travel once we left the ruins if we chose to leave the relative security of them, and that might take us two days. Peter and three of Sir Philip's men, along with Mark, rode ahead of us. Jean and Matthew led the captives and then the rest of us were the rearguard. We rode in silence. In Cedric and the archers' case, it was weariness. We were travelling on a Roman Road and that helped us to move faster but the sound of hooves on cobbles carried for miles in the empty valley that was the Dead Sea. The Turks camped on the ridge would hear us and they would follow. Cedric had confirmed the numbers who would be chasing after us. While they had slept Jean and I had been around the camp to count the weapons which our captives had managed to take. Twelve of them were armed. The rest would have to guard the horses and be ready to pick up the weapons dropped by dead and wounded men! We could afford no passengers.

Peter had secured the ruins although the Jews who lived there appeared grateful that we were Franks and not Turks. I spoke to the headman of the tiny community and gave him silver for cooking pots and food. He had little choice in the matter for the alternative was for us to take them without payment. The men who had no weapons were put to cooking for us. It was more to keep them occupied than anything. Our horses were picketed on the north side of the ruins. While Cedric and his archers found themselves the flat rooves where they would have protection and elevation, the rest of us took to making the southern ruins into our fort. Ruined buildings were robbed of their stone to block all the entrances and broken timber from animal pens were sharpened to make embedded stakes before our walls. Jean organised the captives into making improvised shields from discarded planks and fences. By the time the sun peered from the east we were almost ready.

When Will Green Arrows shouted, "Horsemen from the south!" I knew that we would either have won by noon or the Turks would be despoiling our bodies.

"Get your weapons."

One of the captives shouted, "What about the food, lord, it is not yet ready!"

"When it is, bring it and we will eat while we slaughter Turks!"

That brought a cheer. My words were bravado but when you are outnumbered that is often all that you have.

"Stand to!" Peter's commanding voice boomed out.

We had the captives interspersed between our men at arms and squires. Geoffrey of Lyon was between Matthew and me. He had some planks jammed together to form a rough shield. It would not stop an arrow but it might slow one. I saw the horsemen now. They came, not in a column, but in a rough long line. These were horse archers and could loose from the back of a galloping horse. They were not as accurate as Cedric and his men but I only had eight archers and more than a hundred and fifty were galloping towards us. My one consolation was that they would, eventually, have to dismount and use swords to fight us. Horses cannot climb walls! I viewed our lines. The Turks could envelop our flanks but they would have to dismount to get to us. There were ruined walls and buildings all around. We just had the southern line defended but Cedric and his archers could pick off men if they tried to flank us.

Jean was three men down and, pointing, he said, "You can see the leader. He is the askari with the plumed helmet." I saw the warrior. His face was open and he had a moustache that I could see. "He has the best horse and does not carry a bow. If we kill him then the rest might lose heart. If not..." he shrugged, "it will be a long and bloody day but I, for one, am happy to be here!"

The captives all murmured, down the line, "And me."

I looked at Geoffrey of Lyon. I doubted that he had ever wielded the family sword. He smiled, "I am ready too, Sir William. One day, and soon, I would have ended my life on one of those crosses you saw. This is better for we have a chance, even though it is slim."

I shook my head, "Do not give up hope yet. We have God and right on our side. We do not fight for land we fight for each other!"

Matthew said, "Fear not, Geoffrey of Lyon, Sir William comes from a long line of great warriors. One day I shall be a knight and follow his banner with my own!"

Mark shouted, "And I will too, brother, then the world should shake that we two are unleashed upon them!"

Rafe War Axe shouted, "Well spoken! Your father, John, would be proud of you! When next I raise a beaker of ale with him I will tell him what fine sons he has raised."

Cedric's voice drew my attention back to the Turks! "They are almost within range, Sir William! Brace!"

I shouted, "Shields!"

The captives without weapons took shelter behind walls and the rest of us pressed as close to the wall as we could whilst holding our shields or nailed planks above our heads. Cedric would need no orders and he would aim arrows at the amir if he gave him the chance. I saw that the Turks had halted two hundred paces from us. A line of fifty men had detached themselves. They would race at us and loose arrows both while they charged and when they fell back. I wondered at their range; would they wait until they were close to guarantee hits? They galloped easily and I saw that they controlled their horses with their knees. Of course, they would have to use a hand to turn them. I had faced archers before and trusted in my armour but there was always a part of you which wondered if this time one would defeat the skill of the weaponsmith and plunge through the gambeson and into your body. I lowered my visor and my world shrank to two slits. They waited until they were one hundred paces from us before they loosed. Cedric and his archers had the first strike for the elevation and their war bows gave them greater accuracy at almost twice that range. The horsemen were spread out and so large holes were not punched in their lines but eight arrows each found a mark. One horse pitched its rider forward as it was slain. Four riders fell from their mounts and the other three were wounded.

I saw the amir, with the other two-thirds of his horsemen, wave his sword and a second line rode at us and then the forty-two Turkish arrows flew at us. Three hit my shield and I heard a crack as one hit Geoffrey of Lyon's planks. I also heard cries as men without mail were hit. Even as they turned another five horsemen fell from their horses. Thirty Turkish arrows were sent at us as they turned.

One pinged from Mark's helmet. I knew it was him for he said, "John's father, Henry the Smith, deserves another coin for his work has saved my life, lord!"

"You are hurt?"

"No lord, but it sounds like the bell of the Church in Stockton is tolling inside my head!"

There were more cracks as arrows struck shields, wood and stone. Another cry told me that someone else had been hit. The second line of horsemen was rapidly approaching. I lifted my visor and shouted, "Have the wounded taken away. Replacements!"

The ones who had been cooking were eager to pick up the fallen weapons and improvised shields of the wounded men. Our line was still intact. I looked at Geoffrey who grinned. The arrowhead had come through his planks and was a handspan deep. He lifted his sword and sliced off the head.

This time the horsemen who attacked us had two problems: firstly, they had to slow while they passed between their retreating fellows and secondly, they had to negotiate bodies. They were also aware of my archers' skill. That worry would make them glance at the rooves of the buildings. Cedric and his men had accounted for another three archers before they were out of range.

Baron's Crusade

The second rank's slower charge enabled Cedric and his archers to be even more judicious in their arrows. They aimed at the archers closer to the men who had neither mail nor helmet. This time, when the Turkish arrows struck, there were fewer cries. By the time they had fallen back to regroup, I saw that we had accounted for almost thirty men and horses. Not all the men were dead but there were thirty who would not attack us.

Lifting my helmet, I said, "Replace the wounded!"

A cry came back. "They have all been replaced!"

That told me that we had been hurt, proportionately, more than the Turks. Perhaps the leader knew that for his next tactic showed his determination to end this. He had his whole line charge us. They meant to assault our walls. He had hoped to weaken us with arrows and now he would use his superior numbers to overwhelm us. I saw that the leader, aware that he would be a target, kept himself protected by four warriors who wore full-face coifs. I heard Cedric roar, "Now we bend our backs until our arms burn! His lordship depends on us! I will not be the one to tell Sir Thomas that we lost his son!"

I dropped my visor and watched, again, as Cedric's arrows thinned out the enemy but the sheer numbers who were charging and the fact that some were mailed meant they did not hit as many as they had in the first two attacks. Then the Turks loosed and this time there were more arrows. Thuds, cracks and cries filled the air as their arrows struck home. I had my sword at head height and my dagger was behind my shield in my left hand. This would be a hard and bitter battle.

The Englishman with the executioner's double-handed sword was still alive. I saw that he now wore a mail vest. I had not seen him take it but he must have leapt over the defences to take it from a Turkish body during the lull in the attacks. He was screaming like a Viking berserker. "Come on you heathen bastards! Let me show you how Alan of Chester uses this weapon!" He swung it as four horsemen approached, I saw that they had their arrows nocked. It seemed inevitable that Alan of Chester would die and then I saw one of the men standing next to him had improvised a spear from one of the palings he had found and he rammed that at one horseman. An arrow from one of Cedric's archers took another and then, capitalising on the shock of the two deaths, Alan swung his mighty sword in a long arc. It was so long that it had to be a diagonal sweep and the end hacked into the arm and chest of one of the Turks and then through the head of the other's horse. Certain death had turned into a minor victory and the men around him cheered.

I might have cheered had not the enemy leader closed with me. Fighting just him would not have been a problem but he had four mailed askari with him and their swords slashed at me. I still had the arrows sticking from my shield and when I punched at the horses one went into a horse's eye and it reared. I lunged with the tip of my sword and God smiled on me for it went beneath the skirt of the Turk's hauberk and entered his groin. He and his horse continued to fall back and the leader was forced to move his own horse backwards to avoid being bowled over. Matthew and Geoffrey, although outclassed, fought like tigers. Matthew had become quite skilled and he used his sword as well as any sergeant at arms. Geoffrey's shield was useless against a sword and the first blow shattered it and laid open his left arm. He slashed wildly at the Turk who thought he had an easy victory and hit the Turk's arm. Matthew brought his arm over to hack into the rider's horse and then as another sword came at his head he reacted instinctively and their blades rang together.

An arrow came from the second rank of Turks and I saw it hit Mark in his right shoulder. He cried as he fell, dropping his sword. He held his shield above his head but he was helpless. Matthew should have stayed where he was but it was his brother and he did what any brother would have done. He raced to Mark's side. It left a gap next to Geoffrey and the Turkish leader and one of his bodyguards took their chance and leapt across the gap in the wall for there was neither blade nor spear there and the palings had been smashed to kindling by the previous dead. Geoffrey's sword connected with the Turkish warrior's horse but he was knocked to the ground and lay there, stunned.

"Jean, Philip, we are breached, watch the fore!"

I whirled and ran at the two warriors who had broken through. I leapt over Geoffrey's unconscious body and hit the warrior with my shield and my sword. My sword ripped across his thigh and the weight of my charge, allied to the fact that Geoffrey had already hurt the horse meant that horse and rider fell to the ground. It also made the Turkish amir's horse move sideways and away from me. I brought my sword over to hit the warrior trapped beneath his horse. He wore a helmet and a full-face mail coif but my sword split them and his skull in two.

Matthew shouted, "Watch out, lord!"

I whirled with my shield and sword just in time to block the blow from the amir's sword while brave Matthew hacked through the leg of another Turk who was leaping towards me. His other men were emboldened by their leader's success and our men were hard-pressed. If it was not for Cedric and his bowmen then we would have been swamped. I still held my dagger in my left hand and I ripped my shield and dagger across the amir's horse's throat. I did not kill it but I terrified it and it reared throwing the amir to the ground. He rose to his feet with his small round shield and sword. Two days without enough sleep and little food had weakened me but I knew I had to defeat this leader or everything we had achieved would be lost. I hefted my shield and weighed up my options. His shield was smaller but also lighter. He could deflect my blows without damaging his shield. His sword was not as big as mine but it was sharp. He made my decision for me; he swung at me with his sword while he punched at me with his shield. Alan of Bellingham had often practised such a move with me and I knew how to counter. I met him with my shield, sword and dagger while bringing up my right knee to hit him hard between the legs. I had metal plates on my knees and when I hit the blow hurt him. Our shields were together and I rammed the edge of the shield upward, smashing into his jaw. I was sprayed with blood and teeth. More, I saw his eyes begin to roll and so I pulled back my right arm and rammed the tip of my sword into his open mouth. He fell, dead. When the enemy realised their leader was dead they would fall back!

Of course, a battle is not about two men. His death would dishearten his men but most were too busy fighting to see and it was as I hurried back to the defence that I saw Matthew, standing over his wounded brother and the unconscious Geoffrey, trying to fight three men. It would have been too much for me and although he wounded one, a second rammed his sword through Matthew's body while the third raised his sword for the coup de grace. Alan of Chester's executioner's sword hacked through the three men and, as their bodies fell to the ground, I heard a wail from the Turks as they realised that their lord was dead. They began to flee but our men wanted blood and they did not escape lightly. Arrows struck those some distance from the wall and my men leapt over to hack and butcher all who were close to them. We had won but, as I looked at the dead, I counted the cost.

While men went wild, I ran to Matthew. Alan of Chester knelt over him. I could see that the sword had gone through him and there was much blood. Alan shook his head, "He is a game 'un, Sir William."

Mark was clutching his shoulder and he could not stop himself from weeping, "How is he, lord?"

Before I could speak, Matthew opened his eyes. A trickle of blood dripped from his mouth as he spoke, "I am sorry I left my post, Sir William. I could not let Mark die, he is my brother. He is my father's favourite."

Forcing himself up so that he could speak with my squire Mark said, "Matthew, you must live! You saved my life!"

I added, "And that of Geoffrey of Lyon."

Baron's Crusade

Matthew smiled, "Then perhaps I have made amends for my mistake, lord. I pray you to watch over my brother until you reach home."

"You cannot die, Matty!"

Matthew gave a wan smile, "Nor do I wish to. I would have loved to be a knight. Swear, Mark, that you will be the best knight that you can be for you will a knight for both of us."

"I swear!"

"And lord, I have tried to be a good squire. If I have been at fault then..." His eyes closed and Matthew, the tanner's son, died. No knight ever died better. I looked up and saw my men standing around us; Rafe and Peter had joined us, along with Cedric and my archers.

Cedric shook his head, "It is not right, lord. He had so much to live for. Why did God not take me instead?"

"Because it was not your time. You had better see to the other wounded, Peter. You can do nothing for Matthew. Rafe, collect weapons, armour, horses, and treasure. Cedric, send two of your men to follow the Turks. Make sure that they have gone."

"Aye, lord."

I stood and looked around. There had been many deaths. I saw that Jean lived although his scalp had been laid open to the bone. Sir Philip was also still standing. I called him over, "Sir Philip, a roll call if you please."

"Aye, Sir William." He shook his head, "I am ready to go to my bride now."

I heard murmuring beside me and I saw Geoffrey of Lyon coming to. I knelt next to him, "Lie still until Peter of York can tend to your wounds."

He lay back and said. "Did we win?"

"It is too early to say. We survive, let us leave it at that. Mark, watch over Geoffrey until Peter returns." My father's squire looked as though he was in a daze. Giving him this task might focus his mind.

"Aye, lord."

Peter of York stood and made the sign of the cross. One of the captives had died. "Peter, see to Geoffrey."

"Aye, lord. A sad day yet a day full of glory and heroism; I am uncertain how I should feel but Cedric is right. Any one of us would happily have changed places with Matthew. He was well-liked."

It was hard for me to speak. Matthew was the first squire I had had and he was now dead. I had been comfortable with him. Now, when we returned home, I would have to tell his father and his sister that he had died. The fact that he had died so well would be of little comfort to either of them. Sir Philip and his squire came over. The French knight looked drawn.

"Well, Sir Philip, what is the butcher's bill?"

"Looking at the enemy we have slain it is not as bad as it could have been. We slew over sixty Turks and wounded many others yet our losses are heavy. You lost your squire although your archers and men at arms are whole. I have a squire and three men left. Twelve of the captives died and five were wounded along with Jean. He fought like a lion!"

I nodded for I still could not take in the fact that Matthew was dead. "You and your men did well. You have the honour you sought and I thank you. I know that I could not have done this without you."

"You should rest. I doubt they will come again this night. I will have the food served."

"Aye, the men need it. I will see how Geoffrey is and then we must bury our dead."

Jean wandered over, "It was good to hurt the bastards!"

"I thank you, Jean of Rheims."

"It is I who should thank you. The ghosts of the past are now exorcised and I can return to France." I saw him looking at Matthew's cloak-covered body, "I am sorry the lad died. He was a good warrior."

"I will speak with Peter about Geoffrey and then we will bury the dead."

"This is a good place for the dead to rest, lord. This is where Our Lord walked on the water and is the place the Jews defied the Romans. The dead will sleep well here until the day of resurrection."

There was comfort in Jean's words and I felt better as I walked toward Peter, Mark and Geoffrey. Both youths had had their hurts tended. Peter stood, "Their wounds are not serious but Master Mark will not be able to fight for a week or so."

"If we have to fight again then all is lost."

Geoffrey said, "I am sorry you lost your squire saving my life, Sir William. I feel like a burden now. Many men lost their lives saving me."

"Look around, Geoffrey of Lyon, there was more than you that was saved. Jean of Rheims now has his life back. Sir Philip can return to France and marry. He is freed. You have your life and that is good."

"But what life is there, lord? I have no land and no money. I have no knight to serve and all I know is war."

"My father was like you and he found a life. He became a sword for hire."

"I have heard his story, lord, but he was dubbed, by the King himself. I have nothing."

Mark had been straightening his dead brother's hair for he had seen the other bodies being carried to the graveyard. He looked up and smiled, "My brother, Matty, was a kind brother for he was always looking out for me. He would not wish this sadness and I see an obvious solution, my lord. You need a squire and Geoffrey needs a knight. As Ridley the Giant might say, 'This is fate and was meant to be.'"

When I saw Geoffrey's eyes brighten I knew what answer I ought to give and I did so for John was too young to be even considered for training as a knight. "If you will be my squire, Geoffrey of Lyon, then I shall happily train you to become a knight."

Geoffrey held his sword before him, like a cross, "Then I swear to be the best squire that I can be and serve you unto death."

"No, Geoffrey, for I want no more squires to die. You will serve me until you are knighted. And now, Mark, let us lay your brother to rest with the other brave warriors of Ein Gedi."

The funeral was a sombre ceremony. The Jews who lived in the ruins also attended. Jean told me that our common enemy was the Muslims and they had approved of our heroic defence. The locals left but the rest of us stood around for I let them know I wished to speak to them. The scouts had returned with the news that the Turks had fled east. Another two had succumbed to their wounds before they could even cross the river. We had captured ten horses and we were safe.

"Tonight, we sleep. First, we eat for I know not about you but my stomach thinks that my throat has been cut. Tomorrow we will ride to Jerusalem. The treasure, arms, horses and armour we captured will be sold in Jerusalem and all the survivors of this battle will have an equal share." I smiled at the look of surprise on their faces, especially the rescued men. Most did not know that was my father's way. "Any who wishes may stay in Jerusalem. I will speak with the castellan. For myself, I go to Acre where I shall take ship for England. Jean of Rheims will come with us as far as France but any of you are welcome to share the voyage with us. Indeed, if any so wish it, there will be a home for you in England at my castle." I knew that half of the men before me were English. "If any wish to speak with me then do so but it will be some time before we have our ship."

They all cheered and called my name. I felt embarrassed.

"Away with you, let us eat!"

As I walked back flanked by Geoffrey and Mark, Alan of Chester, although most men since the battle had joked that his name should be

Alan Longsword, hurried up to speak with me. His mail vest was bloody and cut about and he had asked for a Turkish hauberk from the dead. We had given it to him. He said, "Sir William, I am a plain-spoken man and I won't beat about the bush. I served Baron Amaury de Montfort. He would not have come for me. I doubt he even knew my name. There is nothing for me here, France or even England, save by your side. I like the way you lead and fight and I like the care you have for your men. I have not witnessed it before. I have spoken with your men and I would be one of your sergeants."

I smiled, "Honestly spoken and I will give you a place but, on the proviso, that if within a week or a month you are unhappy then you will tell me."

He laughed, "I am an honest man, lord, and I will tell you."

That evening, as we ate, Jean, Peter and Rafe also told me that many others wished to follow my banner. A couple of the Frenchmen were keen to join Sir Philip. The rescue, flight and the battle, it seems, had bonded them. It was likely that I would return home with as many men as I left with. Already Mark and Geoffrey were becoming closer. It was as though Geoffrey had, quite literally, stepped into Matthew's shoes. That night none would let me watch and I slept but it was a troubled sleep for it was haunted by dead men's faces. This had never happened before and, when I woke, I realised why. Men had died because I had chosen to make the rescue. It was not like Elsdon where I had been defending against an enemy. Here I had sought danger and men had died. I had learned a lesson about myself and I was changed.

We left the next morning. I kept my promise and the people of Ein Gedi were given money. Every eye was drawn to the graveyard with the stark newly fashioned crosses marking the graves of our dead.

Although the consensus of opinion was that the Turks would give up it was not beyond the bounds of possibility that they might attempt something on the last part of the journey after we had cleared the Dead Sea and so we were vigilant. We broke the journey up as best we could for we had wounded men but all of us were anxious to spend a night where we would have walls and guards to protect us. We reached Jerusalem just after dark. The wounded were taken to the Hospitallers and we stayed at the expensive inn. It proved to be less expensive for Jean spoke with the innkeeper before he left for the stable where he had worked. He would be leaving and he had his affairs to put in order.

We stayed for three days. We had goods and animals to sell and the healers wished to give our wounded the opportunity to recover. None wished to stay in Jerusalem and so we rode, as a body, north and west towards Acre. The three days of rest and good food in Jerusalem had wrought dramatic changes in the captives. They now looked like the men they had once been. I knew that it was not just the food, the rest and the clothes which had made them change; they had fought together and defeated their enemies. The humiliation and degradation they had suffered were now expunged. They were all tougher thanks to their experience. Geoffrey had been there the shortest time but he told Mark and me, as we rode to Acre, that even if he was surrounded by enemies he would fight to the death and not surrender for he had seen what that meant, here, in the Holy Land.

Chapter 17

The captives were found accommodation in the town of Acre by Jean, who had become their unofficial leader. Sir Philip took his men directly to the port for he was anxious to take a ship and return to his home as soon as he could. That he was unable to leave was not his fault for there were no ships to be had and his enforced presence meant a better ending to this crusade. I took my archers, men at arms and the two squires into the castle. I had expected the castle to be emptier, for King Thibaut, Duke Peter and their men had departed for home, but it was not. Simon de Montfort and his barons had arrived. I realised that was the reason my father had not been there to greet me. He was meeting with the first contingent of the men who would replace us. It gave me the opportunity to show Geoffrey around the castle. Padraig and Richard Red Leg were still using the hospital in the castle. We went to fetch them. Padraig and Richard were as saddened as any by the news of the loss of Matthew.

Padraig looked old, "He was a fine lad and I have shared many a beaker of ale with his father. I have seen enough of travelling, Sir William. When I volunteered for this crusade, I thought to save my soul and to protect the young sergeants at arms. As just four of us remain and Master Matthew is dead, I have failed. Your father has offered me the farm at the Ox Bridge in Stockton and I will take it. I do not know what kind of farmer I will make but it will be better than the warrior I have become."

Mark shook his head, "You are wrong, Padraig! You made us the men we are becoming. The journey is not yet over but you have steered us in the right direction. My brother died not because he was badly trained but because he was doing what you would have done; he was trying to save two of his comrades. He died well. We will all meet again in heaven and my brother will be able to hold his head up when he meets you for he died a warrior and not just the son of a tanner."

"Perhaps."

"Tell me, Padraig, does the arrival of Simon de Montfort mean that we go home now?" Mark was keen to get home now and see his family. The death of his brother had made them far more important than they had been.

He shook his head, "The King's brother, Richard, Earl of Cornwall, travelled a different way lord. I believe there was discord between the Baron and the King's brother but you will have to ask the Earl about that, Baron de Montfort's men are a close-mouthed lot."

I smiled for that was Padraig's way of saying he did not like them. I nodded, "Well, you and Richard can rejoin our men. We make plans to go for it will soon be October and if we do not leave during the autumn sailing then we will be stuck here. If Baron de Montfort is here then we can go."

Padraig grinned, "Those are the words I wished to hear, lord. Your father is with the Baron and his brother. They are in the upper courtyard. Sir Thomas will be pleased to see you."

John and Henry Samuel were waiting on my father and so, when I left Geoffrey and Mark with my men at arms, I went alone through the castle to the upper courtyard. I knew why they were there. At this time of day, it was the coolest part of the castle, for the sea breeze kept it so. The two pages were seated outside the courtyard along with two other squires or pages. I took them to be de Montfort's. I frowned as this was not my father's way.

John and Sam were delighted to see me, "Sir William, your father will be delighted to see you, Uncle!"

"And I am pleased to be back. Rather than cooling your heels here, go and join our men. Mark will tell you all that there is to know." I felt a little cowardly for I was asking Mark to give them the bad news.

John frowned, "And Matthew?"

I gave a sad smile, "Let Mark tell the tale. I have much to tell my father."

One of the squires stood and barred the entrance, "My lord, I was told to bar the entrance of any knight. I must ask you to stay without."

Before I could speak, Henry Samuel stood and faced the squire, "Know your place, squire! Do you not know who this is? This is Sir William of Elsdon!" He swept a hand around, "Ask any in this castle or the Holy Land about him and you will know that you are not fit to lick his buskins! Your master's brother would still be a prisoner but for him."

The squire recoiled in the face of my nephew's verbal attack but I saw his eyes flare with anger, "Peace nephew and cut along." I turned to the squire and spoke quietly but with menace in my voice, "If you were able to stop me then I would be impressed, squire, but you are not, so move yourself from my path for I have had a long ride and I tire of this nonsense!"

The squire nodded and moved. I walked through into the cool air of the lemon-scented courtyard. My father stood and grinned. Simon de Montfort said, without turning, "Did I not make myself clear! I said that…" He stood and turned, "Sir William I…"

Baron's Crusade

My father embraced me and said, "Baron de Montfort is under the impression, now that he has married the King's sister, that he is an important person. He is quickly discovering that he is wrong."

I disengaged and saw that de Montfort had reddened. "He will learn, father, for this is not the court where a baron can grease a palm." I saw that my barb had struck home and de Montfort was not happy. I had made another enemy but I cared not!

"Sit and take refreshment. You are back and I thank God for that but were you successful?"

I nodded, "There is a tale to tell!"

De Montfort said, "But I have not finished!"

My father gave him a cold look, "You mean that you have not finished trying to assassinate the character of Richard of Cornwall before he arrives to take command. I am sorry, I thought you had or were there more poisonous words you wished to add?"

De Montfort stood, "Come, brother, I can see that Sir Thomas is just what I expected, King Henry's lackey!"

I turned to the young Baron and put my hand on his chest, "I will excuse your rudeness once, de Montfort. If there is a second time then you and I will cross blades and not words."

He should have answered my challenge but he did not, "Come Amaury, the air grows foul in here."

Before he left, I said, "Baron Amaury, I managed to rescue one of your men at arms, Alan of Chester."

He looked at me blankly, "I thank you although I cannot put a face to him. Is he well?"

I looked into his eyes; he neither knew nor cared about his men, "He is now for he serves me!"

The Baron nodded, "Then all is as it should be."

They left. My father laughed, "That went well! I confess that I have been distracted in your absence else I would have said that a while ago."

"What is that all about?"

"Richard of Cornwall is unhappy that de Montfort has married his sister. I have yet to speak to the Earl for he has yet to arrive but I think it is because he questions the motives of de Montfort. I think that de Montfort sees this marriage as a way to gain power. Do you know he brought his wife with him? She waits for him at Brindisi."

My shoulders slumped, "Then he does not intend to stay here for long?"

"It seems not, mind you, his brother is unwell. I think his sojourn in Egypt did little to improve his health."

"And the Duke of Burgundy?"

"The Duke felt he had not yet done enough and so he rode south with his men to rebuild Ascalon and make it a fortress once more; I admire him for that and he has more character than the de Montfort brothers. The other lords left as soon as they could. They did not gain the lands and glory they thought. The lords who remain, in the main, are here to carve up the Holy Land. Richard of Cornwall is due here within the week and I will be glad to quit this land." He smiled, "So, tell me of the rescue!"

The smile left his face as I gave him the details. The conditions in which the prisoners were kept and their treatment at the hands of the Muslims both angered and saddened him. When I told him about Matthew, I thought he would burst into tears. I knew then that his wound had changed him. He shook his head, "But there is satisfaction knowing that he died well and that you saved the one man you wished to save. This was all meant to be, my son. Come, I must speak with my men," he smiled, "or should I say, your men for I think that is what they now are."

There were no ships in the harbour. Sir Philip could not take ship nor could we. The men who had been ransomed had taken them all. We would have to wait until Richard of Cornwall arrived and hire those ships. Simon de Montfort kept well away from us but on the second morning after our arrival, I found Henry Samuel and John. Mark and Geoffrey were tending to their hands and faces; they had been fighting.

"What happened, nephew?"

Sam looked shamefaced. "Tell him, Henry Samuel or I shall." Mark had taken over as senior squire and Sam nodded.

"The squires of Baron de Montfort found us and attacked us. They said it was a punishment for the way you treated them."

I began to turn for I would not condone such behaviour. Mark said, "Hold, lord. The wrong has been righted. These hurts are nothing compared with the wounds they inflicted on their attackers. The Baron's squire needed the attention of a healer for John, here, broke his nose and his jaw. He will not be eating well for a while."

I looked at the son of the blacksmith. He had arms like young oaks. "However, Mark, I want you and Geoffrey to go armed and do not let these two out of your sight for if they are like their master, these squires will be vindictive and without honour."

"Aye lord, for Stockton looks after its own."

The next day a small cog arrived in the harbour with the news that Richard of Cornwall, along with the rest of his barons and knights, was a day away, labouring across the sea. My father and I went to the

Castellan to tell him that we would be moving from the castle to quarters closer to the town. The Knights of St. John had a small hospital by the waterfront. It was only used when there were too many brothers to be accommodated in the castle. It was now empty and the master had offered it to us. None wished to stay because the arrival of Simon de Montfort had cast an unhealthy atmosphere over the whole castle.

"In that case let me hold a small feast for you, Sir Thomas. I do not think that the other lords have accorded you enough honour for your actions in the Battle of Gaza and of your son in the recapture of Jerusalem, not to mention the heroic rescue of captives abandoned by their betters."

"You have no need, my lord."

We could not, however, refuse and so we ate in the Great Hall. Our squires and pages also ate with us. Simon de Montfort's squires were there. The one John had defeated had his face swathed in bandages. It was obvious that he would have to endure a liquid diet. The other squire, whom Henry Samuel had fought, bore blackened eyes and a misshapen nose. They had learned a valuable lesson; do not assume others are as ill-trained as you. De Montfort and his brother kept apart from us. My father and I had deduced that Simon de Montfort had been attempting to suborn my father and gain his support to take over the English barons. I felt depressed as we ate for instead of hope with the arrival of Richard of Cornwall, it would be more of the same, plots and politics. There would be conspiracies and there would be alliances. The true purpose of the crusade would be forgotten.

My father sensed my mood. "You have achieved far more than we could possibly have hoped before we arrived here. Yes, there have been losses, but they were fewer than others have suffered. We go home at least as strong as we were when we arrived and, in some ways, richer."

"As strong, father? What of the wound which nearly killed you? What about Matthew?"

He spoke quietly, "I am getting old, William. We both know that. True, William Marshal was older and he still fought for England but my days of fighting are done. Your quest and your journey changed you and now you can take over my mantle. King Henry has promised you a manor in the valley, Seggesfield, and I will hold him to that promise for we served here longer than he asked. I will continue to train you to take over as Lord of Stockton. There is little I can teach you of war; you have shown that you are a master both here and on the borders. You have one son and hopefully, more children will follow. I can indulge myself and be the doting grandfather. Henry Samuel has shown me what we can achieve for the blood of the Warlord is powerful."

His words gave me pause for thought.

The next day we left the castle. The men who would be travelling with us left the inn and our horses, goods and weapons were fetched to the hospital by the water. The mood lightened immediately once we were all together without the hostility from others. The absence of de Montfort and his plots made everyone happier. Our men went into the town to make purchases while my father and I, our squires and our pages watched for the sails of the English ships. There was a stone bench outside the hospital and we sat there, shaded by buildings, to watch as the fleet appeared over the horizon.

"I had planned on staying a few days, William, to acquaint the Earl of Cornwall with the situation. I think I can do that in one meeting. While I meet with Richard of Cornwall I would have you go aboard and meet with the senior captain before others can do so. Negotiate our passage. We have more than enough coin to pay the fleet and I would have us sail all the way to England. I do not wish to have to endure a crossing of France."

"I promised Sir Philip and Jean of Rheims that we would call in at France."

He smiled, "That is easy enough and they can all be in one ship." He shook his head, "You are more like me than you know!"

We knew that the first ship to land would be the one carrying Richard of Cornwall and that would also be the most senior captain, not to mention the best ship. There were other knights waiting to take a ship home and I intended that we would be first to claim passage; we had earned it. As the ship neared, I saw that I recognised her; it was *'Petrel'*. It was the ship which had brought us east. Fate. We stood and made our way to the quayside. I saw the other knights waiting to take ship begin to move towards it but when they recognised my father and me, their shoulders slumped. They would have to take whatever crumbs we left. I knew we were being selfish but our sacrifices had earned us that right.

The gangplank was lowered and, as I had expected, Richard of Cornwall led the barons down the gangplank. As they stepped onto the cobbles, I smiled for their uneven gait showed that their legs were still at sea.

My father bowed and gestured towards the bench we had just vacated, "Your Royal Highness, welcome to the Holy Land. May I offer you a bench? In my experience sitting for a short time helps a lord to regain his composure."

The Earl knew my father and he smiled, "As ever, Sir Thomas, you serve my family well. Has Baron de Montfort arrived?"

There was an undertone in his voice which I knew my father would pick up on, "He is, Your Royal Highness, and while we sit, I can apprise you of the situation. My son, Sir William, will go aboard your ship for we have business to conduct."

"You wish to leave?"

"Your Royal Highness, your brother, the King, asked me to wait here for a year until you arrived. It has been much longer and I am anxious to return to England."

"Quite so. Lead on and get me out of this sun!" My father would tell him of the attempt to suborn him.

The Earl had an entourage of some twenty men. Half would have to bake in the sun while their lord and my father spoke in the shade. It was a situation they would have to get used to. Captain Jack was shouting orders when Mark, Geoffrey and I boarded. We waited while he finished barking out his orders. When he turned and saw me, he beamed, "Sir William, good to see you."

"And you, Captain. We would like to arrange passage to England for my father and me along with our men. Further, we wish another ship to take some of our fellows to France. We will not need above three ships. Can you oblige?"

"Aye, lord and *Maid of Staithes* and *Stormbird* will be available too. After what you did when we were attacked by Frisians, we could not say no but we cannot leave for two or three days at least." He pointed to his sheets and stays, "We had storms and we have to replace rigging and canvas. The autumn storms came early."

I was disappointed but at least we had berths and I knew we could trust the three captains. We negotiated a price and headed back to the hospital. In the time it had taken to arrange the passage my father and the Earl had left for the castle. I went to tell Sir Philip and the others of the arrangement. That done I decided to go into the market and buy more gifts for our home. Geoffrey and Mark came with me. As we headed to the market I said, "Mark, I would buy a gift for your sister. What would she like?" Mark's sister was the firstborn and she was married to one of my garrison. I knew that she kept house for Mark's father and that she would be upset at losing her brother. The gift from the Holy Land might partly make up for the loss.

He pointed to a stall where a man was selling religious artefacts. "If she could have a piece of the true cross then she would be happy."

I shook my head, "The things he sells were made last night in some back street." I pointed to a stall which sold brightly coloured, fine cloth which was superior to any to be found in England. They were used to make garments which were to be worn in a house as opposed to outside. "How about that, made into a dress?"

"Lord, that is too fine for my sister!"

I smiled, "That has decided me! She shall have it and I will have it made into a dress." I went to the stallholder and negotiated for the material and for it to be made into a dress. "I will return tomorrow. It will be ready."

It was not a question and the man understood that. "Of course, my lord."

We had clothes to buy for Geoffrey. He needed a surcoat and we bought that material and, again, arranged for it to be made up. At the same time, I bought four more surcoats for the men who had chosen to follow me. We had coins enough and the promise of another manor back in England meant I would be rich!

It was as we were walking back to the hospital that Mark said, "Lord, we are being followed."

I did not turn but said, "You are certain?" Part of me was annoyed that if he was right then I was becoming lax.

"I think so, my lord, he is good but he is there."

"Then let us get back to the hospital. We should be safe there; although why I should be followed, I do not know. We are leaving!"

"Lord, since John and Sam were attacked, we have been watching. The Baron de Montfort hates you and your father and his men watch us wherever we go although this one is not a Frank."

"And you are sure it was not a Frank you saw following?"

He shook his head, "No, lord, it was a cloaked man, a Turk."

We headed back and went into the hospital. I told Padraig and the others that I had been followed. Three went to the roof to see what they could see while the rest scurried around the outside. They saw nothing.

When they returned Padraig said, "We keep you here now, Sir William, where we can watch you closely."

Fate, however, sometimes intervenes and makes man's plans disappear like morning fog. Henry Samuel returned, "Sir William, your father asks that you use the men to carry the Earl's belongings to the castle."

Padraig shook his head, "Tell him we cannot for Sir William is in danger."

Sam looked terrified, "Danger!"

I smiled, "Padraig exaggerates. I promise I will not leave this bench. Now go obey the Earl's orders."

"Us too, lord?"

"Yes Mark, you and Geoffrey too. I will sit here and you shall see me as you carry the chests and the like from the ships. I can see who slacks!"

Padraig was still not convinced but he nodded, "Let us hurry. The sooner the Earl's war gear is off the ship then the sooner we can be aboard."

Although it did not sit well with me, I rested on the bench. Our men were good workers and soon had disappeared like ants, burdened with boxes, chests and weapons. A beggar shuffled towards me and I took out a copper coin. It did not pay to ignore such requests for the alternative was thievery. Had my men been there then they would have scrutinised him far more closely than I did.

"Alms, lord."

I flipped him a coin and he lifted his head so that I could see his face. It was Al-Shama and he spoke urgently, "Sir William, I do not have long for if I am seen then I am a dead man. There is a price upon your head. An-Nasir Dawud was angered when you humiliated his men, he has hired the assassin brotherhood. You must leave this land now for they always do that which they promise."

"How did you learn this?"

Al-Shama shook his head, "Let us say that there is a Hashashin fortress not far from Damascus and the Emir is no fool. We are not troubled by the assassins and information came to us of the contract. There is an assassin and he will kill you."

"My ship leaves in two or three days."

He bowed and backed off, "Them Sir William, you are a dead man walking. I will pray for your soul."

And just as suddenly as he had arrived, he was gone. I had been told of the order of Assassins or the Hashashini as they were sometimes called. They had once infiltrated Saladin's sleeping quarters and left a poisoned cake on his bedside table and a note was pinned to his bedding. If Al-Shama could get this close to me then the assassin could too. There was little point in telling my men. They were already suspicious of strangers and excessive scrutiny would not help. I would seek the advice of my father. From what I knew these were precise killers. Although poison was a weapon of choice, they would only poison their victim. They had a code which they abided by. They were also happy to die in the commission of their contract. However, as Saladin had discovered, they were more than capable of slipping into a room and using a knife. I had thought my war was over but I was wrong.

I did not see my father again until the evening. He looked tired. He had spent the afternoon helping the King's brother to acclimatise to the country and the politics of the Holy land. It was many months since his wound but he had yet to fully recover. He still had no touch in his hands and while his memory had returned, he found himself weary after long periods of talking. In a perfect world, we would have spoken with Conrad von Schweistein but that was out of the question. My men had not let me out of their sight for they were unsure if the follower was after me or my father. When my father arrived, I shooed them away.

Although weary he knew there was something wrong. "What is amiss, William?"

I told him all. He was remarkably calm about it but he knew the power of the order. He nodded, "The poison threat we can deal with. We will cook our own food and only our squires and pages will touch it. It is the knife in the night which I fear but I have an idea about that." My father was calmness personified. It may have been that he had almost died and been brought back to life but since his wound, he was much calmer. His ideas were simple and I saw how they might work. When he had finished outlining them, he said, "You are right not to warn the others. Let them think that someone follows you. That will keep them alert without making them fear their own shadows. I will speak with Captain Jack. It may be that he can expedite our departure."

If our men wondered what had passed between us, they did not ask. They knew my father too well. He smiled as he addressed them, "We will be leaving as soon as Captain Jack can manage it. I will speak to him later. In the meantime, we stay close to the hospital and that way we can be ready to load the ships as soon as they are ready. It will be crowded on our ships but we have all seen much hardship on this crusade."

Sir Philip was suspicious, "Is there anything I ought to know, Sir William?"

I shrugged, "I was followed this morning by an Arab. My men are wary in case…well just in case. Our pages have annoyed de Montfort's men and both my father and I have enough enemies amongst the Muslims to begin a Holy War. It is just a precaution. We will stay in this hospital until our ships leave."

He looked relieved. "I confess that I am growing used to not having to wear mail. I fear these new knights will have to learn quickly for the heat in this land doubles the weight of the mail."

While my father went to speak with the captain, I walked around the hospital but this time I was looking for ways in which a killer could enter. The exits were not as important for the killer would only have my death on his mind. The hospital was full and although every room was occupied none was overcrowded. All of those within the walls were either English or French; there were no natives. An assassin would stand out if he was seen but, from what I had been told, they were capable of hiding in plain sight! I thought back to the quarry where we had managed that feat, an assassin would find it much easier. My room was next to my father's. The two rooms on each side of us were occupied by our squires and pages. Opposite were the rooms of Padraig and Richard Red Leg. I had all the protection I could wish for. The rooms were more like cells. Each room which was on an exterior wall had an opening and a wooden shutter. The shutter could be barred from the inside. Even though it would make the room hotter I barred the shutter in my cell. While it was still daylight, I examined the room. The only way in was through the door and I could bar that. I began to breathe more easily. I could evade a killer by locking myself in my room.

As I emerged from my room, I smiled for there were men watching me. They had taken the report of someone following me seriously. When my father returned, just before the evening meal was ready, he had good news. "The captain has informed me that we can leave in the hours of darkness, close to dawn tomorrow. He says that we can begin to load the ships at dusk and into the night when it is marginally cooler so we have but one night to endure here."

"How did you manage to persuade him?"

"Gold can be very persuasive. However, when I was aboard a messenger came from the Earl of Cornwall. He wishes to speak to the two of us before we leave. He wants to see us now." My father saw my look and nodded, "Inconvenient, I know. The streets are the last place we wish to be with a killer on the loose. We dress as though for war and wear our mail." He waved over Padraig, "My son and I have to go to the castle. I want you, the new man, Alan, Rafe and Peter to escort us. Wear mail."

"A wise move, lord. I have begun to think that the man who followed Sir William was one of Baron de Montfort's men. If we go to the castle, they may wish harm to you."

When we left, we had one man before us, one behind and one on each side. Alan Longsword was ahead of us and he barrelled his way through the crowds. When we reached the castle, we were taken through to the cool courtyard. Upon reaching it, I saw that Richard of Cornwall was there along with many of his barons but neither of the de Montforts were present.

"Good of you to come, Sir Thomas. I know that you are keen to leave but it is vital that I speak with you first."

"Of course, Earl Richard."

"Firstly, I need to thank you for what you have done for England. Everyone, with the exception of Baron de Montfort, sings your praises, both of you. I have drafted a letter for my brother. He needs to know that which you have done in his name. There will be rewards for all concerned; that I swear. What I need is your assessment of the situation."

My father began and told him of the new Emir in Cairo and the threat he posed. He told of our friendship with the Emir of Damascus and the need to defend what we had. He spoke of the Mongol threat and how we could use that to our advantage. He concluded by saying, "If I were you, Your Royal Highness, I would confirm the truce with the Egyptians and see that Ascalon is rebuilt."

He looked disappointed, "There will be no war?"

My father touched his head, "My wound should tell you how good these Turks are. Wars are best avoided here."

We spoke for a while longer and then left. Earl Richard promised that he would speak to us before we left but he did not mention either of the de Montforts. It was dark when we left and the streets were no less crowded. Our four protectors were even closer than they had been when they escorted us earlier and we reached the hospital safely. Sir Philip had arranged sentries. There were just two doors and he had two men on each door.

The men had not begun eating and, as soon as we entered the refectory, our pages and squires began to serve the food. As much as I wanted to ask if any local had touched or tainted the food, I dared not for fear of making everyone anxious. I took comfort from the fact that there appeared to be a code for these killers. They took pride in just killing their victims! As we all used our own knives to cut the food then the blades could not be poisoned. We drank wine or beer and there was no way that any would have known which would be my preference. I did not enjoy the meal. I ate and I drank just enough to keep up appearances.

My father, seated next to me, laughed as he quaffed half a goblet of wine. He put his head close to mine and said, "If I am not dead in a few moments then we can assume the wine is untainted. Then you can drink enough to make you sleep."

I was not certain if I wanted to sleep but I poured half a goblet and sipped it. Geoffrey frowned when he took away my platter for it was just half-eaten. "What is wrong, Sir William? I have tried to give you that which you enjoy and yet you have eaten little and drunk less. Shall I go and buy another jug of wine?"

I shook my head, drained the goblet and poured more into it. "No, Geoffrey, but I rarely eat a great deal before a sea voyage."

The answer seemed to satisfy him. To take my mind off the killer who waited outside the hospital for me my father spoke of de Montfort. "He is a good soldier; others told me that, and I had no reason to doubt their word. He is supposed to be a good general but I do not like the man. He is too much of a plotter."

I laughed and drank half the goblet, "Then he is in the perfect place. I thought court was bad enough but this is like a nest of vipers. Here the Muslims are preferable to the Christians for you know they will try to kill you while the lords here will smile at you as they stab you in the back."

My father shook his head, "Let us change the subject; knives in the back is not the right topic for this night."

Instead, we spoke of home and what we would do when we reached home. We talked of Geoffrey and Alan Longsword and, inevitably, we spoke of the dead. I had just had three goblets of wine but I could already feel the effects. Some had retired to bed already and so I bade farewell to my father.

Padraig was enjoying the ale for the alewife was English. He raised his beaker, "There, lord, we have kept you safe from de Montfort and tomorrow we head for the cleaner and clearer air of England!"

That set off a heated debate between the French and the English about the merits of their respective countries. My father rose, "And I will retire too." We stopped outside his cell, "I will pray tonight, my son, and I will keep one ear and eye half-open."

"Do not worry. I intend to bar my door! I will be safe!"

Once in the room, I barred it before I did anything else. Then I undressed. I had already lit a good candle which would burn all night. I went to the shutter and checked it was still barred. My room might be hot but none could enter. Before I lay on the bed, I took the precautions my father and I had discussed. They felt foolish now but I did them anyway. I then prayed to God before lying on the cot. I did not think I would get to sleep; for one thing, I was hot and for another, I fretted that, despite all of the precautions, the assassin would get through. Amazingly I slept. It was a dream and nightmare-filled sleep which would not refresh me but then I suddenly woke. It was the need to make water. I rose and went to the large pot which stood in the corner. It was not there. I know it had been there before I visited the castle. Had one of my men emptied it and failed to return it? Then I remembered Geoffrey had emptied it earlier in the morning and he had returned it. I went back to my bed. I would wait until morning. When the cock crowed then I would rise. Sleep would not come and worse, the need to empty my bladder grew until I was convinced that I would burst and wet myself. I shook myself and stood, "William, this is foolish! There are guards on the doors and you have taken preparations. Take a piss!"

I stood and put my dagger in my belt. I slowly and silently slid back the bolt. I listened but could hear nothing from outside. I pulled the door open slowly. The sentries at the front door had shut it but I saw no one in that direction. This was a Hospitaller hospital and there was a garderobe at the end of the corridor. I just had to pass my father's room, Mark and Geoffrey's and I would be there. I saw the glow from the candle behind the closed door of the garderobe. I decided to risk it; where was the harm for the doors were guarded and the shutter secured? Twelve steps never seemed so far to me. I kept whipping around in case my killer was behind me. When I reached the garderobe I entered and bolted the door. It was stiff for few men bothered to bar it. It was a relief to empty my bladder and with that relief came a sense of foolishness that I had been so worried about. I pulled back the creaking bar and opened the door.

The long needle-like dagger that came towards my throat was like a snapping snake. The half-naked assassin was small but he was quick. My right hand came up instinctively and managed to catch the edge. If this was a poisoned blade then I was dead for it scored a cut along the back of my hand. Even though I had deflected it he was strong and the end went into the links on my coif and hauberk. I had felt foolish when I had dressed for war but my father had been right. I punched as hard as I could with my right hand as he tried to pull back the blade for a second, more successful strike. I connected with his jaw but he was a tough man and he barely flinched. The coif and the hauberk's links conspired to hold the blade and allowed me to drag my dagger from my belt. I drew it upwards and the razor-sharp edge tore through the assassin's left arm. It did not slow him and he wrenched his hand free. I suddenly realised that I had been silent.

"Help! Assassin!"

For the first time, this cool killer began to panic. He lunged at my left eye with his dagger and I barely blocked it. The edge sliced across my cheek and blood began to flow. He pulled his hand back for a third strike and then Padraig's sword appeared from the man's right shoulder. Padraig had rammed it up under the ribs. Even though he should have been dead already he still tried to stab me. I sliced down with my dagger and hacked through his fingers. The dagger fell to the ground and he died.

By now every door was open and the sentries at the door had entered. We all looked at the killer. The sentry from the door said, pleadingly, "He did not come from outside on our shift, lord! I swear."

My father took a couple of steps from his cell and looked first at the floor and then at the ceiling. He pointed upwards. "He has been here for hours. He hid up there in plain sight."

"Impossible!"

"No, Sir Philip, for how often do you look up when walking along a corridor? It is dark and he would have been hidden." My father pointed to the ground. There were tiny patches of water. "See where he sweated." He looked at me, "But what I cannot understand, my son is why you left your cell."

"I needed to make water and the pot was not there."

Padraig, who had wiped his sword on the assassin's loincloth said, "Aye and I have been pissing all night!"

"As have I."

"And me."

"And there we have the answer to this puzzle. The assassin doctored the water and the wine. He would have used the root of the dandelion. It is known to make a man want to make water. It did not go against their code for it did not kill but it was clever. By removing the piss pot he could ensure that you would have to go to the garderobe to make water, and by hiding in the ceiling he would wait for you to pass him before attacking. He was a patient man who could hide where none would look." He pointed to the two French sentries, "And you two are lucky. You would have been slain when he left. This is an assassin!"

They both made the sign of the cross. My father and I slept no more that night. Our next sleep would be on the *'Petrel'* as she flew across the Blue Sea, our Crusade was over.

Epilogue

It took two months to reach our home. We parted with Jean and Sir Philip just off the mouth of the Seine. Geoffrey had looked a little sad as his homeland receded into the distance. He was making a new start in a new home but he and Mark had formed a close friendship and the latter had told him of England's delights. Our destination was not York. We would sail to Stockton directly. The letters we carried for the King would be sent south by messenger.

On the voyage, one of the main topics of conversation was the attempt on my life. They could not criticise us openly but I knew that our men, archers, squires and pages were less than happy that we had not told them of the threat. My father remained calm and explained it to them. "Had we told you then each noise in the night would have resulted in confusion for all of you would have thought the assassin had struck. Others might have been hurt and the killer would have had more chance of success. My son slept in mail and coif. An assassin normally goes for the throat. As it turned out the killer was so good, that he almost succeeded. Had William called out as soon as the attack began then he might not have a scar to show his wife and son but perhaps that will remind him of the day he regained his life." He touched the hidden scar beneath his hair, "I know mine does."

We reached Stockton on the afternoon tide. There were no tides to speak of in the Mediterranean and there was something reassuring about obeying the moon and the river. As usual, our slow progress up our meandering river alerted our people. They would know nothing of the crusade nor our losses. For them, this was a joyous day when their menfolk returned. As we rounded the last bend my father said, "I can speak with Matthew's parents if you wish."

I shook my head, "He was my squire and I was there, at the end. It is my task, however onerous."

"Aye, and now your lessons to be lord of Stockton begin."

At the quay were my family and my father. The families of the others would await in the town. It was our way. My wife did not hold my son in her arms. He stood by her side, he had changed from a babe to a child. As the ship neared, I saw her pointing at the ship. I waved and he returned a shy little wave. I said to my father, "Can he have grown so much?"

"It is almost two years since we left. I am guessing that he can speak too."

Baron's Crusade

I could not wait for the gangplank to be lowered but I knew I would have to allow my father to leave first. He stepped off as quickly as he could and my mother ran to him. Theirs would be a tense reunion for he had to tell her of his wound. I followed as quickly as I could. My son, Richard, hid shyly behind my wife's leg. I kissed my wife and then knelt next to the son I barely knew.

My wife said, "This is your father, Richard, give him a hug."

He stepped from behind my wife's leg and held out his arms. I picked him up and when he hugged me tightly around the neck, I thought my heart would burst. In that instant, I knew that I had the hardest task of all to come. I had to tell a father that his child was dead and a sister that she now had just one brother.

I said, "I am home now, my son, and pray God I do not leave again."

We walked into the castle with the garrison and my servants cheering but my smile was a thin one. We followed my father into the inner bailey and then I handed Richard to my wife. "There is something I must do which will not wait." I turned, "Mark!"

Mark had the parcel he had carried from the ship and I walked across to the tanner and his daughter. They were smiling for they could see Mark but then when Mark's father saw my face, he put his arm around his daughter; she was with child. She stared beyond me looking for Matthew. I approached them and she looked into my eyes. I just said, "I am sorry, gammer…"

That was as far as I got for she dropped to her knees and screamed, "Nooooooo!" It echoed around the inner bailey. Every cheer stopped as all eyes turned to the distraught woman and her father.

Mark stepped up to her and lifted her to her feet, "Our brother died a hero and men speak of him with the same respect as is accorded Sir Thomas. I will try to be twice the son and brother I was for I have to live for two." His sister threw her arms around him and they both wept.

His father said, "Thank you, Sir William, for bringing one of my sons back to our home."

He meant no offence but his words cut like a knife to my heart. We had been on a crusade and our place in heaven was assured but for this family, there would be a permanent hole in their lives that nothing would ever fill.

The End

Glossary

a-vikingr- to go raiding
Amir- the leader of an askari column
Askari- a Turkish/Egyptian warrior mailed and armed like a knight or man at arms
Buskins-boots
Chevauchée- a raid by mounted men
Courts baron-a court which dealt with the tenant's rights and duties, changes of occupancy, and disputes between tenants.
Crowd- crwth or rote. A Celtic musical instrument similar to a lyre
Emir- a Muslim leader of some importance
Fusil - A lozenge shape on a shield
Garth- a garth was a church-owned farm. Not to be confused with the name Garth
Groat- An English coin worth four silver pennies
Hospital- more of a hotel than a place for the sick although the sick were cared for
Hovel- a makeshift shelter used by warriors on a campaign- similar to a '*bivvy*' tent
Marlyon- Merlin (hunting bird)
Mêlée- a medieval fight between knights
Pursuivant – the rank below a herald
Reeve- An official who ran a manor for a lord
Rote- An English version of a lyre (also called a crowd or crwth)
sal ammoniac- smelling salts
Vair- a heraldic term
Wessington- Washington (Durham)
Wulfestun- Wolviston (Durham)

Baron's Crusade

Historical Notes

Amazingly the events I made up were not as far-fetched as the reality of this crusade. Duke Peter did raid a caravan which led to the Duke of Burgundy taking a quarter of King Thibaut's army south where they were attacked close to Gaza. Although the King rescued some of them, most of the knights were captured. The fall of Jerusalem was equally bizarre. It had a tiny garrison and fell within a week! I made up the friendship between Sir Thomas and the Emir of Damascus but the Emir did give lands that were not his to the crusaders and the Kingdom of Jerusalem became as large as it had ever been! After the captives were ransomed the Duke and the King returned home and it was only after the King had departed that Richard of Cornwall and Simon de Montfort arrived. Amaury de Montfort lived just a year or so after his release and by 1240 all of the gains made in the crusade were lost. The royal family and Simon de Montfort never got on despite the fact that he was married to the King's sister. If you are interested in the end to this story then read King in Waiting to be published by Endeavour Quill in late 2019.

I also discovered a good website http://orbis.stanford.edu/. This allows a reader to plot any two places in the Roman world and if you input the mode of transport you wish to use and the time of year it will calculate how long it would take you to travel the route. I have used it for all of my books up to the eighteenth century as the transportation system was roughly the same. The Romans would have been quicker!

Books used in the research:

- The Crusades-David Nicholle
- Norman Stone Castles- Gravett
- English Castles 1200-1300 -Gravett
- The Normans- David Nicolle
- Norman Knight AD 950-1204- Christopher Gravett
- The Norman Conquest of the North- William A Kappelle
- The Knight in History- Francis Gies
- The Norman Achievement- Richard F Cassady
- Knights- Constance Brittain Bouchard
- Knight Templar 1120-1312 -Helen Nicholson
- Feudal England: Historical Studies on the Eleventh and Twelfth Centuries- J. H. Round
- English Medieval Knight 1200-1300

Baron's Crusade

- The Scandinavian Baltic Crusades 1100-1500 Lindholm and Nicolle
- Chronicles of the age of chivalry ed Hallam
- Knight Hospitaller 1100-1306 Nicolle and Hook

Griff Hosker August 2019

Baron's Crusade

Other books by Griff Hosker

If you enjoyed reading this book, then why not read another one by the author?

Ancient History

The Sword of Cartimandua Series
(Germania and Britannia 50 A.D. – 128 A.D.)
Ulpius Felix- Roman Warrior (prequel)
The Sword of Cartimandua
The Horse Warriors
Invasion Caledonia
Roman Retreat
Revolt of the Red Witch
Druid's Gold
Trajan's Hunters
The Last Frontier
Hero of Rome
Roman Hawk
Roman Treachery
Roman Wall
Roman Courage

The Wolf Warrior series
(Britain in the late 6th Century)
Saxon Dawn
Saxon Revenge
Saxon England
Saxon Blood
Saxon Slayer
Saxon Slaughter
Saxon Bane
Saxon Fall: Rise of the Warlord
Saxon Throne
Saxon Sword

Medieval History

The Dragon Heart Series

Baron's Crusade
Viking Slave
Viking Warrior
Viking Jarl
Viking Kingdom
Viking Wolf
Viking War
Viking Sword
Viking Wrath
Viking Raid
Viking Legend
Viking Vengeance
Viking Dragon
Viking Treasure
Viking Enemy
Viking Witch
Viking Blood
Viking Weregeld
Viking Storm
Viking Warband
Viking Shadow
Viking Legacy
Viking Clan
Viking Bravery

The Norman Genesis Series
Hrolf the Viking
Horseman
The Battle for a Home
Revenge of the Franks
The Land of the Northmen
Ragnvald Hrolfsson
Brothers in Blood
Lord of Rouen
Drekar in the Seine
Duke of Normandy
The Duke and the King

Danelaw
(England and Denmark in the 11th Century)
Dragon Sword
Oathsword
Bloodsword

Baron's Crusade

New World Series
Blood on the Blade
Across the Seas
The Savage Wilderness
The Bear and the Wolf
Erik The Navigator
Erik's Clan

The Vengeance Trail

The Reconquista Chronicles
Castilian Knight
El Campeador
The Lord of Valencia

The Aelfraed Series
(Britain and Byzantium 1050 A.D. - 1085 A.D.)
Housecarl
Outlaw
Varangian

The Anarchy Series England 1120-1180
English Knight
Knight of the Empress
Northern Knight
Baron of the North
Earl
King Henry's Champion
The King is Dead
Warlord of the North
Enemy at the Gate
The Fallen Crown
Warlord's War
Kingmaker
Henry II
Crusader
The Welsh Marches
Irish War
Poisonous Plots
The Princes' Revolt

Baron's Crusade
Earl Marshal
The Perfect Knight

Border Knight
1182-1300
Sword for Hire
Return of the Knight
Baron's War
Magna Carta
Welsh Wars
Henry III
The Bloody Border
Baron's Crusade
Sentinel of the North
War in the West
Debt of Honour
The Blood of the Warlord
The Fettered King

Sir John Hawkwood Series
France and Italy 1339- 1387
Crécy: The Age of the Archer
Man At Arms
The White Company
Leader of Men

Lord Edward's Archer
Lord Edward's Archer
King in Waiting
An Archer's Crusade
Targets of Treachery
The Great Cause

Struggle for a Crown
1360- 1485
Blood on the Crown
To Murder a King
The Throne
King Henry IV
The Road to Agincourt
St Crispin's Day
The Battle for France

Baron's Crusade

The Last Knight
Queen's Knight

Tales from the Sword I
(Short stories from the Medieval period)

Tudor Warrior series
England and Scotland in the late 14th and early 15th century
Tudor Warrior
Tudor Spy

Conquistador
England and America in the 16th Century
Conquistador

Modern History

The Napoleonic Horseman Series
Chasseur à Cheval
Napoleon's Guard
British Light Dragoon
Soldier Spy
1808: The Road to Coruña
Talavera
The Lines of Torres Vedras
Bloody Badajoz
The Road to France
Waterloo

The Lucky Jack American Civil War series
Rebel Raiders
Confederate Rangers
The Road to Gettysburg

Soldier of the Queen series
Soldier of the Queen

The British Ace Series
1914
1915 Fokker Scourge
1916 Angels over the Somme

Baron's Crusade

1917 Eagles Fall
1918 We will remember them
From Arctic Snow to Desert Sand
Wings over Persia

**Combined Operations series
1940-1945**
Commando
Raider
Behind Enemy Lines
Dieppe
Toehold in Europe
Sword Beach
Breakout
The Battle for Antwerp
King Tiger
Beyond the Rhine
Korea
Korean Winter

Tales from the Sword II
(Short stories from the Modern period)

Other Books
Great Granny's Ghost (Aimed at 9-14-year-old young people)

For more information on all of the books then please visit the author's website at www.griffhosker.com where there is a link to contact him or visit his Facebook page: GriffHosker at Sword Books

Printed in Great Britain
by Amazon